I0657528

The Unwinnable War

Battalion 1 Series: Book 2

Theo Mann

The Invisible Publishing Company

Battalion 1 Series

Contents

Also by Theo Mann (so far)

Chapter 1

Captain Corban Rhodes dragged his vision into focus just enough to see his Striker plunging through the destroyed buildings of a crumbling city.

Massive laser shots struck the few remaining buildings still standing. They pulverized in front of his eyes.

His Striker had to weave back and forth to avoid sprays of falling rubble and pinwheeling wall sections blown out of place.

Rhodes tried to take the controls—but this ship didn't have any controls. Grid lines surrounded his cockpit, covered the ship, and the same grid lines covered him, too.

Two faces hovered in front of his eyes. A bird-like composite of human, animal, and some cartoonish monster hung off on the right side. It talked rapidly to a round, cheery face in the center of Rhodes's view.

"The 249th Platoon is taking up a position between the central business district and the botanical gardens," the first face announced. "Watch out, Rio! You're going to fly into the Dusters!"

"I see them," Rio replied. "Interface with the *Ero* and tell them we're coming in fast."

"The *Ero* already knows we're coming! Oakes is in trouble! He's cut off by laser fire!"

Rhodes summoned all his strength to get his voice working. "Fisher......"

The bird face turned toward him. "You're losing blood, Captain. I'm accessing The Grid to slow it down, but I can't alter your basic organics. We just have to get through the battle and rendezvous with the *Ero.*"

"Don't leave without Oakes," Rhodes husked. "Don't leave anyone behind."

"Hold on!" Rio yelled and swerved to dodge another exploding building.

His grid lines stretched and morphed into different shapes, took the form of a many-legged spider monster, and he bounded off the ground.

He flattened dozens of aliens underfoot, launched himself at another building, vaulted off its side wall, and headed north.

"You can't get to the *Ero* that way, Rio!" Fisher snapped.

"I'm not going to the *Ero!* I'm trying to help Oakes."

"Where are the others?" Rhodes asked.

Fisher adjusted The Grid so Rhodes could see everything more clearly. He should have been the one flying this ship, but he was too injured even to raise his arms.

The Grid pivoted and angled downward to give Rhodes an aerial view of the city of Thaklia.

The Emal had penetrated the city from the east, spread through the streets, and worked building by building to hunt down any Aemon Legion platoons still fighting out there.

The soldiers didn't try anymore to hold the city against the Emal invasion. That would be impossible.

The soldiers just focused on defending themselves while they retreated westward in the direction from which they'd come.

They had their work cut out for them avoiding massive concussions coming from Emal base ships parked on the planes east of town.

The Grid showed Rhodes eight other Strikers zooming through the wrecked landscape. Each ship carried a member of Battalion 1.

Rhodes interfaced with their SAMs. Everyone in the battalion was as injured as he was—or worse.

None of them flew their own ships. The SAMs did everything trying their damnedest to fly the group to safety.

Rio picked up speed trying to intercept Lieutenant Ted Oakes. His Striker Enoch had gotten hit by base gunfire, knocked down, and the Emal swarmed all over the ship.

Enoch's grid lines changed rapidly from one shape to another trying to fight off all the Emal, but they overran him.

He changed into another spider creature like the one Elio used to break into the Emal base ship to rescue the battalion.

Enoch snatched Emal bodies away, sent them twirling off into the mayhem, and weapons erupted from all his limbs, but the Emal still got the better of him.

The aliens climbed on top of him and fired their lasers into his outer housing to cut him to pieces. He changed into a giant spraying lasers from all sides.

All his efforts only seemed to draw more Emal to pull him down. He even tried to fire his boosters to launch away from the planet's surface.

The base ships instantly turned their guns on him, blasted out another building right on top of him, and rock and deadly shards hammered Enoch from above.

The explosion hit plenty of Emal, too, but they didn't seem to care. They stepped on their dead and wounded comrades and used the piles of bodies to climb on top of him.

Rio interfaced with Enoch. The SAM's rugged bear face kept morphing, stretching, and undulating as The Grid changed around him.

The Grid formed the bear's body, but that kept changing every few seconds, too, each time Enoch tried a different shape to overcome the Emal.

"We're coming for you, Enoch!" Rio told him. "We're on our way!"

Enoch roared in fury. Oakes didn't respond at all. He slumped in his cockpit resting his chin on his chest. He had his eyes closed.

Blood saturated his hair and ran down his neck. Seeing Oakes and Enoch in danger snapped Rhodes back to his senses. He had to do something, but Rio was already doing it fast enough for both of them.

The grid lines surrounding the ship morphed again. The Emal must have detected Rio getting closer. The base ships swiveled their laser bombardment in his direction.

Another building evaporated in smoke and dust to Rio's left. He bounded off the ground and soared away to another launch point, only for the base ships to hit a different building right in front of him.

This one blocked Rio's path to catch up with Enoch. Rio would have had to fly around this building to help Enoch. The building detonated in a whizzing fireball of outward pelting shards and debris.

Rio changed his grid lines again, sprang down onto the ground on bouncy cat legs, morphed into another armored vehicle, smashed straight into the wreckage, plowed through it, and burst out on the other side next to Enoch.

The Grid in front of Rhodes's eyes showed him Battalion 1's other Strikers converging on the spot from all over Thaklia. They would get here any second.

Each ship changed shape at blinding speed. Their grid lines morphed and adapted in seconds.

Each Striker extended their wings to soar over obstacles, collapsed into wingless missiles, stretched, compressed, grew different kinds of limbs, changed their weapons configurations, and went through a dozen other transformations with every phase of the battle.

The Strikers' presence electrified the Emal. Thousands of aliens all over the city stopped hunting down the Legion platoons and came after the battalion instead.

The Grid flashed alerts as mobs of Emal flooded to the spot. "We have to get out of here, Rio," Rhodes husked. "We can't let the Emal recapture us."

"I know, Captain!" Rio called over the noise. "I'm working on it."

"Let me help you. I can help you."

"I'm sorry, Captain, but you can't do anything," Fisher interrupted. "We can't risk your injuries causing Rio to malfunction. Just hold on a little longer. We'll get you out. We'll get everyone out."

Rhodes didn't want to just sit here doing nothing, but of course his SAMs were right. The battalion's injuries caused the SAMs to malfunction earlier. None of them could risk it happening again.

The SAMs fought the battle just fine on their own. Rio blasted through the building's eastern wall, twisted back into a Striker, and whizzed over the Emal's heads. He laid down a carpet of scourge gun fire, but he couldn't hit so many teeming aliens.

He didn't try to hit them. His arrival distracted them away from Enoch and left a tiny space between Enoch and the building behind him.

"Get out, Enoch!" Rio called. "Fall back to the *Ero!*"

Enoch bellowed again, flailed his grid lines in all directions, and changed them into whipping lasers to slash the Emal away.

He cut bodies to pieces and sent them flying to free himself from the hordes clambering all over him.

As soon as he cleared them off, he rocketed into the air, changed himself into a Viper missile, and shrieked high into the atmosphere carrying Oakes with him.

The rest of the battalion converged on the spot, but once they got there, the gunfire got too thick.

"Everybody get out and scatter!" Fisher ordered. "We're drawing too many Emal. They know about us. We need to separate so they don't target any of us."

The other SAMs launched into the high cloud and left the city behind, but that only gave everyone a view of the bloodbath going on in the streets.

The Grid showed up perfectly the Emal maneuvering Legion platoons into bottlenecks where the platoons couldn't escape.

The Emal carried out a systematic campaign to hunt down every platoon and eliminate the soldiers with deadly accuracy.

The base ships out on the planes turned their fire back on the streets. The Emal bombarded the platoons one after another and flattened every building to deprive the platoons of any cover.

The platoons retreated from one building to another. The platoons held each line of defense for a few minutes. That was the best they could do before the base ships' bombardment and the steady advance of Emal ground troops drove the Legion farther back.

The base ships stayed where they were on the planes. They didn't need to advance any further to wreak as much destruction as they needed to.

Now the alien hordes moved in to sweep the city clear of any last Legion stragglers. Explosions burst in the dark sky where Emal lasers detonated Legion Dusters and Predators fighter craft.

Those explosions cast a ghostly light over the landscape crumbling to ruin as far as the eye could see. Bodies of Legion soldiers got trapped in the rubble.

The Grid highlighted their failing life signs in ways Rhodes never got to see on the ground. Some of those soldiers were still alive. No one would ever rescue them the way the Battalion 1 project rescued him.

The Strikers blasted skyward and left the battle behind, but only for a minute. The Strikers had to descend to rendezvous with the *Ero* and the other Ravagers parked west of the city.

Rio, Elio, Enoch, Titan, Zion, Stone, Aries, and Teo slowed there in the high atmosphere. Each Striker used his Grid to change back into a ship.

Dozens of Legion vessels surrounded the planet Sulia to carry out the campaign of defending this planet against the Emal invasion.

The SAMs interfaced with each other. The Grid showed Rhodes more than he wanted to know about the injuries each of his people suffered as Emal prisoners.

Lieutenant Dane Rhinehart spoke the words they were all thinking. "We can't just leave them down there. We have to help them retreat out of danger."

"We can't help them," Wild rasped. "Every Emal battle zone turns into this. They're all the same on every planet where the Legion tries to resist the Emal invasion."

"We're supposed to help the Legion," Rhinehart pointed out. "We can't just run away to save our own necks. Only cowards do that."

"We can't even save ourselves," Alyssa Thackery told him. "We barely made it out alive. If we don't go now, we could all die. Then we won't be able to help anyone."

"I'm with Rhinehart on this," Rhodes chimed in. "We're already here. The nine of us might not be good for much, but our Strikers can still fight back. Come on. We gotta do something."

"What did you have in mind, Captain?" Fisher asked.

"The Emal are fascinated by us. They want more than anything to recapture us. We can make them fall back to try to get us—or at least get them to divert away from the platoons while the soldiers retreat the rest of the way to the Ravagers."

"That won't work, Captain," Rocky interjected. "The Legion has never pulled the platoons from a planet this quickly, not even in the face overwhelming Emal numbers. A diversion like that might give the platoons a chance to retreat, but the Legion won't evacuate them off the surface. The Legion will set up here to fight the Emal and try to retake the city. The Legion never gives up on a planet until they've spent at least a month trying to retake it."

Rhodes sighed. He already knew all that. He'd been involved in too many campaigns against the Emal before.

He glanced over at Rhinehart through the interface. Rhinehart glanced at Rhodes at the same time. Rhodes read the same truth in Rhinehart's twisted expression.

Every member of the battalion was bleeding. Oakes and Lauer were barely hanging onto life.

In that moment, Rhodes's adrenaline faded enough for him to feel the sickening pain in his chest. He shivered and then started trembling.

Rio must have detected the same thing. He said, "Let's go," and turned away.

Chapter 2

The Battalion 1 Striker group fell in formation, swooped farther west clear of the battle, and dropped low to skim closer to the ground. They blasted across the countryside approaching the Ravager carries parked west of Thaklia.

Rio interfaced with the *Ero* bridge staff to alert the ship that the battalion was coming in. "We have critically injured crewmen on board. We'll need medical personnel to meet us in the landing bay."

Rhodes started to shut his eyes. The *Ero* medical staff wouldn't be able to help the battalion. The only option was to ship Rhodes and his people back to Coleridge Station.

That meant an eight-week conversion cycle before any of them found someone qualified to treat their injuries. Would any of the battalion survive that trip?

Rhodes was really starting to look forward to dying during a conversion cycle. A harsh, snapping, male voice brought him back to reality with a jolt.

"You can't just abandon those platoons out there to die, Captain! I demand that you go back out there and give them cover while they retreat out of the city."

Rhodes had to summon all his effort to haul his heavy eyelids open. A man's face hovered in front of him on The Grid.

Rhodes went through another torturous thought process before he placed the bushy eyebrows, the lined face, and the deep scowl glaring at him from The Grid. It was Captain Parker Ackerman, Captain of the *Ero*.

His face hung there between Fisher and Rio in the middle of Rhodes's view, but of course the *Ero* captain didn't see the two SAMs.

Ackerman's image showed his neck, shoulders, and part of his chest, too. The image looked like something Rhodes would see if Ackerman had been talking to him through a regular Legion Ravager's communications system.

Rhodes gulped to get his parched through working. Maybe Ackerman could see what a mess Rhodes was right now.

"Did you hear my communication just now, Captain?" Rhodes asked. "My whole party is injured—badly injured. We can't even fly our own ships and two of my men are unconscious. These computer programs are flying our ships. We can't go back to help the platoons. That's your job—and the other Ravagers' jobs. Why don't you launch and give the platoons cover to retreat out of the city?"

Ackerman's face went through a series of conflicted expressions. His eyes dipped like he was looking down at Rhodes's body for the first time.

"Well...." he blustered. "What's the point of you coming out here to fight for us if leave our troops without cover?"

Rhodes took a deep breath. The rest of the battalion listened to his conversation through the interface—except for those members of the battalion who were unconscious. Even the SAMs listened.

"Are you under orders to evacuate the platoons? If I take my people back into danger, get the platoons out of Thaklia, and they make it back to the Ravagers, will you take them off the planet or will you keep them here to go on fighting?"

Rhodes knew the answer as soon as he said the words. Captain Ackerman's features spasmed in some new and creative directions.

His mouth twisted in strange shapes before he worked up the nerve to speak. "I don't make command decisions about what the platoons do or don't do, Captain. You should know that."

"I do know that. I also know that I'm responsible for these people's lives. We barely survived getting captured by the Emal."

Ackerman's jaw dropped. "You got captured....by the Emal.....?"

"We already pulled more than one diversion to give the platoons as much cover as we could. We risked everything and we still might lose some of our people. We're coming in."

Rhodes manipulated The Grid to end the communication. He felt himself about to pass out, too.

He must have lost a lot of blood. Some of his internal organs or components might have gotten irreparably damaged when the Emal tried to remove his implants.

He barely managed to croak, "Get us out of here, Rio," and collapsed back in his seat. He couldn't keep his eyes open a second longer.

Rio didn't say a word. He turned back toward the *Ero* and picked up speed closing with the Ravager line.

The other Strikers followed. No one spoke. Rhodes couldn't look at The Grid anymore. It made him sick—sicker than he already felt.

He really needed to put his foot down and refuse to take the battalion into battle ever again—at least until the doctors and technicians worked out all the bugs in the system. This was getting ridiculous.

What would it actually take—someone getting killed? Oh, what the hell was Rhodes thinking? The Battalion 1 project already killed dozens of people.

Gannon, Poole, Cope, Taylor, and everyone else like them were already dead in this lunatic experiment. They were just as dead if they died in the lab as if they got killed on the battlefield.

All those considerations faded away when the Strikers approached the *Ero*. The ship would take the Strikers on board and Rhodes could forget about Sulia for the rest of his life.

The Emal would conquer this planet long before he and the battalion ever made it back to Coleridge Station. The war would be over—or this part of it. He would never come back here.

He just had to get his people into their capsules. He didn't have to think beyond that. He *couldn't* think beyond that. Just accomplishing that one task looked like an impossible undertaking from here.

He wouldn't have been able to do it at all without Rio and the other Strikers. Some of the battalion would be too injured to walk to their capsules. How would Rhodes get them there? He sure as hell wouldn't be able to carry them—not in this condition.

Relief flooded him on the last approach to the *Ero*. Rio shrieked up on the Ravager line from behind and circled the *Ero* to enter the landing bay.

The launch doors sat open for the *Ero* crew to enter and exit. They worked on the ship, provided support to platoons and officers, set up the command dome behind the battle line, and carried out a dozen other functions to establish the Legion presence on this planet.

Rio flew within a dozen feet of the launch doors when a massive laser shot from an Emal base ship pivoted out of the city. The shot smashed the Ravager right next to the *Ero*.

In seconds, more punishing concussions slammed Ravagers up and down the line. The Emal bombardment hit both Ravagers on both sides of the *Ero*. A third shot struck the dirt right between the ship's landing gear.

The *Ero* toppled away. Rio was flying too fast and veered into one of the nearby explosions.

His grid lines skewed at the last possible second. He yelled a warning, but Rhodes couldn't make out the words.

The prongs locked him to the seat so he couldn't move. He would have been thrown hard against the cockpit dashboard by the impact.

Rio scattered into a jumble of grid lines and barely reformed into a ball before he hit the ground. Continuous explosions sent the ball rolling away from the attack.

Rhodes heard SAMs yelling all over the battlefield. The *Ero* corrected and launched to get out of danger, but it was only one of five of the original fleet of twenty that even made it off the ground.

Enoch and Titan had been in the farthest rear of the Striker group. They stayed Strikers, punched through raging firestorms, and streaked away into the atmosphere again.

Rio's grid lines expanded, straightened out into a long, thin, projectile, tumbled onto its end, and vaulted upward flying impossibly fast. These SAMs could manipulate The Grid so much faster and more easily than a person could.

He changed back into a Striker and whizzed away from the bombardment to rejoin the others.

Rio's face rotated from right to left in The Grid checking on the other SAMs. They talked to each other in a rapid barrage of orders and exchanged information.

All their voices got confused in Rhodes's mind. He couldn't concentrate well enough to distinguish what they were talking about.

So many SAMs talked too fast. He wouldn't have been able to understand even if his mind had been working right. Rio and Fisher gave orders to the other SAMs.

The Grid showed Rhodes exactly how far the surviving Ravagers didn't make it away from the Emal bombardment.

They barely got off the ground before brutal laser fire pounded them back down to the ground. No one would be able to evacuate like this. The battalion couldn't even get near the *Ero*.

Rhodes summoned all his last remaining energy to call over the noise. "Rio! You have to get to the base ships! It's the only way!"

"Not now, Captain!" Rio hollered back. "We have bigger problems right now...."

"The base ships are our only problem." Rhodes dragged himself upright, forced his eyes to focus, and took control of The Grid.

He didn't know if his SAMs could override his will, but Rio didn't intervene when Rhodes took over.

"All of you—follow me!" Rhodes ordered. "We're going after the base ships! It's the only way to draw their fire away from the Ravagers!"

Rhodes blasted away across Thaklia. He didn't have to adjust his grid lines to any stranger or interesting shapes.

The base ships concentrated their firepower on the Ravagers in between laying down devastating shots on the city itself.

The Strikers relied on pure speed, pelted across town, and raced out the other side on a dead run for the base ships—the same base ships the Strikers just worked so hard to overcome to rescue the battalion.

"This is a bad idea," Fisher murmured in Rhodes's ear.

"How do you suggest we evacuate the planet with the Ravagers under bombardment?" Rhodes asked. "Those Ravagers are our only way out of here. Let's go, Rio. Let's do some damage."

Rhodes didn't wait for Rio to fly the ship or run the guns on his own. The cold, sick feeling in Rhodes's middle narrowed his attention to a pinprick.

His mind switched gears. He didn't have to fight for the Legion or the trapped platoons or for anything else.

He fought for survival. That was all. He had to get the hell off this planet and that meant destroying the base ships.

He didn't even know if he had a weapon powerful enough to destroy them—and then he remembered.

The battalion destroyed base ships on Ohait. The battalion detonated base ships by firing into their undersides.

His mind took extra long to process every thought. Of course. That must be why the base ships stayed sitting on the ground during every campaign.

Their armored tops and sides protected them from any weapon the Legion could throw at them. The base ships only exposed their vulnerabilities when they launched.

The thought gave Rhodes a sick thrill. He could destroy these cocksuckers. That would put a dent in their campaign. Nothing else would.

"Follow me!" he called to the battalion.

"What are you going to do?" Fisher asked.

"I told you. I'm going to stop the base ships from assaulting the Ravagers. The Ravagers have to get off the planet."

"What about the platoons?" Rhinehart asked.

Rhodes cast one backward glance at The Grid. Every platoon in Thaklia was pinned down.

"Taking out the base ships is the best way to help the platoons," Rhodes replied. "The Ravagers won't be able to evacuate any platoons if the ships can't land. Let's go. We need to get underneath the base ships and fire Vipers into them from below."

"Below—how?" Thackery asked. "The base ships sit right on the ground."

"Exactly. Copy me—and spread out—one Striker to a base ship. Then circle back and eliminate the others."

Chapter 3

R hodes tilted Rio down toward the ground, picked up speed, and let gravity take over.

The Emal base ships saw the Striker group moving in. Sure enough, the Emal turned their lasers on the incoming battalion, but that only played into Rhodes's hands.

He compressed his grid lines into another long, thin, snake, stabbed into the ground at blinding speed, and set off twisting, coiling, and writhing through the soil heading for the nearest base ship.

The battalion scattered in a fan of similar whip lines. They tunneled underground with each Striker heading for a different base ship.

The base ships cut their fire when the Strikers disappeared. The Emal must not understand what the battalion was trying to do.

The Emal turned their bombardment back on Thaklia. That gave Rhodes and his people a clear run straight to their target ships—and under them.

"Keep going!" Rhodes ordered. "Don't slow down! Fire your Vipers and get clear of the blast!"

He said those words just as he chewed his way under the first base ship. He didn't slow down at all. In fact, he tried to speed up. He had to get away from the ship before it detonated.

He took a split second to fire his Vipers straight up into the ship's underside. He barely made it clear in time before the ship exploded in an almighty thump.

The concussion hit the ground right on top of Rio. The blast knocked the Striker off course, but he and Rhodes were already burrowing farther away.

The base ship erupted in a rippling fireball. More explosions went off all over the planes as each member of the battalion fired underneath their target ships.

The surviving ships wheeled their laser cannons backward trying to defend themselves, but they couldn't see their enemy.

The *Ero* and the other surviving Ravagers gunned their engines and launched into orbit to rejoin the Legion fleet waiting there.

Rhodes didn't give himself a chance to check the position or status of the stranded platoons. He couldn't help them.

This was turning into an exact repeat of every other planet the Legion tried to defend against Emal invasion.

Every one of those battles ended the same way—with dozens of Legion soldiers trapped, stranded, and dying on the ground with no hope of rescue.

Rhodes couldn't stop that now. He might be able to slow it down a little bit.

Then again, he might not be able to slow it down at all. In fact, he became more certain with every passing minute that he couldn't.

These implants didn't change the outcome of the entire war. Nothing could change that. What was the point of all this anyway?

He circled back and locked his sights on the next base ship in line. This was all he could do and he would damn well do it.

He finished off another base ship and turned to the last one in line. The rest of the battalion was busy detonating the others in rapid succession.

The last five rotated their laser cannons in all directions trying to target something—anything.

The Emal finally must have figured out that these burrowing objects under the ground were causing all the explosions.

Rhodes and his people had pulled that trick one too many times. Now the Emal got wise to the game.

Rhodes raced through the topsoil heading for the last ship. The few remaining Emal vessels fired into the ground. Their lasers traced back and forth burning deep fissures in the sod.

They tried their best to track the battalion, but each Striker kept dodging underneath another base ship where the cannons couldn't hit them.

A laser scorched Rio in the tail. Rhodes tried to pick up speed and dove under the last ship. It protected him, but that on its own presented a problem.

He couldn't shoot into this ship's underside or blow it up as long as he was using it to hide. He had to go out into the open as soon as he unloaded on it.

He fired his Vipers, dove out into the fields, and ran into four more lasers skating all over the place. One of them sliced across the sod right above his head and then the base ship exploded.

Rio screamed out as the heat burned him. "Pull out!" Rhodes ordered. "Everybody out!"

He launched Rio into the air, changed back into a Striker, and put on speed gaining altitude.

He made it thirty feet off the ground before he saw the battle. He'd gotten so distracted by destroying the base ships that he didn't see the situation in Thaklia until now. He didn't see anything beyond the few inches of Grid right in front of his nose.

The *Ero* and the other Ravagers made it off the planet just fine. They hovered in orbit with the rest of the Aemon Legion fleet. None of those ships came down to the ground. They stayed out of Emal weapons range.

That left the grounded platoons completely cut off. None of the Ravagers descended even to offer the platoons any support. Forget about evacuating. The Legion really planned to leave these soldiers here to die.

The battalion burst out of the ground heading for the clouds. Rio and the other Strikers could rendezvous with the *Ero*. Rhodes and his people could go into their conversion cycles and forget all about the Sulia campaign.

A smart man would have done exactly that. Rhodes got a hundred feet off the ground and his vision widened to take in the rest of The Grid—the parts he ignored while he attacked the base ships.

The battalion took out the base ships. They no longer bombarded the city from afar, but they'd already done untold damage.

Only a few charred hulks remained standing in a landscape of rubble, smoking, twisted embers, and crushed bodies.

The base ships left plenty of Emal swarming all over the city. The 249th, 278th, and 217th Platoons fell back before the alien onslaught.

The platoons leap-frogged one painstaking mile after another trying to get back to the western side of town.

None of the commanders in charge of those platoons realized the awful truth yet. The Ravagers weren't waiting for them there to save these platoons.

The 249th took shelter behind a debris mound, fired at the advancing Emal, and held the aliens down while the 278th and the 217th retreated behind the 249th.

Then the 217th found a line of fortifications where a tall building had toppled onto its side. Its few remaining walls offered enough protection for the platoon to set up another defense point there.

They opened fire on the Emal and gave the 249th cover to retreat. The three platoons jumped each other's position one after another, but nothing they did stopped the Emal. Nothing could.

Rhodes reacted without thinking. Captain Ackerman made a big noise about Rhodes and the battalion leaving these platoons stranded. Now Ackerman was the one doing it.

Rhodes twisted the grid lines into another many-jointed bounding spider, sprang off the ground, and vaulted straight into the city.

This form could cover the distance almost as fast as an airborne Striker. He leapt off walls, buildings, and over the rubble piles. He sailed from one mound to another barely touched the ground.

The battalion charged in behind him. He didn't take the time to check their vital signs. He already knew it was bad, but it wouldn't get any better by running away. What difference did eight weeks matter either way?

He adjusted his weapons configuration and extended his lasers, thermal cannons, scourge guns, and seeker missiles—one weapon from each of his multiple limbs.

He charged up behind the Emal and opened fire on them. Other monsters in different forms fanned down the Emal line carving a path through them.

"Get Ackerman down here NOW!!" Rhodes called to Fisher. "Tell him the base ships are gone. Now's his chance to do the right thing by lifting off these crews!"

"You heard what Wild said!" Fisher hollered back. "The Legion doesn't want to pull out just yet."

"Tell him to get down here or General Brewster will hear about Ackerman abandoning our battalion down here without evacuation," Rhodes fired back.

None of the SAMs said anything else to protest. Rhodes and his people were too busy mowing down Emal as fast as they could go.

The Emal turned back to defend themselves. That gave the platoons the time they needed to stream through the streets. The platoons didn't have to slow down to find sheltered points.

The soldiers picked up speed and eventually took off running. They stopped and looked around in despair when they saw the hulks of dozens of burned-out Ravagers waiting for them.

The soldiers floundered in confusion for a minute. Some of them even looked behind them into the city, but the Emal were too busy fighting the battalion.

Rhodes crawled closer behind the Emal's position. He savored the feeling of using his lasers to carve these aliens to pieces the way they carved him to pieces.

He shouldn't have thought of the Emal like that. They weren't evil. They just wanted their territory back—territory the Treaty of Aemon Cluster stole from them. He couldn't blame the Emal for that.

His feelings got away from him. These were the cocksuckers who tried to tear his implants out. They would have killed him to take the implants' technology.

The Emal didn't even know how to use the implants' technology. They probably just wanted to study it.

How much differently would the Emal act if they knew these nine individuals were the only ones of their kind in the whole Legion?

How much more dangerous would the Emal become to Battalion 1 once the Emal figured out these nine were the only ones out there?

The Legion pinned all its hopes on Battalion 1. The Emal could eliminate the Legion's most powerful weapons by killing these nine soldiers.

The Emal wouldn't care about stealing the implant technology then. The Emal probably wouldn't have wasted their time and effort capturing the battalion. The aliens would have killed Rhodes and his people on the spot.

Thinking that made him attach the Emal twice as hard, but he still couldn't defeat them by slicing down hundreds of the aliens in front of him.

More would come. The Emal could always send more.....and more.....and more.

Bodies and flying limbs soared out of the mass of aliens in front of him. Blood and gore soaked the ground under his feet, but he still couldn't see the end of the swarm.

The Emal abandoned the platoons and surged back on the battalion. The Emal already knew the platoons were helpless, trapped, and powerless to defend themselves.

The Emal could cut down Legion platoons any time they wanted to. The Emal did it all the time. They'd been doing it one planet after another ever since they first invaded.

Rhodes advanced a little further. His fury and adrenaline pushed him to the breaking point, but he couldn't keep this up forever. He already sensed his energy fading. He used his last shred of strength to save these soldiers.

At that moment, the *Ero* plummeted out of orbit coming in fast. The platoons erupted in cheers and charged out onto the western planes to race on board the ship.

Rhodes couldn't stop shooting at the Emal—not that he tried too hard. His brain refused to shut down.

He didn't think he could even concentrate well enough to adjust the grid lines to change himself back into a Striker.

He was already entering an altered state of consciousness—if he hadn't been in one all along.

The edges of his vision contracted a little more. His awareness of the wider battle shrank. Was he about to pass out right now?

Rio took over, flexed his jointed legs, and rocketed out of the battle heading for orbit. The rest of the battalion did the same thing.

The SAMs transformed back into Strikers burning a vapor trail away from Sulia to rejoin the Legion fleet.

Chapter 4

Rio and the other Strikers gained altitude leaving Sulia behind. Battalion 1 had to wait there with the rest of the Legion fleet while five Ravagers touched down on the planes west of Thaklia, took the stranded platoons on board, and then launched.

The Emal surged westward trying to catch up with the fleeing platoons, but Battalion 1 bought the platoons enough time to load up first.

The Emal bombarded the Ravagers with lasers, but all five zoomed away out of sight before the Emal could do any more damage.

"That looks like the end of that city," Dietz muttered. "What a colossal waste."

"Captain Ackerman is sending us clearance to rendezvous and land on board the *Ero*," Rio reported.

"How generous of him," Wild growled.

Rhodes tried to answer, but his voice and his brain wouldn't connect with each other. Now he felt really sick.

He must have passed out for a few seconds—or longer. He came to his senses sitting in the cockpit while Rio and the other Strikers sat parked in the *Ero's* landing bay.

They were alone. None of the platoon soldiers were here anymore.

Rhodes couldn't get himself to sit up, stand up, or even disconnect himself from his Striker to disembark. He didn't dare to use The Grid to check how bad his injuries were.

He must have faded out again, because when he opened his eyes, he discovered Rhinehart bending over the cockpit. The cover was open.

"We're taking you to your capsule, Captain," Fisher told Rhodes. "Then you can sleep."

Rhodes tried to say something, but a wave of brutal pain gripped him all over when Rhinehart lifted Rhodes's shredded body out of the Striker.

Rhodes heard himself screaming. He really wished he could pass out again, but this time, he stayed conscious for the whole horrible ordeal.

Rhinehart lifted him down to the floor, tried once to set Rhodes on his feet, and Rhodes's knees buckled.

He had trouble dragging his vision into focus. For the few seconds when he could actually make out the rest of the bay, he spotted some members of the *Ero* medical staff standing off to one side.

Their expressions told him all he needed to know.

Rhinehart changed his grid lines into another jointed arthropod-type creature. The medical staff drew back grimacing in terror, but the battalion ignored them.

Rhinehart picked up Rhodes and carried him through the ship to the hold the battalion used as their barracks.

Rhinehart lowered Rhodes into his capsule. "Rest easy, Captain," Rhinehart told him. "We'll see you on the other side."

Rhodes didn't ask what that meant. He didn't expect to survive this.

At least he wouldn't have to wake up from this nightmare. He would go to sleep and stay that way—forever. What a blessed relief that would be.

Rhinehart straightened up and the capsule cover started to close. Rhodes didn't see any of the rest of his people. They must have all gotten into their capsules, too. They needed it. They were all as injured as he was if not worse.

Rhodes stared up through the transparent cover at Rhinehart standing by his bed. Bruises, torn flesh, dried blood, and exposed bone showed around Rhinehart's facial implants. How bad were his injuries?

Right then, the prongs locked into Rhodes's head and body. He jolted from the intense charge taking hold of him.

He closed his eyes and lost sight of Rhinehart. Rhodes couldn't lose sight of Fisher, though.

The SAM hovered in front of Rhodes's vision—where Rhodes couldn't ignore him even when Rhodes closed his eyes.

Rhodes didn't want to ignore Fisher—not anymore.

Rhodes took a deep, shuddering breath. Even breathing hurt.

"Just in case I don't see you again....." Rhodes husked. "I want to tell you.....thank you for your help down there, pal—and for all your help—with everything. I would appreciate it if you could interface with Rio and thank him for me, too."

"You're welcome, Captain." Fisher cocked his head to one side. His bright eyes drilled Rhodes with unusual intensity. "You will survive this, Captain. We will see each other again."

"Well.....thank you anyway. I don't know what I would have done down there without you. I really thought I was going to lose it when I couldn't hear you."

Fisher smiled. He had a calm, steadfast, reassuring smile. He didn't blush or squirm or smirk like a person would when someone complimented them.

"It is very nice to hear you say so, Captain," Fisher murmured.

Rhodes sank deeper into the bed. Relief flooded him—but he also felt the pain more acutely now than he did in the heat of battle.

Pounding, bone-crushing agony washed through his chest and midsection. That pain escalated with every passing minute.

He tried to tell Fisher that he really needed to pass out now, but just then, the conversion cycle started and Rhodes lost consciousness for real.

He woke up in the hospital. He was lying in a different capsule, so he must have been back at Coleridge Station.

He felt much worse than he had when he woke up from every other conversion cycle. He felt much worse than he did when he first woke up from stasis.

The pain in his body had only faded slightly. It didn't drive him insane. It just gnawed at him with a constant, maddening ache—as if it would never go away.

Maybe it wouldn't. Maybe he would stay like this forever, too. That would be the cherry on top of the cake—if this mind-numbing pain nagged him every waking minute for the rest of his life on top of the rage and frustration caused by his implants.

He didn't try to sit up. He just lay on his back hating his life. Not even the curiosity of wondering how his subordinates were doing could make him get up.

He was still lying there when Fisher expanded from his usual place at the corner of Rhodes's vision.

"Welcome back, Captain," Fisher murmured. "Your systems are registering a physical pain response."

"No shit, pal," Rhodes snarled.

Fisher cocked his head the other way. "You are in emotional distress due to your physical pain response. I'll alert the medical team."

Rhodes looked away, but of course Fisher never went away. "How are the others? Are they okay?"

"They are all in recovery the same way you are. Dietz, Oakes, and Rhinehart are all out of their conversion cycles. Rhinehart is still in bed, though. The others are all still in their conversion cycles. Their records indicate the medical staff is still working to repair the damage to their implants and organic tissues before waking them up."

Rhodes snorted. "Did Dietz suffer any damage at all? Did the Emal damage him when they tried to remove his implants?"

Fisher angled his head to the other side. He examined Rhodes extra closely. "Why do you ask that? Of course Dietz suffered damage. Everyone did."

"What damage did he suffer?"

"The Emal removed one of his legs and also tore the implants out of one of his arms. His records indicate he suffered a severe pain response both under the Emal's treatment and when the doctors reattached the implants."

Rhodes looked away again and compressed his lips to stop himself from saying anything. He didn't want to talk about Dietz—probably because Rhodes didn't know what to think about Dietz.

Dietz was the one who got Rhodes on board Rio after the base ships took out the whole battalion. Everyone in the battalion was alive right now because of Dietz.

Why did Rhodes think the Emal would spare Dietz? Why did Rhodes delude himself into thinking Dietz suffered any less than the rest of his comrades?

No one deserved to suffer the way they did at the Emal's hands. Nothing Dietz had ever done earned him that kind of torture.

Fisher didn't pry any further into Rhodes's thoughts on the subject of Dietz. Fisher had been privy to all Rhodes's conversations with his subordinates about Dietz. Fisher already knew what Rhodes thought about Dietz—the good and the bad.

"The question is what we can do about your physical pain response," Fisher went on.

"Is there anything we can do about it?" Rhodes groaned. "I should know better even than to ask that."

"The swelling around your implants may subside in time...."

"Which is another way of saying it may *not* subside in time," Rhodes interrupted.

Fisher adjusted his position and pulled up a Grid outline of Rhodes's body. Fisher rotated it and pivoted it in front of Rhodes's eyes.

"Your implants all appear to be functioning within normal parameters...."

"I've heard that before."

"Therefore, we should conclude that the problem lies in your organic tissue."

"Can you detect anything about that that *isn't* functioning within normal parameters?" Rhodes asked.

"Only the swelling I mentioned."

"Can't you give me something to take the edge off the pain? Can't you just dial down my pain response—or give me an analgesic or something?"

"I can't, but the doctors may be able to. You can ask them yourself. They're on their way here now."

Rhodes shut his eyes and turned his head away. "I can't wait."

"You don't have to wait. I just told you they're on their way here. They'll be here in less than two minutes."

"It's an expression, pal. It means I'm really starting to dread ever seeing any doctor ever again. It seems like, no matter what they do, they only wind up making the problem worse."

"I don't see how they can make the problem worse by lessening your pain," Fisher remarked. "Anything is better than this."

Rhodes gulped down the urge to lose his shit again. This pain wasn't as bad as it had been during the battle on Sulia.

The constant, unrelenting ache somehow made it so much worse. He would almost rather have his implants torn out for real than live with this.

Chapter 5

Rhodes really, really didn't want to see Drs. Neiland, Irvine, and Montague again. He couldn't decide which was worse—living with this gnawing pain or submitting to whatever moronic plan the doctors came up with to try to improve his state.

He shut his eyes again when the door opened and footsteps crossed the floor coming closer. He had no choice but to open his eyes again when the footsteps stopped next to his capsule.

He blinked for a second when he looked up at two completely different doctors. One was a tall man in his thirties.

He had sandy brown hair, pale blue eyes, and freckles, but he didn't look like an overgrown child like General Brewster.

This man had a serious air like Colonel Kraft's. This doctor didn't act at all delighted to be dealing with Battalion 1.

The other doctor was much younger. He couldn't have been over thirty. He looked like he might be twenty-six or twenty-seven at the most.

He had plain brown hair, soft brown eyes, olive skin, and a deep, thoughtful expression. He studied Rhodes way too closely—almost as if this kid could see everything going through Rhodes's mind.

"Good morning, Captain," the older doctor began. "How are you feeling today?"

"I'm in pain—and who the hell are you? I've never seen you before."

"I'm Dr. Nicholas Osborne. This is Dr. Felix Trudeau. We both just joined the Battalion 1 project. We've been assigned to monitor your recovery on our final approach to Coleridge Station....."

Rhodes's head shot up. "I'm not at Coleridge Station now?"

"No, you and the rest of your battalion are still on board the *Ero*. Your injuries were too severe for you to survive the trip in stasis, so General Brewster sent us out to treat your injuries, repair your implants, and monitor your recovery on our last week's approach to the station."

"So.....you're going to hand us back over to Montague, Irvine, and Neiland as soon as we get there? Is that it?" Rhodes asked.

"Dr. Trudeau and I will stay on the Battalion 1 medical staff once we arrive at the station. We're permanently assigned to the project going forward."

Rhodes studied both men. Did they get taken from their families just like Colonel Kraft and everyone else? Was that the hidden subtext Dr. Osborne wasn't saying out loud?

He hesitated and then went on, "If you'll allow me to examine you, I'll determine where the pain is and hopefully we can do something to relieve it."

Rhodes clenched his teeth and looked away. "Fine. The pain is everywhere—in all my implants—all the implants below my neck, that is."

Osborne bent over the control panel on the side of Rhodes's capsule and started pressing buttons. "Your systems are all reading within normal parameters besides that."

"I know that," Rhodes snarled. "My SAM already told me."

Osborne looked up and his eyes brightened. "What else did your SAM tell you?"

"He said you might be able to either dial down my pain response or give me an analgesic for it."

Osborne frowned at his controls. Trudeau tapped away on a remote device. "There is still quite a bit of swelling in your organic tissues."

Rhodes locked his jaws to stop himself from saying that he already knew that, too. This pain really aggravated his nerves. The fuse on his temper was rapidly burning down to a volcanic eruption.

Osborne crossed the room and adjusted something on a panel of computer components attached to the wall.

Rhodes shut his eyes and turned away. He didn't need to see this. He no longer trusted anyone on the Battalion 1 medical staff to do jack shit for him.

He stiffened when Trudeau put his device aside and bent over Rhodes's capsule. Trudeau brought out another device and moved two electrodes close to Rhodes's chest.

Rhodes had developed a pathological revulsion of these devices and the people attached to them, but he was too weak to fight back.

He just had to lie there and take it while Trudeau fiddled with something on Rhodes's chest plate.

He jolted when the electrodes touched his implants and then a rush of sweet relief nearly made him collapse as the pain faded.

"There are some misaligned components in your peripheral processing core," Trudeau murmured under his breath.

He had a soft, gentle, thoughtful way of speaking—almost like he was talking to himself or someone Rhodes couldn't see.

"The components aren't registering sensation properly. We can modify that so they don't feed you such a powerful physical pain response to the swelling in your organic tissue."

Trudeau straightened up, made eye contact with Rhodes for a split second, and turned away to go back to working on his remote device.

"The captain's neural core itself has taken damage, too," Osborne called over his shoulder. "The Emal trying to remove it distorted some of the connections. That may be why the core is sending such a strong response."

"He seems like a very good doctor," Fisher remarked. "They both do."

Rhodes didn't answer. He didn't know how much these two doctors understood about the SAMs. He didn't want to start talking to someone they couldn't see.

He also didn't want to start trusting them—or any other doctor. If they fixed him and eased his pain enough for him to function—that was just them doing their job, wasn't it? They had a long way to go to earn his trust.

They kept tinkering with him until Dr. Osborne came back over to Rhodes's capsule. "I think we shouldn't make any further adjustments for today, Captain. If the adjustments we've made just now give you any relief, I think we should leave them and see if anything happens as a result—either good or bad. Do they give you any relief?"

"Yeah," Rhodes murmured. "Yeah, it feels much better."

Osborne consulted his own device. "Your records indicate that most if not all the adjustments and modifications to your systems have caused unforeseen consequences—some of them catastrophic."

"That's one way of putting it."

"Then I suggest we pause and see if these modifications cause any unforeseen consequences, too. If they don't, we can fine-tune later." He frowned at his device some more. "In the meantime, it appears you still have some time before you fully recover. Feel free to stay here—or, if you're feeling strong enough, you can return to your hold."

"Is anyone else down there?" Rhodes thought about it. "I can't interface with the other SAMs."

"The interface is offline for now. We weren't sure if the malfunctions you suffered on Sulia would be transmissible between you and your subordinates. We're keeping the SAMs isolated for now."

"Then how did my SAM know which of my subordinates was out of stasis?" Rhodes asked.

"You would have to ask him, but I suppose he can access the *Ero's* logs, crew rosters, and passenger complements." Osborne put his device down and leveled Rhodes with a direct gaze. "I'm glad you're feeling better. If you need anything, you can contact me through the ship's internal communications system."

He and Trudeau left and Rhodes did his best to relax in his capsule. He still felt terrible, but at least it wasn't as bad as it was just a few minutes before.

"I wish they'd let me interface with the others," he muttered. "I don't like staying isolated."

"Better to stay isolated than for malfunctions to spread through the battalion," Fisher pointed out.

"It would be nice to have something to do. I hate being in the hospital."

Fisher inclined his head to one side. "Your physical pain response is much less now."

"Have you been able to figure out what caused all the malfunctions on the planet?"

"Apart from what we already know about the injuries and damage to everyone's implants? As far as I can tell, the SAMs got scared when their hosts got injured."

"Then why didn't you and Rocky malfunction? Zen didn't malfunction, either."

"Maybe something in our personalities made us more resilient to the situation."

"Are you saying your personality or Zen's personality is more resilient than Dash? Oakes is a hardened soldier. He shouldn't have reacted like that."

"Oakes is, but Dash is brand new. He's never been in combat before."

"What about you?" Rhodes countered. "You've never been in combat before."

In a very rare show of disturbance, Fisher looked away. "I'm afraid it's only a matter of time before I react the same way, Captain. I hate to bring it up when the battalion is already going through so many problems and malfunctions."

Rhodes sighed and shut his eyes again. He could do that without shutting out Fisher. "I've been thinking the same thing."

"So far, all our malfunctions have been mechanical. What happens when I have an emotional malfunction and it affects you? You could become completely incapacitated the same way Oakes did."

"I know," Rhodes murmured. "I guess we just have to deal with it when the time comes."

"It would be better if we found a way to avoid the situation altogether. You malfunctioning in battle puts the whole battalion in danger."

"Me malfunctioning in battle only puts the whole battalion in danger if we all malfunction at the same time," Rhodes pointed out. "One of the others has always pulled me out of it each time."

"So what do we do if it happens to all of you at once?" Fisher asked.

"I wish I knew, pal," Rhodes murmured. "I don't have any answers."

Fisher fell silent. He kept angling his head from one side to the other and studying Rhodes way too closely.

After a few minutes, Fisher shrank to an invisible dot in the corner of Rhodes's field of view. Fisher didn't ask for permission nor did he ask if Rhodes wanted Fisher to go away.

Fisher just did it. He left Rhodes alone with his thoughts.

Good old Fisher. He always sensed when Rhodes needed time to himself.

Fisher was still there. He would always be there, but he disappeared when Rhodes needed him to.

Rhodes didn't realize until now how exhausted he felt. The pain he experienced when he first woke up drained him more than he expected—or maybe he was just still weak and sick from the conversion cycle.

He relaxed in bed without trying to do anything. He didn't want to think, but he found it impossible not to.

He really wished he could talk to his subordinates, even though the interface—but at the same time, he didn't want to talk to anyone. He just wanted to rest and that's what he did.

Chapter 6

Rhodes opened his eyes after another conversion cycle, and after a few more minutes of lying on his back, he pushed himself up to sit on the edge of the mattress.

Fisher didn't reappear. He stayed silent and invisible.

Rhodes sat slumped and looked down at his feet. Now what was he supposed to do?

Fisher still didn't make himself visible. Rhodes would have expected Fisher to make his presence known by now.

He still didn't show up when Rhodes got to his feet and took a few unsteady steps around the room. The doctors put him in a private room by himself. He would have preferred being in the same hold with his subordinates.

The minute he thought that, he accessed the interface with the other SAMs without meaning to. He didn't think he could.

He automatically connected with Dash and Rocky. Interfacing with them caused Rhodes to interface with Oakes and Rhinehart at the same time.

Rhinehart was just sitting up on the edge of his own capsule in another private room in the *Ero's* medical bay.

Dietz and Oakes were in the battalion's capsule hold. Dietz was working on the computer terminal. Oakes sat at the table writing something on a piece of paper.

Rocky turned his horse head in Rhodes's direction. "Captain?" Rocky looked around. "Where's Fisher? He isn't damaged, is he?"

"I'm not sure where he is or what he's doing. He was fine the last time I woke up." Rhodes turned his attention to Rhinehart. "How are you, Lieutenant?"

"I feel like trash, Sir. I really wish I could go back to sleep, but that will only make me feel worse."

"Are you in pain? Is everything working?"

"I'm okay," Rhinehart croaked. "My face hurts, but the doctors say that's just swelling and it will go away."

Rhodes widened his interface. He could access The Grid now, too. He located Rhinehart's room, passed down a corridor, and entered it to find Rhinehart sitting up the way Rhodes had just seen in the interface.

Rhinehart burst into a grin when he saw Rhodes. "I didn't think you'd make it, Sir."

"Neither did I. I might even have wished a few times that I didn't make it."

Rhinehart laughed.

"Thank you for bringing me in," Rhodes went on. "And thank you for taking over when I got hit. It makes me feel better to know I have people like you who can step in if anything happens to me."

Rhinehart curled his lip at the surroundings even though no one was here for him to curl it at. "This operation doesn't inspire a lot of confidence, does it, Sir?"

"No, it doesn't." Rhodes jerked his thumb over his shoulder. "I'm going to check on Dietz and Oaks. Are you feeling strong enough to come with me?"

"I might as well."

Rhinehart heaved his big body off the capsule and hobbled across the room. His presence gave Rhodes another excruciating wave of relief. Someone was back.

Oakes and Dietz were fine, too. Rhodes saw that through the interface. Now the battalion just needed to get the other five back.

Then they'd be in business—but not before the doctors and technicians figured out everything that went wrong during the last battle.

Rhodes and Rhinehart limped out of the medical bay and headed for the battalion's capsule hold.

"Have you heard anything about when the others get out of stasis?" Rhinehart asked.

"I haven't heard anything—but I didn't ask. I've just been trying to get back on my feet myself."

Rhinehart nodded. "Me, too."

"Did the Emal damage your implants at all?" Rhodes narrowed his eyes at Rhinehart's face. "You do still look a little puffy around the eyes."

"I had a splitting headache when I woke up. The doctors thought it was just the swelling, but Rocky said it wasn't. He said it was a problem, so they fixed it." Rhinehart glanced over his shoulder to make sure no one was listening.

The *Ero* crewmen streamed back and forth past the two men. None of the crew so much as glanced at Rhodes and Rhinehart.

"Those two doctors are so much better than the three at Coleridge Station," Rhinehart murmured under his breath. "I'm so glad they're coming back with us."

"We'll still be stuck with Neiland, Montague, and Irvine," Rhodes pointed out. "They aren't going away."

"I wish they were," Rhinehart snarled.

Rhodes didn't get a chance to answer before the two men entered the capsule hold. Oakes jumped up when he saw them. "Sir! I didn't know you were up and around."

He shook hands with both of them and then Oakes and Rhinehart hugged.

Dietz stopped what he was doing and came over to them smiling, but it was a suspicious smile with no warmth in it. He didn't try to get closer to Rhodes or Rhinehart.

"Welcome back, Sir," Dietz began. "It's good to see you back on your feet."

"Thank you, Sergeant—and thank you for helping me on the planet. You saved the whole battalion."

"I've been trying to tell him that," Oakes chimed in. "He won't listen."

Dietz squirmed and shuffled his feet. "Naw. I was just trying to save my own ass and I needed the rest of you to make it happen."

"Well, we all made it back this time," Rhodes cut in. "Let's go down the hall and see what's happening with the others."

Rhodes used his interface to find the rest of his subordinates. For some reason he couldn't figure out, the *Ero* crew put all five of the battalion members in one room together. Rhodes and Rhinehart were the only ones who got private rooms.

It couldn't be because Rhodes's and Rhinehart's injuries were so bad. If that was true, Rhodes would have been the last to wake up.

That didn't matter, though, because they all made it back in one piece—or as good as. Rhodes could accept just about anything else as long as they all survived.

There wasn't a lot to see beyond the readings on each capsule. They all read as normal. The soldiers inside went on sleeping. Rhodes couldn't talk to them.

He wouldn't have been able to do anything if he saw anything wrong with them anyway, but at least he could satisfy himself that all his people were okay.

They would always be okay as long as they lay there sleeping in their capsules.

He wished like anything he could keep them like this. He wished he could protect them and somehow stop the Legion from sending them back into danger.

Nothing would prevent it. These people were alive right now for only one reason—so the Legion could put them in danger again.

Rhodes would rather have gone to face that danger alone if it meant protecting these people. He would gladly have died a thousand times over to protect them from what he knew was coming.

What was coming was a whole lot more of everything that happened on Sulia. The Legion would keep fighting the Emal. It was an unwinnable war.

The Legion would keep throwing their best soldiers in front of the Emal guns which meant the Legion would keep throwing Battalion 1 in front of the Emal guns.

That was Battalion 1's whole reason for being. It was the battalion's only function.

Which was worse—dying on the battlefield or suffering the tortures of the damned both on and off the battlefield?

Would Rhodes be willing to suffer the tortures of the damned to protect his comrades in the 249th?

If someone asked him during his life, he would have replied with an enthusiastic yes. He would have been the first to sign up to suffer any torture to protect even one of them—to give even one of them a chance to get off the battlefield alive.

He lived his life that way and he died that way.

Things sure looked different from this side of the line. He'd been suffering the tortures of the damned ever since he woke up with these implants.

He was the damned now. The whole battalion was. They were writhing in torment in this special little version of Hell.

He was damned to this dimension of Hell for the crime of trying to sacrifice his life to save his comrades in the 249th. That's how he got into this mess in the first place.

Was it really worth it? He was really starting to question that now.

He should have just blown his brains out and gotten it over with if he really wanted to die. He didn't save the 249th from anything. He just signed them up for more hopeless battles against the Emal.

He never would have come here if he did that. He wouldn't have to go through any of this.

Oakes startled Rhodes out of his thoughts by nudging him. "Sir? Are you ready to go?"

Rhodes looked up. He'd been standing next to Lauer's capsule staring down at the man's rough, bearded face.

Rhodes couldn't come to any conclusions here because there were conclusions to come to.

He only had two options—end it or keep going. If he didn't end it, he had to keep going. That was the only truth.

Thinking about ending it accomplished nothing. He wasn't ready for that yet, which meant he had to keep going.

He was just turning away from Lauer's capsule when Fisher expanded from the corner of Rhodes's vision.

Fisher looked around the interface. "Captain! You're awake!" Fisher frowned. "Where are we?"

"We're still on board the *Ero*. The rest of the battalion is still in stasis. Where have you been, Fisher?"

Fisher cocked his head and studied every part of The Grid inside the interface. "I'm not sure, Captain. I didn't realize you were out of stasis. I just came back online this moment and here I am." He scrutinized Rhodes. "How long have you been awake?"

"Only a few minutes. Why did you come online before and not now?" Rhodes asked. "You were fine the first time I woke up."

Fisher inclined his head the other way. "First time? You woke up a first time? So this isn't the first time you've been awake?"

"How could it be when we aren't in the lab?" Rhodes asked. "I'm walking around the station without you. I've been on my own this whole time wondering where you were."

"Ah, yes. Of course." Fisher frowned and looked around in confusion. "I can't explain it, Captain."

"You better not be malfunctioning again." Rhodes turned to the other SAMs. "Are any of you malfunctioning? Have any of you suffered any problems since you woke up?"

"No, nothing," Dash replied. "Everything has been functioning within normal parameters."

"We've been fine, too," Zen added.

Rhodes checked on Rocky. "Do you detect anything out of the ordinary in Rhinehart?"

"I'm still detecting swelling around his facial implants," Rocky replied. "Some of the neural junctions are registering a physical pain response, but other than that, he seems to be fine."

The three men looked fine from the outside. "I don't like this," Rhodes muttered.

"I'm sure it's nothing, Captain," Fisher told him. "I'm back now and I'm functioning normally."

"You aren't functioning normally if you didn't come online when I came out of my conversion cycle. Something isn't right there."

"Don't go looking for problems that aren't there," Oakes chimed in. "Who cares as long as he's working, right?"

Rhodes dropped the subject, but he still didn't like it. The smallest irregularity in any of the SAMs gave him a very bad feeling.

He couldn't do anything about it now. He wouldn't be able to do anything about it until it exploded in his face and the whole nightmare started over again.

He was just about to turn away a second time and leave the lab when Drs. Osborne and Trudeau walked in.

Osborne raised his eyebrows. "Is there a problem?"

"My SAM just came online," Rhodes replied. "I've been walking around the station, talking to my subordinates, and visiting these people while my SAM has been offline. He also doesn't remember when I first came out of stasis. He was working fine then. Now he thinks this is the first time he's come back online. Something's wrong with him."

Trudeau consulted his device. "I'm not reading any malfunction in any of your systems."

"That's what everyone says right before one of us malfunctions," Rhodes fired back.

"It's nothing, Captain," Fisher murmured. "I'm sorry it happened. I'll try not to let it happen again."

"It isn't your fault, pal," Rhodes told him. "This had nothing to do with you."

"We can't do anything about it until something goes really wrong," Osborne replied and turned to the remaining five capsules. "It's time to wake up the others anyway. It's fortunate that you're here now. I'm sure your people will be happy to see you."

Chapter 7

D r. Osbourne went down the line of capsules tapping on one control panel after another. The readings changed and the covers opened.

Rhodes, Rhinehart, Oakes, and Dietz lined up and watched Lauer, Thackery, Henshaw, Fuentes, and Coulter start to stir.

They groaned, rubbed their heads, and asked where they were. The two doctors explained it to them.

They eventually sat up enough to look around and see their comrades standing there waiting for them.

Lauer heaved a heavy sigh. "Captain! I thought you were dead."

"No such luck, Lieutenant."

Lauer snorted. "Maybe we all would have been better off."

Osborne walked away. "Everything seems to be functioning within normal parameters. You can take the battalion back to the capsule hold. We'll be landing at Colcridge Station in a few days. Once we get there, we'll run some more tests to find out what caused you all to malfunction on the battlefield. You can rest and recover until then."

He and Trudeau left. Lauer glared after them. "Who the hell are they?"

"Two new doctors on the Battalion 1 project," Rhodes replied. "They seem like they're all right."

"They aren't all right if they're doctors on the Battalion 1 project," Lauer snarled. "They'll just screw things up the same as ever."

"I'm sure things are screwed up enough on their own, Lieutenant," Rhodes replied. "Come on. Let's get out of here."

He checked each person and each SAM, but Osborne was right. Everyone seemed to be working the way they should.

The five patients got painfully to their feet and hobbled back to the capsule hold where they all went straight back to their capsules.

Rhodes and Rhinehart joined Dietz and Oakes at the table. "What have you two been doing to occupy your time while the rest of us have been asleep?" Rhodes asked.

Oakes shrugged. "Not much of anything. There isn't a lot to do around here—the same way there isn't a lot to do at Coleridge Station."

"I've been keeping track of my family through the terminal," Dietz replied. "I might not be able to communicate with them, but I can keep an eye on them from afar. It's better than nothing."

Rhodes glanced over at him. Rhodes realized in that moment that he'd never taken the time to find out if Dietz even had a family.

Why wouldn't he? He must have some relatives out there somewhere.

Why did Rhodes go out of his way to dehumanize Dietz? Rhodes didn't understand himself.

He'd been too consumed with finding everything wrong with Diez even to ask the most obvious question.

Rhinehart stared at Dietz, too. "Damn, man! Good idea! Why didn't I think of that? I should have checked on them before. I could have been seeing everything they're doing!"

Oakes grimaced and looked away. "I don't know how you can stand it. I can't look. I don't want to see what they're doing. It's bad enough just knowing they're out there."

"The system loads up pictures and everything," Dietz added. "It's the next best thing to being there."

"But it isn't being there," Oakes argued. "We can never be there ever again. How do you live with that?"

Dietz shrugged. "I wasn't there when I was deployed with the Legion, either. I lived through pictures from home and watching them on the terminals. It isn't so much different now. We sent letters back and forth—but not very often. I can trick myself into thinking I just sent them a letter and it's been a while and they just don't have time to write back—or they already wrote me and I don't have time to write back. It's not that much different."

"It's different," Oakes snarled. "It's very different."

"No one is asking you to look," Rhodes told him. "If you don't want to look, don't look."

Oakes turned on him. "I don't see you looking."

Now it was Rhodes's turn to look away. "No, I couldn't look."

Oakes waved at Rhodes and pointed at Dietz. "You see? I'm not the only one. Do you think I want to see my wife getting together with another man? Do you think I want to see obituaries for my parents dying and school reports of my son getting in trouble for getting in fights?"

"So you're just gonna live without it?" Dietz asked. "How do you live with that?"

Oakes glared at him for a split second, stood up, and stormed out of the hold. He switched off the interface so none of the others could see where he was going.

Rhinehart sat silently through the whole argument. Dietz glanced over at Rhodes. "It isn't like he can say I'm doing anything wrong by looking."

"No, you aren't. I can't fault you for wanting to stay in touch, even from a distance. You keep doing your own thing. He'll deal with it in his own way."

"Or not," Rhinehart murmured.

"Just do what you gotta do." Rhodes stood up. "It's going to be hard on all of us. Just do whatever you have to do to cope with it. None of us can ask for anything better than that."

He would have liked to leave the hold, but he didn't want to go anywhere near the *Ero* crew.

Their reaction—or non-reaction—unnerved Rhodes more than the soldiers' hostility. He would rather have someone outright hating him than ignoring him and pretending he didn't exist.

Oakes was right. There was just as little to do here as anywhere else. Dietz went back to work on the terminal. Oakes returned half an hour later and went back to writing something on a piece of paper.

Rhinehart went into The Grid where Rocky showed him a detailed schematic of all Rhinehart's implants.

They held a long, complicated conversation about how all Rhinehart's components worked, how the fusion generator fed power to Rhinehart's implants, and how it reproduced Rhinehart's weapons so fast.

Rhodes should have listened. He'd always wondered about this stuff, but he couldn't get interested in it.

It would have been more accurate to say the subject made him sick. The revulsion and fury he felt when he first woke up—it started to creep back into his soul.

He didn't realize it until he and the rest of the battalion woke up from their next conversion cycle.

Thackery, Henshaw, Coulter, Lauer, and Fuentes woke up, too. The whole battalion was back together again.

Rhodes sat on the edge of his capsule and stared at his mechanical feet. He hated them. He hated everything about this life. He hated himself most of all.

Being this half-robot infuriated him. How dare the Legion do this to him?

He seethed in silent fury....and then he realized. He'd been calm yesterday. He'd been fine while he visited his subordinates in the lab. He didn't hate himself then—not any more than he already did.

He stood up and turned from right to left. The feeling didn't go away.

He wanted to destroy something. He wanted to pulverize every one of these capsules and tear each of his subordinates apart to stop this project before it got any worse.

This hold didn't have a washroom, so he crossed the room to the terminal desk. No one was using it.

He sat down and programmed it to make the screen a reflective surface. He stared at his reflection.

The sight of his implants sent him into a rage. He stood up so fast that he kicked the chair over.

He didn't bother to pick it up. He stormed across the hold and paced back and forth. He had to get rid of this rage somehow.

He scrambled for some way to do it safely. He couldn't come up with any idea other than going to the training room and going into some Grid battle scenario.

Not even that would satisfy him. Nothing would satisfy him other than killing everyone involved in this project.

Fisher expanded himself in front of Rhodes's eyes. "Good morning, Captain. I trust you had a good conversion cycle."

"Something's wrong, Fisher," Rhodes snarled through gritted teeth. "I'm having an emotional disturbance."

Fisher cocked his head. "I'm not detecting any malfunction...."

"WILL YOU STOP SAYING THAT?!!" Rhodes thundered.

Everyone else in the hold jumped, spun around, and stared at him. Rhodes wheeled away, but there was nowhere to go. He was stuck with this.

His fury broke his ability to control it and he lashed out for a split second before he found a way to stop himself. He punched his fist at the only target available.

His knuckles smashed the concrete wall next to him. That impact brought him back from the brink just enough to stop himself from hitting anything else.

He would have liked to smash the whole *Ero* to pieces. He would have liked to kill everyone on board.

This rage bursting out of him right now—it just kept escalating. It built with every passing second.

He clenched his teeth and snarled in a deadly undertone. He didn't trust himself to speak any louder than that. "I'm telling you something's wrong," he muttered.

"I believe you, Captain," Fisher replied in his calmest, most soothing murmur. "I'm alerting Dr. Osborne. He's on his way now."

Rhodes clamped his mouth shut to stop himself from answering. He didn't trust Dr. Osborne nor did Rhodes trust himself around Dr. Osborne.

Thank the stars that Dr. Neiland, Dr. Irvine, nor Dr. Montague was here—or General Brewster. Rhodes really would have lost it on any of them.

"Your stress levels are reading somewhat similarly to what they were when you first came online at Coleridge Station," Fisher informed him while they waited. "They're elevated, but they're still within normal parameters."

"They aren't within normal parameters!" Rhodes spat.

"I realize that, Captain," Fisher breathed. "I'm sure the doctors will do everything possible to eliminate the cause of the stress."

Rhodes already knew they wouldn't. They would have to remove his implants to eliminate the cause of the stress.

He didn't say that out loud. Rhinehart, Oakes, and Lauer gathered around Rhodes. "What's wrong, Captain?" Lauer asked.

"I'm malfunctioning," Rhodes growled through gritted teeth. "Fisher called Dr. Osborne."

Rhinehart accessed the interface and immediately switched it off when he felt Rhodes's fury. "Holy shit! This is bad!"

"If one of us is malfunctioning, we can expect others to malfunction, too," Oakes decided. "We're going to have to keep a close eye on things."

"Maybe this has something to do with the delay when Fisher came back online," Rhinehart suggested. "Fisher was the only SAM who suffered a delay. Maybe this will stay isolated to the captain."

"I'm not detecting any malfunction in my programming," Fisher remarked.

Thackery, Henshaw, Fuentes, and Coulter gathered around, too, but just then, Drs. Osborne and Trudeau rolled in.

Rhodes had to fight himself all the way down the corridor to the lab. "It's getting worse," he snarled through locked teeth. "You might need to take me offline."

Osborne paused in the middle of the corridor and raised his device. He opened his mouth to say, "I don't think that's necessary....."

Rhodes overreacted again, seized the doctor by the elbow, and marched him the rest of the way to the lab.

Rhodes saw himself acting violently toward the one man who was supposed to be helping him. Rhodes couldn't stop himself, though.

Rhodes felt the last shreds of his self-control starting to disintegrate. He shoved Osborne into the lab a lot harder than he should have.

Osborne stumbled once and spun around to confront Rhodes—as if Osborne would be able to stop Rhodes if he did try something.

Trudeau hung back out of range and stared at Rhodes with huge eyes.

Osborne tried to play it off and waved toward the stool next to his computer components. "Take a seat, Captain. We can work this out."

Rhodes ignored the gesture and crossed instead to the capsule standing on the other side of the room. It was the same capsule Rhodes had been using while he was in stasis.

He sat down and started to stretch out. "What are you doing, Captain?" Osborne asked. "You don't need to go into another conversion cycle."

"I'm going to kill someone if I stay like this." Rhodes waved him away. "Get to work and fix it. I don't care what you have to do. Take me offline if you have to. You'll be able to do it quicker if I'm like this."

The prongs stabbed into Rhodes's head and back. He wilted in relief when they locked him in place. He couldn't go anywhere now.

He could have unlocked himself if he really wanted to, but he finally got the message across to the two doctors.

They gaped at him in horrified disbelief for a second and then attacked their machines.

Trudeau made the first move by immobilizing Rhodes. He wouldn't be able to get up now even if he wanted to.

ler kept rotating right and left looking at nothing on Rhodes's internal Grid. "I'm still not detecting any unusual brain wave patterns."

"Maybe the problem is in your programming," Rhodes muttered. "Did you ever think of that, pal?"

Osborne turned around and raised his eyebrows. "What programming?"

Rhodes had to take a deep, steadying breath before he trusted himself to speak. "Check Fisher's programming functions first. He didn't come back online when I woke up from my second conversion cycle. He was offline for almost twenty minutes and he didn't remember me coming out of stasis. Maybe the malfunction is with him."

"I think I found the problem," Trudeau announced without turning around. "The SAM's interface with your behavioral protocol is feeding back on itself. It's only supposed to allow him to monitor your emotional state for any disturbance. Now it's feeding back and causing the disturbance he's supposed to detect."

"That explains why he can't detect it," Rhodes muttered.

Fisher cocked his head to one side. "Are you sure about this, Captain? I don't like the doctors tinkering with my programming."

"Now you know how I feel, pal," Rhodes snarled.

"I'm removing the distortion and correcting the feedback," Trudeau reported. "Let me know if it gets any better."

It did. The rage started to fade and Rhodes sank back on the mattress with a shuddering sigh.

The feeling of wanting to wreck something didn't go away, though—not completely. It dwindled to a low, simmering resentment against everyone and everything involved in this project, including Rhodes himself.

Trudeau finally turned around to study Rhodes. "Is that any better?"

Rhodes couldn't look at this kid. "I guess so."

"Do you feel like sitting up, Captain?" Osborne asked.

Rhodes didn't want to sit up. He didn't want to do anything. He hated everything about this.

Did that hatred come from Fisher's malfunction—or just from the nightmarish reality itself? How could this resentment ever go away when Rhodes really did resent the project?

He couldn't stay in this lab for the rest of his life, so he sat up on the edge of the capsule.

He was just about to push himself to his feet when a high-pitched scream stabbed him in the brain.

In a split second, all the other SAMs interfaced with him. The battalion had slackened their habit of always staying interfaced with each other to keep an eye on each other.

Everyone in the battalion had been on constant watch for any malfunction. All of that went out the window when they got injured on Sulia.

Waking up from such a long conversion cycle broke the routine. Everyone stayed out of each other's heads while each person went through their own personal recovery.

Now all the SAMs burst into Rhodes's head in an instant—and they all malfunctioned at the same time.

Henshaw kept screaming in Rhodes's ear. Each of the SAMs malfunctioned in a different way. Each malfunction affected that individual differently.

Keon's grid lines kept twisting across his face, distorting the SAM's panda appearance, reforming, and smearing somewhere else.

Henshaw collapsed on her knees in the capsule hold, clutched her head, and screamed herself hoarse every time Keon's grid lines changed his appearance.

Rocky bared his teeth and snarled at Rhinehart through The Grid. The horse head sprouted fangs and its eyes stretched upward into two glowing red slits.

Rocky bared his teeth at Rhinehart until he backed away. He bumped into the wall, but he couldn't get away from his murderous SAM.

Oakes projected a Grid copy of himself into the interface. The lines that formed the copy's outline snatched Dash out of thin air and the two figures wrestled, yanked, and fought each other inside The Grid.

Coulter collapsed on the hold floor spasming, twitching, and convulsing in pain. Murphy hovered there in space watching Coulter howling in torment. Murphy didn't react. He didn't do a thing to intervene or to help Coulter.

Fuentes huddled in a ball the way he did when he first woke up. He sat on the table, pulled his knees to his chest, and cast terrified glances at the rest of the battalion.

Crushing fear, self-hatred, and revulsion flooded Rhodes coming from Fuentes. Van hovered in front of his eyes yelling at him in some language Rhodes couldn't understand. It didn't sound like any Preinean language he'd ever heard before.

Rhodes tried not to see all his subordinates suffering these catastrophic malfunctions all at the same time.

His hands flew to his head, but the agony and torture overwhelming each of them rushed back on him. He grimaced as all their pain and distress hit him full force.

He'd never shared his subordinates' thoughts or emotions like this. Now it all poured through the interface. He felt everything as if it came from himself.

Trudeau rushed him. "What's wrong?"

"They're malfunctioning!" Rhodes choked and groaned as a torrential wave of physical pain smashed into him. It came from Coulter.

Osborne sprang back to his controls. "Who is malfunctioning?"

"All of them!" Rhodes fought to breathe. "They're......" He broke off in a scream of terror coming from Henshaw.

Osborne and Trudeau scrambled over their machines. "I'm not picking up anything...." Osborne began.

Rhodes cut him off with a roar as Dash overcame Oakes's grid lines. Dash extended his own lines to surround Oakes, wrestled him to the floor, and Dash started throttling Oakes to a bloody pulp.

Dash expanded to a huge size. His grid lines stretched and formed whipping alien limbs that strangled Oakes, pounded him into the floor, and started burrowing into Oakes's mouth.

"Shut them down!" Rhodes bellowed. "Shut them down now!"

"WHO!!" Osborne yelled back.

"All of them! Shut down all of them—NOW!"

Trudeau hovered in front of Rhodes's eyes trying to examine him. Rhodes barely saw him, and right at that moment, Fisher transformed in front of Rhodes's face.

Fisher had been hanging there in his usual place. Now he morphed into a monster as hideous as any Rhodes had ever seen. Fisher grew fangs, his eyes stretched out to become pointed slits, and he rushed Rhodes with all those teeth bared.

Rhodes screamed again and reared back to get away from the SAM. The next minute, another catastrophic surge of fury seized Rhodes. This dwarfed anything he experienced before.

He lunged for the SAM to kill it no matter what. Rhodes broke away from the prongs holding him down, shot out his arms, and levitated off the bed trying to seize Fisher before the SAM killed him first.

Rhodes became distantly aware in some other part of his brain that his mechanical hands were closing on Trudeau instead.

At that moment, something happened outside Rhodes's awareness and he lost consciousness completely.

Chapter 8

Rhodes woke up and instantly recognized Dr. Neiland's lab at Coleridge Station. He collapsed back on the mattress in his capsule. He couldn't decide if he was happy about being back here.

He groaned when he remembered everything that happened on the *Ero*. Sweet Jesus! Could he and his subordinates look forward to more of this....well, forever?

What if the doctors and technicians never worked out all the bugs in the Battalion 1 project? What if Rhodes and his people kept suffering from these malfunctions for as long as they survived this disaster?

Why would it be any different? Implanting these devices into living tissue couldn't end well. It would always cause problems, either physically or mentally.

The human body and mind weren't designed for this. The battalion members' bodies and minds would continue to reject the new reality.

Then there were the SAMs. Just how much of this had to do with them?

How much control did they really have over each battalion member's behavior and thought process? Did it even matter anymore which of them malfunctioned or why?

The SAMs weren't alive. They might be self-aware, but they weren't human. Whatever else they might be, their thought processes were incompatible with human nature.

They couldn't possibly be anything else. They were machines—computer programs. The two systems would always conflict.

Rhodes didn't understand much about the Battalion 1 project, but he understood one thing. Whoever designed this whole lunatic scheme didn't plan for the SAMs to have to deal with strong, raw human emotions.

Whatever genius came up with this must have thought the battalion members would have no emotional reaction to anything that happened to them.

Whoever designed this must have believed that the battalion members would have no emotional reaction to getting these implants, much less losing their families and their basic humanity.

That on its own was incredibly short-sighted of the project designers. They really showed their incompetence by not taking into account that the battalion would end up going into combat.

Going into combat always brought up powerful emotions—both during the combat itself as well as before and after. The project designers never thought of that.

Fisher reappeared immediately this time as soon as Rhodes opened his eyes.

"Captain," Fisher murmured. "I am so sorry about what happened before. I feel awful about attacking you the way I did."

"It wasn't your fault, pal," Rhodes husked. "I know you didn't mean to."

"How can you ever trust me again? How can you trust that I won't do it again?"

"I don't have any problem trusting you, pal. You look fine now. You're back to normal."

Fisher looked away. "You're much more generous than I would be."

"How can you even say that? I attacked you, too. I would have killed you. I wanted to."

"I know you did," Fisher murmured. "I felt that when it happened."

Rhodes tried to look somewhere else, but he would always have to look at Fisher. Fisher would always be right there in front of Rhodes's face. "I'm sorry about that."

"You malfunctioned," Fisher pointed out. "You can't blame yourself for that."

"You malfunctioned, too. What did you think—that you were somehow immune to malfunctions even though all the other SAMs have been suffering malfunctions all this time? You know you aren't immune. You said so yourself. You were the one who told me it was only a matter of time before you malfunctioned and it affected me."

Fisher hesitated for a second. "I'm afraid I did think that. I told you that, but I never really believed it. I somehow convinced myself that I wouldn't malfunction simply because I am your SAM and you're the battalion's commanding officer. I somehow convinced myself that I was too important to malfunction—and that you were too important. I didn't let myself think it was possible that I could let you down like this."

"You didn't let me down, pal. Shit happens. It happens to the best of us." Rhodes dragged himself out of bed. "What are the others doing?"

"I'm not sure, Captain. I can't interface with them."

Rhodes's head shot up. "You can't? Why not?"

"I'm not sure, Captain. The interface simply isn't working."

"Where are they?" Rhodes immediately realized his mistake. Fisher wouldn't be able to find that out without the interface.

Rhodes dropped into The Grid, but it didn't tell him anything, either. It read Coleridge Station all around him, but The Grid only showed the normal station personnel. The Grid didn't indicate the location of any Battalion 1 people, not even Rhodes himself.

He was just about to stand up and go looking for his people when Dr. Irvine, Dr. Montague, Dr. Osborne, and Dr. Trudeau walked into the lab.

Rhodes cast a suspicious glance around, but he didn't see Dr. Neiland. Irvine and Montague were just as bad, but Rhodes had developed a special vendetta against her.

"How are you feeling, Captain?" Dr. Osborne asked.

Rhodes stifled the urge to snort. "I'm about as good as you would expect. Did you cut me off from the interface?"

Dr. Irvine spread both hands. "Everyone in Battalion 1 suffered catastrophic systems malfunctions. We thought it best to keep you isolated from each other until we can iron out the wrinkles."

"And did you? Did you iron out the wrinkles?"

"That remains to be seen, now that you're out of your conversion cycle."

"So what did you do? What caused the malfunctions?"

Osborne went over to the central stack of components and started tapping on them. "All your SAMs suffered errors in their base programming during your battle on Sulia. It appears that going into combat affected them in ways no one was able to foresee."

Rhodes compressed his lips. Of course no one foresaw those problems. No one in the Battalion 1 project had even been looking for them.

"We've corrected the errors in the programming," Dr. Trudeau added. "You shouldn't suffer from any further malfunctions."

"I'll believe that when I see it," Rhodes fired back. "I think what you mean is that you corrected the problems that you know about—the ones that caused this particular set of malfunctions. Obviously you couldn't correct any problems you haven't foreseen."

Trudeau lowered his eyes. "Of course, Captain. That is what I meant."

Dr. Montague looked down at the remote device in his hand. "Is your SAM functioning normally, Captain? Is he exhibiting any unusual changes?"

"No, he seems fine and he's acting normally, too."

"He's reading some emotional distress," Osborne called over his shoulder from his stack of equipment. "This is unusual. The SAMs aren't programmed to experience emotional distress."

"Why not?" Rhodes demanded. "They're self-aware. It makes sense that they would have a range of emotions and reactions to their circumstances."

"They're programmed to help the individual soldier cope with emotional disturbance. The SAMs aren't programmed to cope with emotional disturbance of their own." Trudeau looked up. "What's wrong with him? Why is he disturbed?"

"He says he feels guilty about attacking me earlier when he malfunctioned. He thinks he violated my trust and I won't be able to trust him again."

"That's odd. The SAMs aren't programmed to feel guilt or shame over their actions at all."

"Why not?" Rhodes repeated. "They're self-aware. They should have a full range of emotions."

"They aren't programmed to have any emotions at all," Dr. Montague interrupted.

"Then something must have gone seriously wrong," Rhodes replied. "The SAMs feel fear, so they must feel everything else, too."

"If you could just lie down, Captain." Dr. Irvine moved in. "We need to make some more adjustments."

Rhodes didn't want anyone making any adjustments to anything, but he would do just about anything to prevent another catastrophe like the last one—or like all the rest of them.

He started to lean over to lie back down on his mattress when Fisher crumbled before Rhodes's eyes.

The SAM's features contorted in a grimace of misery and he broke down sobbing right there.

He spasmed and jerked as the grid lines twisted his face in all the wrong directions—except that they were all the right directions. They formed all the most perfect expressions of someone falling apart in despair.

"Fisher!" Rhodes choked. "What's wrong?"

Fisher broke out in a few more sobs, and just as fast, he erupted in rage. At least he didn't change back into a monster full of fangs.

His grid lines burst apart as he expanded. He bared his teeth in a feral snarl and bellowed in fury.

His face rotated from right to left like he was struggling to break out of something holding him back.

Rhodes jolted away as Fisher's image rushed closer. "Whoa!" Rhodes yelled. "What are you doing to him?! Stop!"

"We aren't doing anything!" Dr. Osborne yelled back. "We haven't even started making the adjustments yet!"

"You're....." Rhodes began and broke off when Fisher collapsed again. His grid lines all went limp and flopped down to land in a pile.

They would have landed on the floor except that there was no floor in The Grid.

The lines slumped into an inert mound of lines right there in front of Rhodes's horrified sight. "Fisher!" he husked. "No!"

Just when Rhodes feared the worst, the lines bounced up and re-formed Fisher's normal face again. He blinked at Rhodes in that quick, bird-like way of his.

"Fisher?" Rhodes croaked. "Are you okay?"

"I'm fine, Captain. Why do you ask?"

"You....you malfunctioned again."

"I don't think so," Fisher replied. "You must be mistaken. I'm functioning according to my programming. All my systems are operating within normal parameters. I would remember any malfunction."

Rhodes opened his mouth to reply, but he could already see that Fisher didn't even remember what just happened.

At that moment, another agonizing wave of crushing grief seized Rhodes by the guts. It nearly made him buckle from the sheer weight of agony.

He almost broke down in despair, too, but just as fast, his feelings changed to stupid, hysterical, irrational mirth.

He had to bite his lip to stop himself from bursting out laughing right now. This whole ridiculous situation was too stupid to take it seriously a second longer.

He understood at some deeper level that he was malfunctioning again. He turned to lie back down on the mattress before anything else went wrong. He wanted to lock up with his capsule so he wouldn't be able to react to whatever this feeling changed to next.

He made it to a forty-five-degree angle to his mattress when this unstoppable groundswell of emotion erupted in a volcanic blast of pure murderous rage.

This time wiped out his previous fury and turned him into a raving psychopath in the blink of an eye. He didn't even have a chance to try to stop himself.

Something beyond himself shot him off the capsule. This other force moved all his limbs without him doing anything, trying anything, or deciding on anything.

Dr. Irvine happened to be standing closest to Rhodes's capsule. Rhodes swiped his mechanical right arm to one side and sent Irvine flying. He slammed into the wall and flopped unconscious on the floor.

The other doctors got out of Rhodes's path just in time for him to storm over to the central stack of computer components.

He could have destroyed them instantly by firing his Vipers into them, but he wanted to feel everything—or whatever part of him was doing this wanted to feel everything.

He charged the stack, extended both fists in front of him, and plowed straight through the equipment.

Screens and block processors exploded all around him, but that wasn't enough. He tore his way through the stack ripping everything apart with his bare hands.

He burst out the other side, swatted wires and conduits out of his face, and looked around for what else he could destroy.

He would never stop destroying. He would destroy the whole station. He wanted to tear the whole world apart.

He wasn't close enough to anything here, so he bent over, punched both fists into the floor, and roared in fury when he tore the floor plates up with his bare hands.

He hurled them into the walls, smashed more equipment, and sent the technicians running for cover.

He spotted Osborne and Trudeau on the other side of the room. They attacked what controls they could while they tried to shut Rhodes down, but nothing worked.

The small part of his brain that could still form rational thought had to admire them for having the courage to stick around.

Rhodes didn't see Dr. Montague anywhere. He must have bolted and left these two behind to try to save the situation.

Rhodes couldn't damage the lab fast enough by walking around pulverizing the equipment with his fists. He needed more—always more. Nothing would ever be enough to satisfy this rage.

He dropped into The Grid. It still worked.

He took off at a blinding run, measured the grid lines covering the walls, and straightened his arm on one side.

He hit the wall still running at his top speed and carved a path of destruction around the lab until he got to the other side.

His rage made him do all this, but he also felt something outside himself turning him, moving his limbs, and even directing his thoughts. Was he even doing any of this?

Osborne and Trudeau had to dive out of his way when he ran past them. They huddled together in the middle of the lab for protection. Flying sparks and shrapnel twirled in the air.

He got back to where he started and went to work tearing the wall components apart one brutal piece at a time.

He could take until doomsday to finish off this place and everything in it. He never wanted to see this lab or Coleridge Station again.

He turned his back on the rest of the lab so he could give the job his undivided attention.

He was in the middle of destroying a pile of processor units when a jet of fusion torched him in the back.

The Grid activated. He didn't have to turn around to see two dozen Legion soldiers standing across the lab.

They unloaded their Jackhammers on him, but the shots didn't damage his metal housing.

He unleashed three Vipers back at them and blasted all those soldiers out into the corridor. He turned around, stormed across the lab, and raised both his arms to wipe them all out with his lasers and scourge guns.

He actually hoped in that moment that someone sent more soldiers after him so he could kill them, too.

What was wrong with him? He only ever wanted to protect Legion soldiers. That was his job. He never wanted to harm his own comrades.

None of that meant anything right now. He wanted them dead in the worst, most torturous way possible.

Which weapon should he use to torment them as much as possible before they died? Should he use his thermal cannons to torch them to death? Should he blast their bodies to smithereens with his Vipers?

He made it halfway across the lab before another catastrophic smash hit him from somewhere. The Grid expanded for a fraction of a second—just long enough for him to read a Ravager in orbit over Coleridge Station.

The ship fired down at the station, punched through the ceiling, and a charge of electric voltage hit the walls and floor. The charge shut him down in a split second and he blacked out again.

Chapter 9

Rhodes woke up and groaned again when he remembered what he did. He tried to shut his eyes, but he couldn't block out the sight of Fisher in front of him.

Rhodes cringed when he saw his SAM—his friend. Rhodes didn't want to face the aftermath of destroying the lab the way he did.

"How are you feeling, Captain?" Fisher asked again.

Rhodes looked away. "I feel like I don't want to be here."

"Unfortunately, that option is no longer available. General Brewster ordered your weapons to be taken offline until the doctors and technicians satisfy themselves that you're no longer a danger to anyone."

"I'm sure I don't need weapons to do it, pal," Rhodes growled. "Corporal Poole killed himself without using weapons. I suppose it's just as well. I'm not going into battle any time soon. Better for me to not have any weapons. I can live with it if it means no one gets killed."

Fisher hesitated for a moment of tense silence. When he spoke, he used the same calm undertone as always. He expressed no emotion at all when he said, "Someone already did get killed. Dr. Irvine is dead."

Rhodes collapsed back on his mattress with a broken sigh. He clamped his eyes and his lips shut and looked away, but those words stabbed him in the heart.

"I should have known," he choked. "I should have known. Some-one was bound to get hurt one of these days. Too many things have been going wrong."

Fisher cocked his head to one side. "You're experiencing another emotional distress response. Why? You did not kill Dr. Irvine. I did."

Rhodes spun around fast. "You?!"

"I took control of your movements and responses and made you destroy the lab. I malfunctioned exactly the way you said. I had an emotional reaction and I used The Grid to cause you to attack the lab." Fisher inclined his head the other way. "Didn't you feel it while it was happening? I sensed you trying to resist and stop yourself....but I may have been mistaken."

"I.....I thought I was the one doing it. I felt.....something outside myself.....but I thought I was just mad. I didn't know...... I'm so sorry, Fisher."

"Why are you sorry? You've been in stasis all this time because of me. I'm surprised they brought me back online at all after what happened."

Rhodes ran his fingers through his hair. This was the worst yet. "I am, too, honestly. I'm surprised they brought either of us back online."

"They had no reason to take you offline. You were the one who put yourself into a conversion cycle when you saw yourself spiraling into a violent rage. You wouldn't have attacked Irvine or the lab if not for me." Fisher looked away. "I would have expected them to take me offline and give you a different SAM."

"I don't want a different SAM. I want you. You must have mal-functioned again. In fact, I know you did. You wouldn't have attacked the lab otherwise. The doctors must realize that."

"I hope you're right, Captain," Fisher murmured. "I would hate for something like this to happen again."

Rhodes would bet any amount of money that it would happen again, but he didn't say that out loud.

He couldn't even blame Fisher for this. Rhodes wanted to destroy the lab. He enjoyed it.

Fisher probably didn't have to try too hard to control Rhodes. Rhodes doubted he resisted very much if he resisted at all. Maybe Fisher just said that to make Rhodes feel better.

He was one malfunction away from doing exactly the same thing without any help from Fisher or anyone else.

Rhodes didn't even need a malfunction to do it. His own hopeless fury over this situation could make him snap any second now.

He was too weak to get out of bed now. He must have been in stasis for a long, long time the way Fisher said.

Rhodes would get his strength back soon enough. Then what?

He was more of a danger to himself and others now than he'd ever been. He didn't trust himself to stop himself if he really, really wanted to do something.

"Is there any word on the others?" he asked.

"They're all in long-term stasis, too—or they were," Fisher replied. "The station records indicate that everyone in the battalion has suffered malfunctions."

"Wonderful," Rhodes muttered. "I can just imagine."

"None of them required a Ravager firing on them to shut them down, though. That special honor goes to you alone."

Rhodes snorted. He really didn't want to talk about this anymore.

He didn't blame Fisher at all. At least he was functioning now. He didn't show any further sign of emotional disturbance.

Rhodes was too grateful for his SAM to hold this latest incident against Fisher. Malfunctions could and would happen to everyone. This one just turned out to be worse than the others. That wasn't Fisher's fault.

Rhodes stayed where he was until the nausea passed. Then he got to his feet and shuffled around the lab for a while until his strength started to return.

He was back in Dr. Neiland's lab—the same lab where Rhodes woke up from his first stasis. The Legion must have rebuilt it while he was asleep.

Rhodes didn't ask how long he'd been unconscious. One of these days, the Battalion 1 governing body would decide to leave him like that. Then everyone would be much better off, including Rhodes himself.

He finally worked up the energy to leave the lab. He was back at Coleridge Station, which meant he could go back to the battalion barracks.

The rest of his people would go back there as soon as they got out of stasis, too. Going there would be the quickest way to see them—wherever they were.

He really needed them right now. He needed other people in the same boat as himself.

They wouldn't hold Dr. Irvine's death against him and Fisher, either. Everyone in the battalion wanted Dr. Irvine dead.

Fisher read his mind. "Dr. Neiland isn't on the station roster anymore, Captain. Her record indicates that she resigned from the project."

Rhodes snorted. "Lucky her. Where do I go to resign?"

"At least you haven't lost your sense of humor."

Rhodes walked out of the lab and stopped dead in his tracks when he stepped into the corridor. A squad of ten armed Legion soldiers stood there waiting for him.

They all wore riot gear and carried Jackhammers. He didn't recognize any of them from his recent rampage.

Two of them flanked the lab entrance. Another two stood across the hall facing him.

The rest spaced themselves out on both sides to surround him heading in both directions.

He shouldn't have been surprised by this, but their presence didn't even intimidate him—not even with all of them bristling with weapons.

He could have taken them all out with his bare hands. Did they even realize how badly he outmatched them?

He felt nothing but pity for them whether they knew or not. He wasn't here to hurt them or even to resent them for guarding him. Even that made a sick kind of sense.

He decided to ignore them and set off down the corridor heading for the barracks. He just wanted to see his subordinates. He didn't care about anything else.

He tried to access The Grid on the way there, but the interface still didn't work. The Grid of the station worked the way it always did, but it still didn't return any information about anyone in the battalion, including Rhodes.

"It's kinda spooky, isn't it?" Rhodes remarked to Fisher on their way down the hall. "It's almost like the brass is getting ready to take us offline for good."

"I'm starting to see things your way, Captain," Fisher murmured. "Maybe that would be for the best—for everyone concerned."

"We're a ways past that now, pal," Rhodes pointed out. "Dr. Irvine is still dead."

"Dr. Montague has requested transfer to the station's personnel medical wing. He no longer works for the Battalion 1 project, either. Osborne and Trudeau are our only doctors now."

"Good," Rhodes replied. "I won't say I trust them completely, but at least I don't suspect them of malicious intent."

"Did you suspect Neiland, Irvine, and Montague of malicious intent? I didn't. I thought they were merely incompetent—or perhaps too inexperienced and ignorant of their subjects to do the job justice."

Rhodes sighed. "You're right, pal. I guess I didn't suspect them of malicious intent, either. Osborne and Trudeau don't strike me as being quite as ignorant or incompetent, though. They seem to take the job more seriously."

Rhodes and Fisher didn't have a chance to discuss it further before Rhodes walked into the barracks.

Whatever he might have been hoping to find here went right out the window. All his subordinates were already here. So here Drs. Osborne and Trudeau.

Rhodes saw right away that nothing had been fixed. He was the only person present who was functioning—at all.

Dr. Osborne was trying to do something to Thackery's cranial implant while she glared at him and smacked his hands away from her head.

Rhodes distinctly heard her yell at him to get the fuck away from her.

Her voice was one of the few he could distinguish in a sea of noise. Dietz and Coulter stood across the room bellowing at each other at the tops of their lungs.

They gesticulated wildly. The miracle was that they hadn't resorted to violence yet, but it would happen soon if things kept escalating like this.

Rhinehart was in the act of overturning the terminal desk when Rhodes walked in. The terminal went flying and Rhinehart went to town on both the table and what was left of the terminal.

He scooped up sections of the table, tore them to pieces, and then lifted the terminal above his head to smash it onto the floor. He stomped it under his feet until he reduced it to tiny fragments.

He kept bellowing in rage the whole time. When he finished, he swung both fists and pounded them into the wall.

Lauer lay sprawled face down on top of his capsule. He kept his head buried under his arms while he thumped his fists onto the cover again and again.

He smashed in the transparent cover, but he didn't seem to notice. He kept striking again and again with no awareness of what he was doing.

An agonized yowl of broken misery echoed off the cover from his mouth pressed against the device's metal housing.

Fuentes sat huddled in a fetal ball in a corner of the barracks. His lips, cheeks, and body trembled with anguished emotion while he watched his comrades fall to pieces all around him.

He kept jerking, spasming, and trying to shove his way farther back into the corner, but he was already as far back as he could go.

Oakes stood over him in a guarding posture. Oakes planted his feet wide apart and glared out into the room. He clenched his fists at his side and gritted his teeth ready to attack anyone who came too close to Fuentes.

Dr. Osborne bent over Georgie Henshaw. She lay flat on her back on the floor and she was out cold.

He worked frantically over his remote device trying to do something, but she never responded.

Rhodes took in the whole scene in a split second, but that didn't help him decide what to do. He didn't know which of his subordinates to approach first.

He had to admire the two doctors for getting involved in this. They could have retreated for their own safety, especially after what happened to Dr. Irvine.

They turned out to be braver even than these armed soldiers. Another twenty stood guard all around the barracks, but none of the soldiers intervened to stop Lauer and Rhinehart from destroying Legion property.

The soldiers guarding Rhodes didn't enter the room. They stayed near him—as if he was somehow more dangerous than the rest of these people.

Rhodes took a deep breath and stepped into the room, but he still didn't have a clue what to do or say first.

Oakes and Fuentes didn't seem to be in any danger. Rhodes wouldn't have been able to help with whatever was wrong with Henshaw, either.

He headed for Coulter and Dietz to break up the fight.

Before he could get there, Rhinehart finished demolishing what was left of both the terminal and the table.

He spun away, and without looking where he was going, he charged for the capsules, too.

Rhodes recognized that crazed look in Rhinehart's eyes. Rhinehart wanted to destroy everything in sight.

Rhodes dodged in front of him and stopped Rhinehart in his tracks. "Stop, Lieutenant. You don't want to do that."

"YOU BASTARD!!" Rhinehart bellowed. "GET OUT OF MY WAY!!"

He seized Rhodes by the shoulders and hurled him aside. Rhodes tried to stand his ground, but Rhinehart's size and strength overpowered Rhodes easily.

Rhodes would have pitched across the floor, but he stumbled and caught his balance.

Rhinehart charged to the nearest capsule, which was Fuentes's, grabbed the open cover, and tore it off with one massive jerk of his powerful arms.

The cover went flying into another corner—away from anywhere it might hurt anyone. Then Rhinehart attacked the capsule tooth and nail. He smashed down on it with both fists and roared in mindless fury as he wrecked that, too.

Rhodes braced himself to dive in and try to stop the destruction, but he didn't. He stopped where he was and watched.

The doctors and soldiers didn't stop Rhinehart, either. They didn't stop him from destroying the terminal and they didn't stop him from destroying Fuentes's capsule.

Oakes didn't intervene, either, not even knowing that Fuentes needed this capsule to survive.

Osborne kept trying to do something to Henshaw through his device. Trudeau was getting more and more desperate to do whatever he was trying to do to Thackery.

Rhodes didn't see anything wrong with her, but when she tried one more time to swat his arms away, she collapsed backward, toppled off the bench, and hit the floor.

Trudeau pounced on her, did something to her cranial implant, and then he started frantically working on his device, too.

He cast a few petrified glances around the barracks. The wild terror in his eyes said it all. These two doctors were more than aware of everything going wrong in here right now.

Thackery and Henshaw must have been suffering from the most dangerous malfunctions. That must be what knocked them out.

The other members of the battalion might be getting violently enraged and destroying Legion property, but they weren't in any danger of dropping dead from whatever was wrong with them. Fuentes even had Oakes guarding him.

Rhodes decided to take a page from the doctor's playbook. He left Lauer and Rhinehart alone, went over to Coulter and Dietz instead, and stepped between them.

Rhodes pushed them apart and pointed behind Coulter. "Go over there, Eddie. Back off!"

Coulter got in Rhodes's face. "Don't you fucking tell me what to do! This asshole tried to attack me!"

"I don't care what he did!" Rhodes yelled back. "You're both malfunctioning! Now get the hell over there NOW!! Back off, Dietz! Go over there!"

He pushed them farther apart and steered them into opposite corners of the barracks. They must have been at least partially rational because they did it, obeyed him, and separated to opposite corners.

They kept glaring at each other until Dietz turned his back and faced the wall.

"He's a scumbag," Coulter snarled in Rhodes's ear. "I swear I'll tear his fucking head if he looks at me sideways again."

Rhodes opened his mouth to say again that Coulter only felt that way because he was malfunctioning.

At that moment, another broken roar split across the barracks. So much other noise echoed off the walls that the sound didn't startled Rhodes at first.

Before anyone could move, Fuentes sprang to his feet and charged across the barracks. He made it halfway to Thackery before Rhodes realized what was happening.

Fuentes's anguish and terror from a minute before erupted in animal rage. He bellowed in fury and picked up speed heading straight for Thackery.

Rhodes leapt forward to stop him from attacking her, but Fuentes wound up sprinting straight past her and he collided with the wall.

He hit it with such force that he pulverized it to rubble in seconds, charged through, and took off running down the station's corridors.

He vanished out of sight before anyone realized what was happening. Both doctors looked up.

The sight snapped Rhodes out of his shock. He pointed at Osborne. "Keep doing what you're doing and help her! I'll go after him!" He waved to Oakes and the soldiers. "Come on! Let's go!"

Chapter 10

Rhodes clambered through the hole in the barracks wall and glanced right and left down the Coleridge Station corridors.

He didn't have to wonder where Fuentes was. Sections of destroyed walls, injured people, and the sounds of screams led the way to the left.

Oakes caught up with Rhodes in the corridor. They took off running in that direction with a dozen soldiers on their tails.

"Where is he going?" Rhodes asked Oakes.

"How should I know?" Oakes countered.

"Did something happen in the barracks before I showed up?"

"Nothing you didn't already see," Oakes replied. "I was worried Rhinehart, Coulter, or Dietz might put Rudy in danger, so I stood guard to protect him."

Rhodes glanced over at Oakes. Everything else about him seemed to be functioning normally.

"Did you malfunction?" Rhodes asked.

Oakes raised his eyebrow. "Which time?"

"Now. Why are the rest of them malfunctioning and not you?"

Oakes shrugged. "Who the hell knows why any of this is happening? Did *you* malfunction?"

"Which time?" Rhodes asked.

Oakes snorted. "Got it."

The two men faced front to follow Fuentes's track. It burst through more walls and left people trampled and cowering in fear along the way.

Rhodes climbed through a few more breaches before he spotted Fuentes ahead. He was crossing the concourse to the other side of the station.

"He's heading for the loading dock!" Rhodes waved to the soldiers. "Get around in front of him and head him off. It looks like he's trying to escape from the station!"

The soldiers split up, raced down two different side wings, and left Oakes and Rhodes to run on alone.

Rhodes tried not to notice the soldiers finally leaving him alone. If he wanted to escape from Coleridge Station, now would be the perfect time to do it. Everyone was preoccupied with Fuentes.

Rhodes didn't want to escape from Coleridge Station. He didn't want to go anywhere. He had nowhere left in the known universe to go.

No one was out there waiting for him to come back—not like this. His family would have been more horrified to see him alive than they were to hear about his death in combat.

Oakes and Rhodes burst onto the loading dock and spotted Fuentes a hundred yards down the platform.

A bunch of transport freight craft, Dusters, and a few random Predators lined one side of the dock.

A single Ravager sat parked on the other side. It had its engines running as it prepared to launch.

Fuentes stood in the middle of the platform. His body convulsed in all directions before he managed to lurch one painful step closer to the Ravager.

Rhodes took a step forward. How dangerous was Fuentes? What was he even doing here?

At that moment, the interface switched on and Van's fuzzy, feline face appeared on The Grid right next to Fisher.

She twisted her grid lines all around Fuentes's body, restrained his arms against his sides, and wrapped the lines around and around his legs to stop him from moving.

He struggled with all his might, snapped a few lines, and took one more step before she wrestled him back under control.

Rhodes couldn't figure out how she activated the interface. It was supposed to be offline, but she did it somehow.

"Help me, Captain!" she rasped. "Rudy is trying to kill himself!"

Rhodes opened his mouth to ask how Fuentes planned to kill himself with a full-sized Ravager, but Rhodes didn't get the words out.

Fuentes gave one more violent jerk, tried again to take another step, and toppled onto his side. He couldn't raise his arms to break his fall.

He landed hard on the platform and his metal housing made an echoing crash through the loading dock.

Rhodes and Oakes charged forward to get to him in time, but the instant they started running, Fuentes overcame his SAM's best efforts.

He roared in fury, tore his limbs out of the grid lines, and took off at high speed heading for the Ravager.

The engines thundered louder as the ship fired up to lift off the planet.

Fuentes activated The Grid. The lines spread all over him and he changed shape.

Van made one last heroic effort to stop him and failed. He morphed into one of the many-jointed creatures the battalion used on Sulia, bounded across the platform in a split second, and soared onto the ship's upper hull right above the engines.

He landed there and transformed back into a man. He turned around, straightened up, and a peaceful smile spread over his face.

The Ravager's engine noise throbbed off the dock walls with the noise of thunder. The ship would launch any second now.

Fuentes only had to jump off at the moment of launch. The engine wash venting from the exhaust manifold would incinerate him instantly. It would all be over.

Van kept the interface active through the whole disaster. Her lines kept snaking around Fuentes's body trying to wrench him away from the manifold. Her efforts only made him smile more broadly. She couldn't control him.

Rhodes considered for a second if he shouldn't change into some vehicle or creature to jump up there. He should be the one to talk Rudy down, but Rhodes didn't do that.

He'd been telling his people from day one that he wouldn't hold it against them if they chose this route. Who was he to stop Fuentes from ending his miserable life? Rhodes really wished he could end his own.

Oakes didn't move, either. The engines fired and the soldiers fell back.

The ship lifted off the dock and Fuentes spread his arms to jump. The engines exploded in twin jets of fire. He sprang off the hull and started to fall toward the flames just as the engines ignited to full power.

At that moment, a blinding streak blasted across the loading dock, zoomed between Fuentes and the manifolds, and snatched him out of thin air.

Rhodes barely had time to register one of the battalion's Strikers whizzing past. Rhodes blinked....and there was Fuentes locked inside the cockpit.

The Striker circled and landed in front of Rhodes. Fuentes went ballistic, pounded the cockpit cover with his fists, and when that failed, he attacked his own face with his fingernails.

His mouth opened in a wordless roar of agony and hopeless despair. How many more times would Rhodes see that expression before this whole nightmare came to an end?

Fuentes dug his fingernails around the edge of his facial implant. He bellowed again and started to pull when a powerful thump went off inside the cockpit.

Fuentes collapsed into the seat, unconscious. Van disappeared off the interface. Rhodes didn't even get a chance to thank her for at least trying to save Fuentes.

The Ravager gunned its engines, rocketed off the loading dock, and climbed away into space. It left a heavy silence behind it.

Rhodes stared at Fuentes lying in the cockpit with his eyes closed. Was he really better off alive if he wanted so badly to end it?

Right then, Rio appeared on the interface next to Fisher. Rio smiled just as cheerily as ever. Not even this could dampen his mood.

"I got here as soon as I could, Captain." The SAM cocked his head in concentration. "Fuentes's vital signs are stable. He's functioning normally again."

Rhodes sighed. "Thank you, Rio. You saved his life."

"Van interfaced with Teo and asked us to come and get Fuentes. I was the closest, so I came."

"We need to take him back to the lab," Rhodes replied. "Put him down and I'll take him from here. You can go back downstairs with the other Strikers. I really appreciate your help, Rio."

"Of course, Captain. It's good to have you back."

"I wish I could say the same thing, pal. Thank you. I'll take Fuentes from here."

Rio's grid lines changed. They became flexible and almost liquid. They parted and lowered Fuentes's unconscious body onto the dock platform before the ship reformed into a Striker.

The ship took off and Rio vanished off the interface. Rhodes stared down at Fuentes for a minute before Rhodes decided what to do with him.

The kindest thing to do would be to put Fuentes down right now. He would never wake up or have to deal with the aftermath of this latest catastrophe.

Rhodes would never be able to do that. He knew that now. He wouldn't stand in the way of one of his subordinates taking the only way out left to them, but he wouldn't do it for them.

If dying meant that much to Fuentes—or any of them—he had to do it himself.

Too bad Van and the other SAMs overcame the interface and called in the Strikers in time to save Fuentes.

Fisher understood now why Rhodes would want to end it. The other SAMs obviously didn't agree. Why should they? They wanted to live. Rhodes couldn't blame them for that, either.

The Strikers would be the hardest to convince. They spent their time in the landing bay downstairs.

Fisher and the battalion's personal SAMs spent their time riding around inside these people's heads. Of course they understood better, but Van wasn't ready to go there.

Rhodes couldn't know what went on between Fuentes and Van. He obviously hadn't come to the same understanding with her that Rhodes came to with Fisher.

Would Fisher try to stop Rhodes from ending his life? They never really had that conversation except for when Fisher said he understood.

Rhodes sighed, picked up Fuentes, and carried him back to Neiland's lab. No one was here. Osborne and Trudeau were still in the barracks doing God only knew what with Thackery and Henshaw.

Rhodes dreaded going back there. He didn't want to watch his whole party go down in flames.

He laid Fuentes in the capsule, locked the kid into the prongs, and shut the cover. Rhodes adjusted the controls to put Fuentes into an indefinite conversion cycle.

He wouldn't wake up until the doctors deliberately adjusted the cycle back to the way it was and woke him up on purpose.

Maybe they wouldn't wake him up at all. Maybe they would leave him like this—forever. Would that really be so bad?

Rhodes turned away and found Oakes standing there watching him. Oakes stared down at Fuentes for a long time, too.

Then Oakes's eyes flicked to the control panel. He saw.

The two men shared a moment of deep eye contact before they both left the lab. They didn't talk all the way back to the barracks.

They walked into a scene almost worse than the one they left. Every other member of the battalion lay unconscious on the floor—Thackery, Henshaw, Dietz, Lauer, Rhinehart, and Coulter.

Drs. Osborne and Trudeau went from one person to the next checking everything on their devices.

"What happened?" Rhodes gasped when he walked in. "Are they ....?"

"They were becoming dangerous—to themselves and each other," Trudeau replied. "Dietz and Coulter started arguing again and then they started shoving. Coulter slammed Dietz's head against the wall. Rhinehart started trying to destroy Lauer's capsule while Lauer was still trying to destroy it himself. They would have started fighting....so we decided to shut them all down."

"What about Thackery and Henshaw?" Rhodes asked. "What's wrong with them?"

"Their SAMs were dysregulating their vital systems, so we shut down the two SAMs. Thackery's and Henshaw's systems are working fine as long as we keep the SAMs offline. We'll take all of them back to the lab until we can readjust all of them."

"What about.....?" Rhodes and Oakes exchanged another glance. They were the last two left.

Rhinehart and Lauer had destroyed all the capsules in the barracks. The two of them had reduced the place to a wasteland of wrecked electronic components all over the floor.

"I'll send two new capsules down for you and Oakes," Osborne replied. "You have nothing to worry about. You two can stay here."

Rhodes glanced over at Oakes. Oakes glanced over at Rhodes. The words, *You have nothing to worry about,* meant exactly nothing right now.

The two men had everything to worry about. How long could they stay in these barracks before one of them suffered another nightmare malfunction?

One of them could kill the other. No one would be able to do anything about it.

The Legion soldiers seemed to have the same idea. They returned to the barracks and stood guard over Rhodes and Oakes as if the whole battalion was still here.

A bunch of technicians came down from the lab and carried the rest of the battalion away. The crowd filed out of the room and left Rhodes and Oakes alone with their guards.

The soldiers faded into the wallpaper. Rhodes and Oakes were alone together—as alone as they possibly could be.

"So.....what do you feel like doing?" Rhodes asked.

Without moving or saying a word, Oakes switched on the interface between himself, Rhodes, Fisher, and Dash. Oakes and Rhodes looked back and forth between the two SAMs.

"Is everything all right, Captain?" Dash asked.

"I wouldn't go so far as to say that," Rhodes replied.

Oakes headed back to the table—the table Thackery where had been sitting when Rhodes first showed up. It was the only table still standing. It was the only stick of furniture left in the whole barracks.

Oakes slung his leg over it, sat down, and pulled toward him a pencil and a piece of paper lying there.

"What are you working on?" Rhodes asked. "Are you writing a book or something?"

"I thought I'd try drawing the way you do." Oakes passed his pencil across the page. "I don't seem to be able to get the hang of it—not like you do."

"It just takes practice." Rhodes looked over his shoulder and then sat down. "Do you want me to give you some pointers?"

"Naw, I don't feel like it." Oakes pushed the paper away and made a face. "I don't feel like doing anything."

"Do you want to play The Ship, The Captain, and The Crew?"

Oakes shrugged. He refused to make eye contact. "I guess we have nothing else to do."

"I'm sure they'll send us another terminal before long."

The words barely got out of Rhodes's mouth before a cleaning crew entered the barracks. They started sweeping up the mess, throwing away all the twisted scraps of destroyed capsules, and then some technicians wheeled in two more for Rhodes and Oakes to use in their next conversion cycle.

"I guess we're a battalion of two now," Rhodes pointed out.

"Until something else goes wrong with one of us," Oakes muttered. "It would really be ironic if the whole program ended like this—with all of us malfunctioning, going offline, or ending it one after the other. You gotta wonder how long it would take these jokers to take the hint and stop trying."

Rhodes didn't answer. He got the dice off the bookshelf. For some unknown reason, Rhinehart had left the bookshelf intact. He didn't try to destroy that or any of the books on it.

Rhodes rolled and jotted down his score on the paper Oakes had been using. Oakes rolled. He didn't even bother to score his turn. Rhodes did it for him and went again.

"I really wish I could," Oakes muttered under his breath. "I keep telling myself to do it. I just don't do it, though. I don't know why."

Rhodes didn't ask what Oakes meant. Rhodes already knew because he'd been thinking exactly the same thing.

Chapter 11

Rhodes stepped into Colonel Paxton Kraft's office. General Kenneth Brewster, Colonel Kraft, General Hyde, Colonels LeClerc and Neff, and Admiral Pulman were already there.

They stood around the central table waiting for Rhodes to show up. He halted in the doorway and didn't approach.

"Come on in, Captain," Admiral Pulman called. "We're all anxious to debrief you about the Sulia campaign."

Rhodes stiffened. "Why do you want to debrief me about it? You can see everything that happened on our SAMs' feed."

"We still need to discuss it with you," General Hyde replied. "We need to evaluate what went wrong, what went right, and how we can learn from this to do better next time."

"Everything went wrong," Rhodes replied. "The only thing you can learn to do better next time is not to throw good platoons in front of the Emal—but you'll never learn that. You would have learned it a long time ago if you were going to learn it at all."

"We aren't here to talk about what the Legion does with the regular platoons," General Brewster told him. "We're only here to talk about how things worked out with Battalion 1."

"You know how things worked out with Battalion 1," Rhodes repeated. "You can see the way things worked out. We're having all these malfunctions now because of what happened during the Sulia campaign. Don't you get that?"

"Explain it to us anyway," General Hyde urged and waved at the table. "Please come in. We're all anxious to hear your report."

Rhodes still took at least a minute to make up his mind to walk into the room. He probably wouldn't have entered it at all if Colonel Kraft hadn't been present.

Rhodes couldn't forestall the inevitable, though. Talking to these people was the best way to make sure it never happened again—if that was even possible.

He stopped next to Colonel Kraft. Kraft never talked to Rhodes in the presence of these much more senior officers. Kraft kept quiet the way Kraft always did.

His presence steadied Rhodes. He could tolerate this because Kraft was here.

"Now please tell us what happened," General Hyde went on. "We understand you coordinated with one of the platoon captains and formulated a plan to defend the eastern side of the city while the platoons traveled through Thaklia from the *Ero* landing site."

"So what if I did?" Rhodes asked.

"You weren't under orders to coordinate with the platoon captains."

"I wasn't under any orders at all. No one informed me about what the battalion was supposed to do. I talked to him and he told me he was supposed to take the platoons all the way through the city and defend the eastern side. I offered to go ahead of him and hold the enemy there until he established fortifications for his platoons."

"You weren't authorized to make that call," Admiral Pulman interjected.

Rhodes rounded on him. "I don't give a shit if I was authorized to do it or not."

"Your insubordination is unacceptable, Captain," the admiral growled. "You're still subject to military protocol. You still have to follow the chain of command."

"What chain of command?" Rhodes fired back. "I just told you I didn't receive any orders—from anyone. We were deployed on Sulia to defend Thaklia from the Emal and that's what we did. So that makes me insubordinate? What are you going to do—strip me of my command? Go right ahead. Do you I look like I care?"

"Battalion 1 still needs to function as a military unit," General Hyde cut in. "The Emal are becoming more entrenched on Sulia. The Legion is mounting another campaign to reclaim the planet....."

"Reclaim the planet!" Rhodes blurted out. "Are you insane?! Sulia is gone. Just give it back. You'll never reclaim it. The Emal are unstoppable. Surely even a bunch of dunces like you can see that."

"As General Brewster said, we don't make decisions for the wider Legion," Admiral Pulman replied. "The Legion will mount another campaign to retake Sulia and Battalion 1 will support the platoons...."

"No, we won't," Rhodes snapped. "Battalion 1 isn't going anywhere."

Admiral Pulman's head whipped around real fast. "You're flatly refusing to deploy?"

"Under the circumstances? Absolutely I'm refusing to deploy. My people can't even walk down the goddamn corridor without malfunctioning. One of my guys just attempted suicide—again—and the rest are either murderously violent, emotionally unstable, or their SAMs are out of control. No way would I let you send any of us into combat like this—much less on a suicide mission back to Sulia. You're out of your flippin' minds if you think I'd agree to that."

"You don't have to agree," Colonel LeClerc chimed in. "We can send you without your consent."

"You can't send us anywhere if we're all dead or permanently in stasis," Rhodes spat back.

General Brewster interjected just then with his usual brainless optimism. "The important thing is that the battalion is ready to deploy when you're needed. I'm sure the doctors will correct any malfuncti ons....."

"What could possibly lead you to that conclusion?" Rhodes countered. "Fuentes has been in stasis for over three weeks since his suicide attempt. If the doctors were capable of correcting his malfunction, they would have done it by now."

The senior officers confirmed Rhodes's worst fears by exchanging glances with each other. So that's how it was. The doctors couldn't correct Fuentes's malfunction—probably because he wasn't malfunctioning.

He was having a normal human emotional reaction to a life-destroying event. He lost everything, including his humanity, and he couldn't live with it. Now he wanted to end it. Rhodes couldn't blame him.

"Unfortunately, the doctors can't find any malfunction in Fuentes to correct," Colonel Neff murmured. "That's why the doctors weren't working on him when he fled the barracks. All their readings on him were coming back normal. They didn't consider him critical—unlike the others."

"Then that goes to show how much the doctors know," Rhodes replied. "Fuentes was in serious emotional distress before he fled the barracks. He was barely hanging on."

"His responses and stress levels were reading the same before he fled the barracks, while he was on the loading dock, and the readings are still the same now when he's in stasis. The doctors can't correct a problem they can't detect."

Rhodes waited for someone else to say something. "So what are you telling me for? It isn't like I can fix whatever is wrong with him."

"We ask you to try," Colonel LeClerc replied. "We ask you to try to convince him to return to the battalion as a contributing member of the team."

Rhodes waited again, but no one said anything else. "You're the man who just said you would deploy me against my will to carry out a suicide mission. Give me one reason why I should cooperate with you."

"The only other options are that we either leave Fuentes in stasis indefinitely or take him offline for good," General Hyde replied. "I'm sure you wouldn't want that."

"Why in the name of God would I want him back in the battalion? He wants to die. Just take him offline."

"We can't waste a good soldier," General Brewster replied. "We've lost too many in this project already. One soldier who wakes up and can function in The Grid is too valuable to waste."

"Function?" Rhodes snorted. "You actually call what Fuentes is doing functioning? Are you stupid?"

"So you won't even try?" Colonel LeClerc asked. "We expected better of you, Captain."

"You obviously haven't even looked at the feeds from Sulia," Rhodes countered. "You obviously don't know the first thing about how or why we malfunctioned down there—or what we went through as a result. The Emal tried to rip our implants out."

Every officer at the table squirmed. "We know that," General Hyde murmured.

"So I won't let you send us back to Sulia to let it happen again—not unless you can come up with some convincing way to make sure it doesn't happen again. You'll have to come up with some way to make sure none of it happens again—and that includes all the malfunctions. The SAMs shut down from elevated adrenaline levels—which were normal for battlefield conditions."

Admiral Pulman bent over his device and tapped on it. "Yes, about that...."

"Then the SAMs malfunctioned again when my people got injured. Some of the SAMs refused to function at all because they became pathologically afraid of their hosts' injuries."

"That may be because their hosts had no direct combat experience before this campaign," General Hyde suggested.

"That just goes to show how little you know what you're talking about, lady," Rhodes snapped. "It happened to experienced, trained Legion soldiers with plenty of combat experience—and it *didn't* happen to experienced, trained Legion soldiers with plenty of combat experience. How much combat experience the host had didn't have anything to do with how the SAMs reacted. This project is a massive exercise in incompetence."

"Then how do you suggest we deal with Fuentes and the others?" Admiral Pulman asked.

"I just told you how to deal with Fuentes."

"You can't seriously expect us to just take him offline," General Brewster exclaimed. "Do you have any idea how much we've already invested in each of you—both monetarily and in other resources?"

Rhodes only shrugged. "We're already dead, so it doesn't really concern us. Fuentes will never be fit for deployment—not ever. You never should have entered him into this program, but it's too late to go back on that now. The only solution is to cut your losses and take him offline now before he causes even more problems for the rest of us later."

"So you won't even try?" LeClerc demanded. "You won't even try to convince him?"

"Nope," Rhodes replied. "If you put me in the same room with him, I'll tell him that, as soon as you activate his weapons to go into battle, to use them to end his life. That's the best thing for him now."

"I don't believe I'm hearing this!" Brewster muttered.

"I already said the same thing to Rhinehart, Coulter, and Fisher," Rhodes replied. "I'll say it to the rest of them the very first chance I get."

"Who's Fisher?" Colonel LeClerc asked.

Rhodes inhaled to read this jackass the riot act for making decisions about a battalion he knew absolutely nothing about it, but right then, Colonel Neff interrupted.

"Actually, I agree with Captain Rhodes on this one," he breezed.

Everyone at the table spun around to stare at Neff. "You do?" Rhodes gasped.

"Not about taking Fuentes offline," Colonel Neff explained. "I agree with you about not sending the battalion back to Sulia—not under the circumstances. I agree with you about not sending the battalion anywhere under the circumstances—not until we establish with a wide degree of certainty that these malfunctions are contained and unlikely to happen again."

"I agree," Colonel Kraft added. "We took the battalion's success in the training sessions for granted. We were bound to run into unforeseen problems on the battlefield and that's what happened. That's why we decided to deploy the battalion against the Emal in the first place—to test this technology against a real enemy. We got lucky that we retrieved the whole battalion alive. It could have been a lot worse.

It's thanks to the battalion's cohesion as a team and Captain Rhodes's leadership that we even have a battalion to continue working with."

Rhodes stared at Kraft in stunned disbelief. Someone was actually sticking up for Rhodes and the battalion.

"Of course we can't send the battalion back into combat until we work out all the malfunctions," Colonel Neff went on. "That would be unthinkable."

"But what about the Sulia counteroffensive?!" General Pulman exclaimed. "We can't just leave the platoons without help."

"The platoons would be just as defenseless if we sent Battalion 1 back to Sulia the way they are," Colonel Neff pointed out.

"But we're no closer to solving these malfunctions," General Hyde pointed out. "The counteroffensive is scheduled for three weeks from now. We would have to arrange training sessions to test the adjustments...."

"Then you obviously have a lot of work to do. You don't need me for that." Rhodes turned away. "I won't do anything, plan anything, or accept any orders until I start seeing my people back in the barracks with smiles on their faces. Until then, this battalion is dead in the water."

He walked out of the office. He actually enjoyed being as rude as possible to these morons. They deserved a lot worse. Battalion 1 was dead in the water before it even got started.

Going on another campaign sounded like Rhodes's idea of Hell. It would be his worst nightmare.

The officers wouldn't take Fuentes offline. Rhodes already knew that. They would manipulate his SAM and Fuentes's neural systems.

Then they would send him back to the battalion where he would become Rhodes's problem again. What would Rhodes do then?

Fuentes turning his weapons on himself would be by far the best outcome Rhodes could hope for.

It beat the hell out of Fuentes turning his weapons on his comrades, other Legion soldiers, or maybe the station staff. Rhodes could just imagine the fallout from that.

Rhodes returned to the barracks where he found Oakes waiting for him. The soldiers still stood guard over the two men even though nothing had happened in three weeks.

Oakes took one look at Rhodes's face and snorted. "I thought so."

Rhodes collapsed at the table. Oakes's artwork had been steadily improving under Rhodes's instruction these last three weeks. "They're out of their natural minds."

"And this is news?" Oakes sneered. "I mean...look at us, man. This is some psycho's bad dream."

"They want to send Fuentes back to the battalion," Rhodes told him.

Oakes sniffed at nothing. "I'll make sure to keep my weapons charged just in case he tries something else."

Chapter 12

O akes and Rhodes sat at the table in their barracks and worked on their drawings. Covering one page after another with drawings was practically the only thing they did all day.

The two men occasionally took walks around the station, but seeing other members of the station staff robbed the experience of its former pleasure.

Being around normal people spoiled the experience. Taking a walk around the station no longer provided the relief and solitude the men craved. Taking a walk around the station only made the alienation and despair worse.

Rhodes pointed his pencil at Oakes's drawing. He was drawing a picture of a little girl swinging on a swing under a big sprawling tree.

"Try tightening up your lines there," Rhodes told him. "Your trunk is too wide. It's taking up too much of the negative space."

Oakes darkened the line of the trunk and glanced over at Rhodes's page. Rhodes was drawing a view of the barracks in front of him.

Oakes's expression changed when he saw what Rhodes was working on. Rhodes never drew anything that might remind him of his past.

Despite Oakes's assurance that he didn't want to check the terminal to see what his family was doing, he always ended up drawing domestic scenes of children playing or otherwise enjoying their lives.

Neither of the two men commented on this, but Rhodes caught Oakes's expression changing a lot when he saw Rhodes's art.

He always drew scenes from the present—either people or SAMs in the battalion, views from different parts of Coleridge Station, or sketches of equipment, ships, or landscapes he'd seen on deployment.

He and Oakes stayed interfaced with each other the way they did before the Sulia campaign. Rhodes had changed his opinion on himself and the other members of the battalion needing privacy.

He didn't want privacy. It somehow seemed rude to try to hide anything from people whose very lives depended on how stable his mental state might be at any given moment.

His mental state, Fisher's mental state, and how well both of them were functioning at any given time—all of that was as much Oakes's business as Rhodes's own. Oakes had a right to know at any moment of the day how well Rhodes and Fisher were functioning.

Rhodes would have gotten very suspicious and nervous if Oakes suddenly decided to stop interfacing with Rhodes and Fisher. Rhodes would have immediately suspected that something was wrong.

Rhodes didn't want Oakes thinking that about him. Rhodes wanted Oakes to know everything. Rhodes wanted Oakes to be the first to know in case something went wrong.

Then Oakes might actually be able to do something about it—like maybe put Rhodes down before he killed someone else.

He didn't feel guilty about killing Dr. Irvine. He just wanted to take every possible step to make sure it never happened again.

Oakes and Rhodes spent all their time together. What one did, the other did. If one of them took a walk around the station, the other went with him just because.

They hardly ever talked, though. There didn't seem to be much to say anymore.

Dash and Fisher didn't talk much, either. They just hovered there in The Grid watching whatever Rhodes and Oakes were doing.

Rhodes didn't discuss Dr. Irvine's death with Fisher again. Rhodes kept an eye on Fisher for any sign that Fisher still blamed himself for Rhodes's rampage.

Fisher never showed any emotional reaction to anything—not anymore. He might have been hiding it or the doctors might really have corrected whatever caused him to take control of Rhodes in the first place.

Rhodes didn't believe anymore that Fisher would have been able to hide anything from him. Rhodes would have known the instant anything went wrong with Fisher.

They'd become linked in a whole new way since Dr. Irvine's death. Fisher no longer showed any surprise or even any aversion to the idea of Rhodes or one of the other battalion members taking their own lives. Fisher had finally gotten the message.

Rhodes lost track of time these last few weeks. Time lost all meaning without meals, activities, and social interactions to break up the day.

The hours between conversion cycles blurred into one continuous blank space. Rhodes felt nothing, experienced nothing, said nothing, did nothing—was nothing. His life was over.

He remained suspended in this kind of purgatory. The doctors might as well take him offline. He was as good as dead anyway without something to do.

He pushed away his drawing of the barracks and pulled a blank piece of paper toward himself. Now he had to decide what to draw next.

He tried not to notice Oakes lingering over his picture of the girl on the swing. He always did this when he got closer to completing one of his drawings.

He passed his pencil over the lines he'd already drawn. He pretended to strengthen and darken them to adjust certain parts of the image, but he didn't really change anything.

He almost stroked the image with his pencil. That was his way of touching the subject without actually touching them. He sat there staring at the children in his drawings for much longer than he needed to.

Rhodes pretended not to see that and concentrated on his own paper. His pencil hovered over the sheet, but right then, the barracks door opened and Henshaw walked in.

Rhodes nearly tripped over the bench trying to stand up too fast. "Georgie! You're back."

She made a face somewhere between a smile and a grimace. "They just let me out. I just woke up from stasis."

He hustled over to greet her. Oakes left his drawing and crossed the room, too.

Henshaw entered and then Rhinehart, Lauer, Coulter, Dietz, and Thackery walked in behind Henshaw.

Rhodes devoured each of them with his eyes. "Are you all okay? Did they fix whatever malfunctions you had?"

Coulter shrugged. "Who the hell knows what they did? I guess we just have to wait and see how it all works out—until it all goes to shit again."

Oakes surveyed the group. "Rudy isn't here."

"He might not come back," Rhodes told the others. "The brass is considering taking him permanently offline."

"I hope they do," Thackery muttered. "That guy is the last thing we need around here."

"You can't blame him for malfunctioning," Henshaw pointed out.

"He didn't malfunction," Rhodes replied. "That's why he isn't here. The doctors can't find anything wrong with him. He was reacting normally to his circumstances. I'm sure we've all thought about doing the same thing."

The others shuffled their feet. Rhodes studied each face in the group. Each of them looked haggard, drained, and depressed—even more than they should have been after getting out of a long conversion cycle.

Few of the group would hold eye contact. When they did, they only did it for a few seconds before they looked away.

"How do you all feel about interfacing with each other?" he asked. "Oakes and I have been interfacing with each other—just to keep an eye on things. How do you all feel about doing the same thing?"

Thackery nodded. "I'm in. I don't want to be alone anymore."

"Definitely," Rhinehart replied. "It's the safest way for all of us."

Rhodes surveyed the others. Coulter nodded and Lauer said, "Yeah, let's do it."

Rhodes interfaced with all of them and they all established connections with each other.

Their joint interface connected to The Grid. Rhodes checked each of their SAMs. They looked and acted the way they should. Everything seemed to be working properly.

All the fight seemed to have gone out of each of them. None of them showed much spark about doing anything, not even Dietz.

The SAMs didn't jump into conversation, either. No one spoke unless they absolutely had to.

Coulter, Lauer, and Rhinehart accompanied Rhodes and Oakes back to the table. The five men sat down and the new arrivals complimented Oakes's artistic development.

Dietz went over to the computer terminal. Henshaw and Thackery meandered around the half-empty barracks. "Where are our capsules?" Thackery asked. "I want to lie down. Where are we supposed to go through conversion cycles without capsules?"

"I'm sure the brass will send some down for you, now that you're out of the lab," Rhodes replied. "You can use mine in the meantime if you want to. I'm sure it will work just as well for you."

Someone would have turned this into a joke in the past, but no one said anything about it now. No one made any noise about Thackery using Rhodes's capsule.

Only a few moments of silence passed before the technicians came in wheeling a bunch of new capsules for the rest of the battalion.

Thackery and Henshaw stood off to one side watching the technicians hook the new capsules up to the wall.

Thackery waited until the technicians left and Dr. Osborne came in to adjust the controls on all the capsules.

She got into her capsule right away, lay down, and went into a conversion cycle even before he finished fine-tuning it.

He kept working on her capsule for a long time before he moved on to the others.

Henshaw hung back watching every move he made. Dark circles surrounded her one eye. Her cheek looked sunken. Everyone in the battalion looked that way.

Rhodes had been checking his reflection in the washroom mirror every morning as usual. He didn't notice himself looking so worn out, but maybe he wouldn't notice it in himself.

He didn't notice Oakes looking different, either, but maybe Rhodes got used to that the way he got used to them not talking.

If Oakes looked drawn and bowed down by his circumstances, Rhodes would have considered that normal considering everything that happened. Rhodes would have considered that normal for himself, too.

He didn't really know what to think about any of this anymore. He'd given up trying to figure it out.

Rhinehart and Coulter asked him about what the brass planned to do with the battalion. Rhodes repeated the discussion that happened at his last meeting with the governing body.

Dietz and Henshaw listened from a distance, but they didn't get involved. No one acted at all surprised by any of this, not even Rhodes's suggestion to take Fuentes offline.

"They'll send us back into combat," Rhinehart murmured under his breath. "The Legion has invested too much in us to just let us sit here doing nothing."

"The only question is if they'll send us before or after they work out these malfunctions," Rhodes replied. "They said the counteroffensive was starting in three weeks and that was two weeks ago. If you all come back to full functioning, the brass might decide to deploy us pretty soon."

Coulter sighed. "This is a really bad idea. So they corrected the malfunctions. That doesn't mean we won't suffer new ones once we get out there."

"There's no way to test us under battlefield conditions without sending us into battlefield conditions," Lauer pointed out. "Training sessions don't mean a thing."

"If they reactivate our weapons for training, will they leave our weapons active afterward?" Oakes asked.

Rhinehart glanced over at the soldiers. They never left the barracks. "How much longer will the brass keep us under guard like this? Are we prisoners here or what?"

"We always have been," Wild muttered through the interface. "We aren't any more prisoners now than we were before."

That killed the conversation again. Rhinehart, Lauer, and Coulter started playing The Ship, The Captain, and The Crew, but they didn't talk trash to each other or laugh or joke around. They hardly talked at all, not even to tally their scores.

They passed the dice around the circle in a dull trance. Henshaw fidgeted in a corner of the room and then, after fifteen minutes, she went into a conversion cycle, too.

The four men stayed awake a little longer before they did the same thing. Would they feel better after their cycles?

Rhodes couldn't bring himself even to care about that. He was finally adjusting his own sense of reality to this new horror. None of these people would ever recover or go back to normal. Normal didn't exist for them anymore.

This brooding, depressed silence actually felt more normal than the easy comradery the battalion enjoyed before. This dark, distant silence somehow matched the circumstances better.

The rest of Rhodes's people were finally responding appropriately to their situation. They were settling into it for the long haul—for as long as it lasted.

They conserved their energy for the ordeal ahead. Making light of it or trying to find some enjoyment in it—none of those things were possible any longer.

Even the SAMs fell into this gloomy stupor of just trying to survive this in any way possible. That was the best anyone could hope for now.

The four men entered their conversion cycles. Rhodes and Oakes were alone again the way they were before. They didn't talk. Nothing ever changed. It never would change ever again.

Chapter 13

Thackery's capsule cover opened. She came out of her conversion cycle first.

Rhodes barely glanced up from his drawing. He should have been more concerned about how his people would recover from their long stasis.

Thinking about it took too much effort. He wouldn't be able to predict the outcome anyway. He just had to wait and see.

His whole life was a game of wait-and-see now. He couldn't bring himself to care about much of anything.

Thackery didn't sit up right away, so he went back to drawing. He and Oakes had been sitting at the table drawing ever since the battalion came back from the lab.

Rhodes started to slip back into his brainless trance when the door opened a second time. He stiffened when he thought Fuentes might be coming back.

Instead, Colonel Kraft walked into the barracks and stopped next to the table.

He watched Rhodes and Oakes drawing for a second before Kraft worked up the nerve to speak. "Do you mind if I talk to you for a second?" he asked.

"Go right ahead," Rhodes replied without looking up from his drawing. "I'm all ears."

"Don't worry about it, Colonel." Oakes pushed back his bench and stood up. "I'm going to take a walk anyway. See you around, Captain."

"Have a good one, Lieutenant."

Oakes walked out of the barracks and left Rhodes alone with Kraft. Oakes left the interface active, though. He and Dash would be able to hear every word Rhodes and Kraft said to each other.

Kraft waved behind him. "Do you want to take a walk, too?"

Rhodes looked up for the first time. He had been planning to hold this conversation here in the barracks.

He wasn't interfacing with Thackery and Koenig—not yet—but he certainly didn't plan to conceal his conversation from them.

She rolled onto her side facing away from Rhodes and Kraft. She kept her eye closed. If she was listening to their conversation, she didn't show it.

Rhodes shrugged and stood up. "Okay. We can take a walk."

The two men left the barracks. The door was just closing when Thackery and Koenig appeared on the interface next to Fisher, Dash, and Oakes.

She gave Rhodes a knowing look through The Grid. No one in the battalion trusted these officers one inch.

"What's on your mind?" Rhodes asked once he and Kraft started strolling down the hall.

"I wanted to let you know that the brass has decided to deploy you back to the Emal wars."

Rhodes only nodded. "I'm not surprised."

"They won't send you back to Sulia. They plan to deploy you on a different planet. I know it doesn't make any difference. They're also scheduling the battalion for a series of training sessions to test out how well everyone is functioning."

Rhodes nodded again. None of this came as any surprise to him.

Kraft halted there in the middle of the corridor and pulled Rhodes to a halt. "They're also sending Fuentes back to you. I wanted to be the first to tell you. He's getting out of stasis tomorrow."

Rhodes stiffened. "So.....the doctors still can't find anything wrong with him?"

"Unfortunately not. No one in the governing body knows what's wrong with him...."

Rhodes raised his eyebrow. "But other people do?"

Kraft shrugged. "I'm beginning to think the doctors suspect. Osborne made a very detailed study of all the battalion's medical records when he first joined the project. He's studied them a lot more carefully than anyone in the governing body."

Rhodes turned away and started walking again. "I'm not surprised by that, either, actually. He and Trudeau had a much more thorough understanding of our circumstances even than Neiland, Irvine, and Montague. It was almost like those three went out of their way to *not* understand even though they were with us the longest."

Kraft lowered his voice to a confidential murmur. "I also want you to know that Osborne made a very convincing case for taking Fuentes offline—the same way you did. He came very close to resigning in protest over bringing Fuentes out of stasis at all."

"That does surprise me."

"Why should it? No one understands your situation better than Osborne—apart from everyone in the battalion, I mean. He realizes Fuentes is a danger to others as much as he is to himself."

"How are you going to handle that when you activate his weapons systems?" Rhodes asked. "You'll have to activate his weapons to send him through training. Do you plan to leave him unarmed the rest of the time? I don't even know why I ask. It won't make any difference once we deploy in combat. He'll be armed all the time. He'll have to be."

"Osborne asked the brass the same thing. I don't suppose they would have thought about it at all if he didn't bring it up."

"So what's the answer? When do the brass plan to activate our weapons?"

Kraft glanced right and left before he lowered his voice even more. "They already are active. They've been active for two weeks. If anyone in the battalion tries anything, they'll be fully armed and dangerous."

Rhodes looked away, but that only brought him face to face with Thackery, Koenig, Dash, and Oakes all listening through the interface.

Rhinehart and Lauer were waking up from their conversion cycles, too. They weren't on the interface yet, but they would be soon.

Having their weapons systems active didn't change how Rhodes felt about any of them. It would definitely change things once Fuentes returned.

For some reason, Rhodes didn't worry too much about Dietz having active weapons systems. Dietz was the least of Rhodes's problems right now.

Kraft halted in the middle of the corridor again. "You and the battalion are scheduled for your first training session this afternoon—before Fuentes comes back. You'll be able to see how well everyone is functioning. If everything works out, hopefully Fuentes will reintegrate into the battalion. The rest of you will have a stabilizing influence on him. That's what the brass hopes, anyway." He turned away. "I'll send you the full schedule. You can let me know if you have any issues with it."

He walked off and left Rhodes with plenty to think about. Standing around the barracks with fully activated weapons systems was one thing.

Taking them into a training session was another matter entirely. The battalion would have to shoot at their targets.

Nothing would stop any of them from shooting at each other then—if one of them got the crazy idea to shoot at something other than their targets.

He wandered back to the barracks in no particular hurry. He was in no rush to hurry up and get himself or his people shooting at anything.

At least Fuentes wouldn't be with them—not today. That adventure would have to wait until tomorrow—after the battalion found out if they could navigate even a simulated Grid course without someone winding up dead.

Dietz, Coulter, and Henshaw woke up before Rhodes got there. The others informed their comrades about the new schedule. Everyone had plenty to say about it.

Rhodes listened to their conversation through the interface. "How are we ever supposed to trust our SAMs again?" Coulter asked.

Henshaw gasped. "You don't trust your SAM?! How can you even say that, Eddie?"

"Fisher killed Dr. Irvine," Coulter pointed out. "Fisher took control of the captain and turned him into a raving, murderous maniac. The same thing could happen to any of us."

"We have to trust our SAMs!" she exclaimed. "They're all we have. The captain told us that from day one."

"How do we know one of them won't turn on us?" Coulter went on. "Legacy tried to kill you, but Keon could have done the same thing."

"Keon would never try to kill me!" she shrieked. "Don't you even suggest that about my SAM!"

"He might if he malfunctioned," Coulter argued. "I wouldn't think Fisher could hurt anybody, either, but he did."

"That wasn't his fault, though," Henshaw countered. "You can't blame him for that."

"I'm not saying it's his fault. I'm saying it happened and we have no way of knowing if or when it might happen again. It could happen on the battlefield. We could be fighting the enemy and one of the SAMs could turn on us instead."

"We're all thinking the same thing, man," Lauer muttered. "None of us wants that, but we all have to live with the possibility."

Henshaw rounded on him next. "I can't believe you're going along with this. You and Wild have been tight from the beginning."

"This has nothing to do with how I feel about Wild," Lauer told her. "We have to take all potential risks into account and this is one of them. The SAMs will always be a risk—to all of us. Each of our SAMs is a risk not just to the person carrying that particular SAM but to everyone else in the battalion. Accept it."

She threw up her hands and turned away. "I am not going to start thinking that way about Keon—or any other SAM."

"What about Van?" Thackery asked. "She's Rudy's SAM."

"She tried to save his life," Henshaw countered. "She tried to stop him from killing himself."

"That's kinda the point, isn't it?" Rhinehart interjected. "She took control of his movements—or tried to. She tried to override his free will and make him do something he didn't want to do—or stop him from doing what he wanted to do."

"Of course she did!" Henshaw blurted out. "That's her job—to help him and protect him. What was she supposed to do—let him kill himself—and her along with him?"

Rhinehart shrugged. "Why not? It's his decision if he wants to end it."

"No, it isn't!!" she shrieked. "He was malfunctioning! He wasn't thinking clearly."

"He was not malfunctioning," Fisher interjected in his soft undertone. "The brass says the doctors didn't find anything wrong with him either before he fled the barracks, while he was climbing onto the Ravager, or afterward."

"This is crazy!" Henshaw's wild eyes skipped around the group. "I can't believe you're all turning against your SAMs."

"We aren't turning against our SAMs—or I'm not," Rhinehart replied. "It is kind of unnerving, though, how dependent we've all become on them. We can't even fight without them. If they go down, we go down with them. We can't disconnect to keep functioning independently."

"That's a good thing!" she exclaimed. "That's the way it's supposed to be! We're supposed to depend on our SAMs."

"Maybe not this much," Thackery pointed out.

"I don't care what any of you say!" Henshaw fired back. "I'm glad I have Keon...."

"We're all glad we have our SAMs...." Oakes interjected.

"I'm not," Thackery snarled. "I hate the bastard."

Everyone turned around to stare at her. "You do?" Henshaw gasped. "Why?"

"Why in the world would I want some stranger getting in my face all the time and spitting his poison into my ear around the clock?" Thackery snapped. "I can never get rid of him even if he makes himself invisible. He's always there, watching and listening. He'll never go away—and like Eddie says, I don't even know if I can trust him. In fact, I know I can't. I would kill him if I could."

"I know exactly how you feel," Rhinehart murmured.

"The captain feels the same way," Fisher chimed in. "He's too polite to say so, but he still doesn't want me around."

"It isn't like that," Rhodes countered.

"Of course it is, Captain. You're too generous to say it in so many words, but admit it. You would much rather just live your life independently without a SAM. That's human nature. This whole situation with you, the battalion, and the SAMs—it's unnatural. It's contrary to your natural state. You would much rather go back to the way it was before. You can admit it. You won't offend me by saying so."

Rhodes squirmed. Fisher was right. Rhodes would much rather not have had a SAM at all.

He was immeasurably grateful that he got Fisher instead of some other SAM, but that didn't change the fact that this was unnatural. Human beings weren't designed for this.

His silence answered Fisher loud and clear.

"We all feel that way," Lauer murmured. "None of us asked for this."

Rhodes walked into the barracks just then and everyone turned to face him. He was in charge of this battalion. He was the one responsible for dealing with this disaster and coming up with a solution—if there was any solution to come up with.

Chapter 14

R hodes walked into the barracks and looked around at all his subordinates—and all their SAMs. They all waited for him to solve their problems.

He would never be able to do that because their problems were all his problems, too. He couldn't even cope with them himself, much less everyone else.

"What are we gonna do about this, Captain?" Henshaw asked. "We have to trust our SAMs. How can we not?"

"We've gone over this a million times," Rhodes replied. "The only question is how we're going to handle our session this afternoon." He turned to Thackery. "Can you work with Koenig, or do you want to make him silent and invisible and fight on your own?"

"I have to work with him," she replied. "I need his information. I can't keep track of everything on my own. The system feeds too much at me at once. I have to keep track of the whole Grid."

"That's the whole point," Henshaw interrupted. "We're all better off...."

Rhodes raised his hand to silence her. "You made your point, Georgie. We all know how you feel about Keon. I'm not asking you." He turned back to Thackery. "Just tell me what you want to do."

She twisted in her own skin—what was left of it. "What choice do I have?"

"You have the choice to make him silent and invisible. You have the choice not to take his information at all and accept the consequences—including that you might not see something in time. You could get shot and killed—or recaptured by the Emal. That's the risk you would have to take."

She curled her lip in disgust. "Great. So he's holding me as a hostage."

Rhodes turned to Coulter. "What about you and Murphy? Are you willing to work with him?"

"I'll work with him. It doesn't mean I have to trust him."

"No one is asking you to."

"That doesn't solve the problem of what we're supposed to do if one of them malfunctions during a battle—or a training session," Thackery pointed out.

"There won't be anything we can do," Rhodes pointed out. "We just have to deal with it. I don't like this any better than you do, but it isn't like we can do anything to prevent it from happening. If anything, we just have to prepare ourselves for when it does happen."

"Fantastic," Lauer snarled and turned away. "I'm done with this whole conversation. Just tell me when it's time to go. I don't want to talk about this anymore."

Dietz went back to the computer terminal. He didn't say a word during the conversation and neither did Zen. Should Rhodes be worried about that—more worried than he already was?

He took that opportunity to turn to the nine SAMs. They still surrounded him in the interface.

"Is there anything we can do to win back your trust, Captain?" Murphy asked. "I had no idea Eddie felt so strongly about this."

"Be grateful your host doesn't hate you and want to kill you," Koenig remarked. "I thought Coulter was rather circumspect and rational about the whole matter."

"None of you have to do anything to win back my trust," Rhodes replied. "I know none of you did anything deliberately. You malfunctioned. I don't blame you for that or for anything else you did while you were malfunctioning."

"Thank you, Captain," Fisher murmured. "You're very forgiving."

"Will you stop that—all of you? I don't care about any of that. I want to talk about what we're going to do, both in the training session and in actual combat, if one of you malfunctions."

"We won't be able to do anything if we malfunction," Wild pointed out. "We'll be helpless and out of control the way we have been in the past."

Rhodes sighed. "What about taking yourselves offline? Is that even a possibility?"

"Not if we're incapable of controlling our own processes," Wild replied.

"There must be some contingency plan we can come up with."

"I have a suggestion to make, Captain," Fisher interjected.

"By all means, let me hear it."

"I suggest that we assign each of our hosts the ability to deactivate our emotional responses in case of emergency. That would prevent any of us from incapacitating our host with crippling fear or sending one of you into a berserk rage the way we have in the past."

Rhodes spun around. "Can you do that?"

"I believe we can install a protocol in each of our systems that will assign our host the ability to do it."

"Why don't you just go the whole hog and assign our hosts the ability to take a SAM offline if they malfunction?" Rocky asked. "That would be much more effective, especially if the host is still perfectly functional. They can continue to function without a SAM until the SAM gets reprogrammed or repaired."

"What's the point of the host functioning independently?" Keon asked. "What's the point of the host carrying a SAM at all if they can function just as well without it?"

"I don't say the host can function just as well without it," Rocky replied. "I say the host can function better without a malfunctioning SAM than with a malfunctioning SAM. We wouldn't assign the battalion the ability to deactivate their SAMs just because. Thackery wouldn't be able to deactivate Koenig just because she doesn't like him. If a SAM malfunctions to the point of incapacitating their host—so long as the fault lies in the SAM and not the host themselves—then each person in the battalion would be able to function better by taking the SAM offline—even temporarily. It would be better than the entire host shutting down due to a malfunction in the SAM alone."

"That's an idea, but the doctors would have to reprogram each SAM," Rhodes pointed out. "We don't have time for that."

"We have time before the brass deploys the battalion back to Emal wars," Rocky suggested. "It might not happen today or tomorrow, but the SAMs are more likely to malfunction in real combat anyway."

"How much of that could you do right now?" Rhodes asked. "Could you assign each of us the ability to switch off your emotional responses?"

"Why not give the SAMs the ability to switch off each host's emotional responses, too?" Wild suggested. "If it will benefit the hosts to deactivate some function of their SAMs, then logic would suggest that the same might be true in reverse."

"You can't do that!" Keon countered. "You can't just deactivate some function of your host's neural processes."

"Why not?" Wild asked. "Wouldn't the hosts function better in combat without all that raw emotion running unchecked through their veins? It would certainly prevent any malfunctions."

"It might not prevent ALL malfunctions," Fisher pointed out. "It might even cause new ones. Human beings aren't designed to function without their emotions."

Rhodes held up his hand. "We don't have time to argue about this right now. I want each of you to start working on it—but don't install any of these switches yet. Just explore the possibility of installing them. We need to check with the doctors....and everybody....before we do something as drastic as that. In the meantime, we have a training session to prepare for."

The group broke up and everyone went back to whatever they were doing before—or they started to.

Fisher stopped them before they walked away. "I'm taking the captain out of the interface for a few minutes. I want to have a private conversation with him."

Lauer narrowed his eyes at the SAM. "Whatever you have to say to him you can say in front of us."

"I'm afraid it doesn't work that way, Lieutenant," Fisher returned with plenty of icy steel in his voice.

Rhodes had never heard Fisher talk to anyone like that—almost as if Fisher was Lauer's superior officer speaking down to someone beneath him.

"I'm not asking for anyone's permission," Fisher told him. "I'm going to have a private conversation with the captain before the training session. I'm informing you so you won't get alarmed when I take him off the interface."

Rhinehart frowned at him. "Don't we get a say in this?"

"No, you don't." Fisher turned to Rhodes. "If you don't mind stepping out of the barracks for a moment, Captain...."

Rhodes cringed at his tone. Now Fisher was ordering Rhodes around.

Rhodes realized in that moment just how deep his trust in Fisher had grown. Rhodes never once thought Fisher meant him any harm—or that Fisher would manipulate him—or that Fisher wanted to talk to him privately for some underhanded reason.

It never once crossed Rhodes's mind that Fisher wanted to take him by himself so Fisher could malfunction, turn murderous, and harm Rhodes.

Rhodes would never believe that, but he saw plenty of his subordinates giving him side looks. They certainly thought Fisher was capable of that and maybe a lot more.

Why shouldn't they believe it after the way Fisher used Rhodes to kill Dr. Irvine? Fisher could be spilling all kinds of psycho suggestions into Rhodes's ears while his subordinates' backs were turned.

Fisher wouldn't do that. For a start, this was the first private conversation they'd ever had since Rhodes got out of stasis. He'd been interfacing with Oakes the whole time and then with the whole battalion.

Fisher never asked to talk to Rhodes privately before. This must be something serious.

Rhodes walked out of the barracks and Fisher switched off the interface. He did it by himself. He didn't give Rhodes a chance to do it himself.

Rhodes set off walking through the station. Fisher didn't break the silence until Rhodes passed the concourse and entered Coleridge Station's administrative wing.

Too many people in the battalion knew about the loading dock. Too many people went there for privacy. Rhodes didn't want anyone finding him there.

He also didn't want anyone overhearing whatever he said to Fisher. More than two hundred station personnel worked on the loading docks around the clock.

They were all used to hearing Rhodes talking to someone they couldn't see. He didn't think they listened to his one-sided conversations with Fisher, but he couldn't be certain.

Instead, he went to an empty auditorium. He couldn't remember anyone in the station ever using the auditorium for anything, but he didn't exactly keep track of station happenings.

The auditorium was definitely empty now. Rhodes sat down in one of the seats in the far upper corner of the stands before he faced his SAM. "What's on your mind?"

"I'm.....I didn't want to say anything in front of the others, Captain...." Fisher stammered.

"What's wrong? Are you malfunctioning again?"

"No, nothing like that."

"Are you feeling guilty again about killing Dr. Irvine? Is that what this is about?"

"I...." Fisher looked everywhere but at Rhodes. "I....I......"

Rhodes waited. He'd never seen Fisher this uncertain before. He always acted so put-together and controlled in front of the battalion.

"Whatever it is, we can work it out," Rhodes told him. "We've gone through worse before."

"How would I know, though?" Fisher blurted out. "How would I know if I was malfunctioning?"

Rhodes opened his mouth to answer and stopped himself. That was the problem. None of them realized they were malfunctioning—not while it was in the middle of happening.

"I hate to say it, but I agree with Thackery and Coulter," Fisher rasped. "You've always stood up for me. You always put your faith in me—but what if you're wrong? You shouldn't trust me—not after everything that's happened. Your trust is misplaced. You would be setting yourself up for another disaster."

"No! We aren't going to start thinking like that." Rhodes shot to his feet and stormed out of the auditorium on his way back across the station. "We've been through too much already to start doubting each other now."

"But what if Rocky is right? What if there's a way to take the SAMs offline and all of you would be better off without us?"

"Stop that right now!" Rhodes snapped. "You've saved my ass too many times. Your job is to protect me and my job is to protect you. I'm not better off without you and you aren't better off without me. We're a unit now. No one is going to take you offline—not as long as I'm alive."

"What if I malfunction?" Fisher murmured. "What if I don't realize what I'm doing and I put you in danger—or I put someone else in danger? It's my job to make sure that doesn't happen. I might take control of you and make you kill yourself or someone else."

"You would only do that if you malfunctioned. Then it wouldn't be your fault."

"But you would be just as hurt or dead. How can I live with that?"

Rhodes shook his head again. "I don't know where all this doubt is coming from, but you can't start thinking like that. We're going into combat soon. You need to be certain of yourself and me—the same way I need to be certain of myself and you."

"You heard what Lauer said. You have to take all potential risks into account. This is a potential risk. You would be irresponsible not to consider it."

"I am taking it into account, pal. I have considered it and taken it into account and I have come to the conclusion that I'm better off with you than without you—even if you malfunction. Now please stop talking about this. Get your game face on. We have too many other problems to deal with. We can't start doubting ourselves now."

Fisher hesitated for a minute before he asked. "Where are you going?"

Rhodes didn't answer and he didn't go back to the barracks. He went to the lab. It was Dr. Osborne's lab now. He'd taken over the facility that used to be Dr. Neiland's.

Osborne and Trudeau worked together all the time now. Trudeau shadowed Osborne everywhere he went.

Neither of them acted at all surprised by Rhodes showing up unannounced.

Neither of the new doctors ever mentioned or showed by action or body language that they were even aware that Rhodes and Fisher had been the ones who killed Dr. Irvine.

Neither of the new doctors showed any misgivings that another malfunction might cause someone in the battalion to do something similar to Osborne or Trudeau.

Osborne looked up from whatever he was working on. "Can I help you, Captain?"

"I want you to check my SAM and see if he's malfunctioning."

Osborne frowned at his controls. "Is he behaving strangely? Is he doing anything out of the ordinary?"

"That's what I want to find out. I don't really know what's ordinary or out of the ordinary when it comes to a SAM."

"What is he doing?"

Rhodes shrugged. "It's hard to describe."

Osborne tapped on his screen a few times. "I'm not reading any disturbance. All his systems check out."

Rhodes nodded. "I thought so."

"Did you really think it would be any different?" Fisher murmured in his ear. "I'm doing my job."

Osborne studied Rhodes a little more closely. "Is something bothering you, Captain?"

"Not really. Thank you for checking."

He walked back out of the lab. "Why did you do that?" Fisher asked. "Did you really think my doubts were a malfunction?"

"You aren't supposed to have any emotions at all. You feeling guilty about Dr. Irvine was a malfunction."

"I'm not malfunctioning," Fisher murmured. "I'm trying to protect you."

"I know that, pal. That's exactly why I trust you the way I do. You wouldn't suggest it if you weren't trying to help me—and the rest of the battalion."

Fisher hesitated again. "So what do you want to do about it?"

"Nothing. There isn't anything we can do except keep on going. We'll just keep going until we can't go anymore."

Chapter 15

Rhodes dropped into The Grid and looked around at his subordinates. They all looked as gloomy and drained as they did when they first got out of stasis—this time.

Going through a conversion cycle—or even multiple conversion cycles—didn't do anything to perk them up.

The lingering reality weighed on each of them more heavily with every passing day. It almost got worse with every passing hour they had to stay alive.

The interface stayed active when they entered The Grid. The eight SAMs joined the circle in front of each member of the battalion.

"Is everybody ready?" Rhodes asked.

"Ready," Henshaw replied.

"Shut it down at the first sign of trouble," Rhodes ordered. "If anyone malfunctions, get out of The Grid, shut down your weapons, and get out of danger pronto. Understood?"

Everyone nodded. Lauer said, "Yes, Sir."

"Let's go," Rhodes ordered.

He turned away, fired his boosters, and took off through the black Grid landscape. The rest of the battalion flew on his heels.

The landscape changed immediately. Rhodes cringed when it morphed into another Emal deathscape just like Luluna.

Some part of him expected this. The system—or whatever cosmic power decided which scenarios the battalion trained in—they must have realized the Emal presented the battalion's greatest emotional challenge.

The battalion soared over mountains of rubble, twisted bodies, and crashed ships. The grid lines rotated behind Rhodes and adjusted his view of the landscape, every obstacle, and every enemy position ahead.

The battalion approached the front line. "What's the objective?" Rhodes asked Fisher.

"We're supposed to defend another platoon evacuation. Ravagers are coming in to lift off the platoons, but the Emal are pressing too closely for the Ravagers to land."

Rhodes glanced up at the sky. "I don't see any Ravagers. Why do they take so long to descend?"

"They don't want to fly into enemy laser fire."

"So we have to fly into enemy laser fire instead?" Lauer asked. "Stellar."

"This scenario has all the elements that caused us to malfunction before," Rocky pointed out.

"All except real Emal," Oakes added. "We never dealt with a training session where the Emal found out about us and tried to capture us for our implants."

"They could be trying to do it here," Rhinehart suggested, but right then, the laser fire in the distance flickered in the battalion's direction.

"Get down on the ground!" Rhodes ordered. "Get behind the hills!"

Fisher adjusted The Grid in front of Rhodes's eyes. "We're still too far away from the platoons. We won't be able to defend them from here."

"There's another channel behind those hills there," Koenig suggested. "We can fly through the channel, flank the Emal, and attack them from the northeast. That will draw them away from the platoons long enough for the Ravagers to land."

"Don't listen to him, Captain," Thackery interjected. "That channel is a trap."

Rhodes spun around to stare at her. "What makes you say that—and don't tell me it's because Koenig suggested it."

"It isn't that. Look. The Emal have mounted laser cannons on both sides of the channel."

"They're unmanned," Koenig argued.

"Shut the hell up! I'm not talking to you," Thackery snapped and made some modifications to The Grid layout. The whole battalion looked at it through the interface. "If you roll back the readings from previous battles, you'll see that the Emal planted these cannons in that channel before the battle shifted over here. The cannon placements are mechanized. We would fly straight into them."

"How did you figure that out without Koenig telling you?" Rhinehart asked.

She sneered at him and then wrinkled her nose at her SAM. "I don't need him to tell me that shit."

"We could still use the channel," Koenig suggested. "We can just fly over the cannon placements and avoid them."

"You really must be malfunctioning if you expect me to fall for that. The cannons can swivel upward and hit us from any direction." She turned back to Rhodes. "We can't use that channel."

"What about using a different channel?" Fisher asked. "We can use this one farther west. It doesn't have cannon placements and it would accomplish the same thing. It would get us into a protected position where we can flank the Emal."

Thackery made a face at him, too, but she didn't argue back.

Rhodes didn't understand her sudden hostility toward the SAMs, especially her own. He couldn't find any fault with her logic about the cannon placements, though. They really did make that channel a death trap.

"Find us a route through the alternate channel, Fisher," Rhodes ordered. "Lay out a course for us and transmit it to each person's Grid."

"Sending it now," Fisher replied.

The route showed up on The Grid. Thackery didn't complain about it.

Rhodes gave the order and the battalion diverted into the other channel. He kept pivoting The Grid in front of his face, changing the lines, and checking every possible angle for hidden enemies.

The Emal concentrated their firepower on the platoons in front of them. As usual, the Emal pinned the platoons down in the black wasteland.

Lasers, fusion blasts, and the fire from exploding ships gave the only light. Rhodes and his subordinates could see everything in The Grid, but Rhodes found himself hesitating to trust that.

What if Fisher was right? What if Rhodes was making a colossal mistake by trusting both Fisher and The Grid?

Rhodes tried to shake those thoughts out of his head. He couldn't start questioning them now—especially not Fisher.

Fisher and The Grid were the only tools Rhodes had to work with. If he got rid of them, he had nothing left.

The battalion got halfway up the channel before lasers erupted from all the way down on the very floor. They blasted scrap metal out of the way before the lasers burned upward into the night.

The rubble must have buried the cannon placements. The debris concealed the guns until the battalion flew directly over them.

Four lasers fired at the battalion and two of them hit Thackery. She tumbled out of the sky and pitched at terminal velocity toward the ground.

Coulter yanked out of formation immediately and dove after her. "Don't go down there, Eddie!" Murphy yelled, but Coulter was already plummeting straight for Thackery.

He wound up flying straight into another laser barrage. They converged and smashed into him, too, just as he caught Thackery out of the air.

He broke her fall, but at too great a cost. He fell through another volley of shots that pinwheeled him and Thackery head over heel.

They crashed down on the ground at the very bottom of the channel. They landed close enough to the cannon placements themselves that the lasers couldn't hit either of them here. That was the only thing that saved them.

"Murphy! Koenig!" Rhodes snapped. "Are you both still online?!"

"We're fine," Murphy growled. "Coulter is injured and Thackery is unconscious."

"Stay where you are," Rhodes replied. "We'll accomplish the objective and end the training session. That's the quickest way to get you out of The Grid. We can't risk coming down to get you right now."

"Go," Murphy muttered. "These two aren't going anywhere."

Rhodes checked The Grid once to make sure Thackery and Coulter were all right. Coulter had laser burns on his abdomen and the organic side of his shoulder. Other than that, he was fine.

Thackery's vital signs read normal. She was just unconscious. Both SAMs were fully operational, though, so her injuries couldn't have been very severe.

Rhodes dragged his awareness back to the battle. He could think of plenty of things he wanted to say to both Thackery and Coulter when this was all over.

That would have to wait, though.

"Scan the rest of the channel and see if you can locate any other placements," he told Fisher.

"There are four of them. I'm bringing them up on The Grid. You can avoid them by flying higher up the hillsides on both sides. That should avoid the motion sensors."

Rhodes obeyed without a word. He didn't allow himself to think of Fisher as his superior officer.

It would have been more accurate to say that Rhodes no longer cared if Fisher was his superior officer.

At least someone around here might actually be qualified to make decisions for the \ battalion. Rhodes sure wasn't—or he didn't feel like he was.

Listening to someone else and following Fisher's orders gave Rhodes one of the greatest senses of relief he'd ever experienced in his life. He trusted Fisher a hell of a lot more than he trusted any other senior officer involved in this war.

He swooped high over the hillsides, but never high enough to alert the Emal of the battalion's approach. He swerved wide to avoid the last placement.

The Grid showed the Emal line ahead. They bore down even harder on the Legion platoons. The Ravagers hung off in orbit. Lasers flew thick and fast. The Ravagers couldn't descend without getting destroyed.

Rhodes gunned his boosters. "Get the Ravagers down here now!" he ordered. "Spread out and draw the Emal away from the platoons!"

His subordinates scattered to the four winds. It would have been really helpful to have eight people attacking the Emal right now instead of six.

He stuffed down his annoyance and concentrated everything on getting the Emal's attention.

He didn't use his Grid this time or change into a giant glowing alien. No one in the battalion did.

They plunged in gunning all their weapons at the Emal on the western flank. Rhodes flew straight ahead while his subordinates fanned down the line to cover as much territory as possible.

Rhodes unloaded with his scourge guns. The gun blasts lit up the night. They got the Emal's attention better than anything—except maybe Viper explosions.

He unloaded one Viper after another. They detonated down the line and the Emal spun around to face the battalion.

The Grid gave Rhodes a perfect view of the Ravagers sinking through the dense cloud. The Emal opened fire. That left a clear space for the Ravagers to land and start taking the platoons on board.

Eight members of the battalion might not have been able to stand up to the Emal numbers. Six definitely couldn't.

The Emal overran the battalion in seconds. Whoever programmed this training session definitely didn't include the part about the Emal trying to capture the battalion for their implants.

Rhodes's mind shifted gears. He came up with an imaginary explanation that the Emal no longer wanted to capture the battalion. The aliens just wanted to destroy the only Legion weapon that posed a threat to the Emal invasion.

None of that mattered because the battalion couldn't hold its own against the Emal horde. Thousands of aliens surged away from the escaping platoons and smothered the battalion in no time.

Lasers wheeled back and forth across the battlefield, but they didn't concentrate on the platoons anymore.

Base ships in the far rear on the Emal side turned their guns on the battalion. Every shot killed countless Emal, but the aliens didn't care.

A punishing smash hit Rhinehart thirty yards away from Rhodes. Rhinehart screamed and crumpled under a tide of alien bodies.

"Rhinehart!" Rhodes bellowed, but Rhinehart vanished off the interface along with Rocky.

Rhodes spun around to fight his way over there, but he couldn't move with so many Emal in the way.

He scrambled to locate Rhinehart on The Grid, but Rhinehart wasn't there anymore.

"He's gone, Captain!" Fisher yelled over the noise. "The Grid must have returned him to Coleridge Station!"

"We gotta get out of here! How much longer before the Ravagers lift off?"

Fisher said something in response, but Rhodes didn't catch it as another bone-crushing smash of cannon fire struck on his right.

Lauer went down and he vanished off the map, too. Wild went with him. That left four people—Rhodes, Henshaw, Dietz, and Oakes.

The Emal swarm overwhelmed the four even easily, now that the aliens no longer had so many people to target.

Rhodes went into a frenzy shooting as many Emal as he could. He got so preoccupied with shooting every weapon in his arsenal that he forgot to check on the rest of his people.

He swiped his own lasers back and forth across the horde. He unleashed one Viper after another.

So many Emal packed around him that the Vipers exploded right on top of him. Their blasts pounded his implants and nearly knocked him down.

He couldn't let himself fall under these aliens. They would cut him to pieces.

He spun his laser to the right carving a path through hundreds of bodies. Countless more Emal surged at him from right behind the aliens he just cut down.

Their eyes surrounded him on all sides. He couldn't see anything beyond all those eyes staring back at him.

Without warning, a catastrophic smash hit him from somewhere. It flattened him in a split second....and he came to his senses back on the plain, black Grid. The war-torn landscape was gone.

Chapter 16

R hinehart grabbed Rhodes's arm and pulled him to his feet. "Are you okay, Sir?"

Rhodes shook himself. "I'm fine, Lieutenant. Did we accomplish the objective? Did the Ravagers lift off?"

"The Ravagers made it out," Fisher replied. "That's what ended the training session. It just cost all your lives in the process. If this had been real, only Coulter and Thackery would have survived."

Rhodes glanced around the circle. Thackery, Lauer, Coulter, and Rhinehart all appeared unharmed. "Are all of you okay?"

"I came back here," Thackery replied. "Eddie said I got hit, but I don't think I did. I think The Grid took me out of the session and replaced me with something else—something that made you think I got hurt."

Rhodes confronted her and Coulter. "What the hell were you two thinking? You agreed to work with your SAMs. You can't go questioning everything they tell you in the middle of a battle."

"Koenig was wrong about the first channel," Thackery argued. "I couldn't let him lead us into a trap."

"I couldn't let her fall to her death," Coulter pointed out. "She would have died from that fall if that battle had been real."

"*You* could have died," Rhodes countered. "You should have listened to Murphy."

"His job is to protect me, but he would have put another battalion member in danger by doing it." Coulter shrugged. "Anyway, I made it."

"You both agreed that you would work with your SAMs," Rhodes went on. "None of us can afford for you to get taken out because you don't listen to your SAMs' information."

"We agreed to work with them," Coulter returned. "We told you we wouldn't trust them."

"Then what's the point of going into battle with them at all? Just make them invisible and silent if you aren't going to listen to their recommendations."

"What are we supposed to do—obey them blindly and never question their judgment?" Thackery fired back. "We've already seen that they can't be trusted."

"If you really want to hear my opinion, then yes, I say you should obey them blindly and never question their judgment," Rhodes replied. "That's what I'm doing."

"You do?" Lauer asked. "You obey all Fisher's recommendations and never question him—ever?"

"Not in a combat situation—no, I don't. Are you crazy? He told me to fly up along the hillsides and he was right. He can process information in The Grid a lot faster than I can. I don't have time to run through hours and hours of battle data the way he can. He can do it in a split second. If he tells me to fly somewhere to stay away from laser cannons, that's what I'm going to do. I would be stupid not to."

"What if he gives you a questionable order?" Coulter asked. "Would you obey him then?"

"Do you mean an order like, say, 'Don't fly into enemy laser cannons?' Is that the kind of questionable order you mean?"

"You can't expect us to believe that Fisher has never done anything questionable," Thackery interjected.

"We know he has," Oakes chimed in.

"I never said he hasn't," Rhodes replied. "I know he has, but the middle of a battle isn't the time to start questioning his every word. I won't question him at all unless I have some reason to think he might be malfunctioning. Neither Murphy nor Koenig was malfunctioning when they made those recommendations."

"But Koenig was wrong about that first channel," Thackery pointed out.

"That isn't why you ignored his recommendation," Rhodes countered. "You ignored his recommendation because you resent having a SAM. If your positions were reversed and he was the one telling you the channel was unsafe because the Emal had planted laser cannons there, you would have rejected his recommendation and flown straight into that channel. You would have gone out of your way to do the opposite of whatever he suggested."

Rhodes turned to launch into a similar reprimand of Coulter. Rhodes saw himself reprimanding them in front of the whole battalion.

Rhodes intended to do exactly that. He had to make an example of these two.

"This whole session proves my point—just in case any of you haven't already gotten the memo," he went on. "We all have to make a choice—live with the SAMs or not. I've already made my choice. I won't give up Fisher. Hell no."

Thackery looked away.

"I don't see anything wrong with Murphy or Koenig," Rhodes told them. "As far as I'm concerned, you two were the ones who stepped out of line. I don't see anything wrong with either recommendation that either SAM made during the training session."

"You don't see anything wrong with Koenig telling us to fly into enemy laser cannons?" Thackery countered.

"So Koenig made a mistake based on incomplete information. So what? A mistake like that could happen to anyone."

"Murphy would have let her die," Coulter argued. "I couldn't let that happen."

"I definitely took Murphy's side on this one. That fall wouldn't have killed Thackery—not even if the battle had been real instead of a Grid training session. You alive and helping the battalion against the Emal would have been much more useful to accomplishing the objective than you crashing and burning along with her. Murphy did his job by protecting you. You were the one in the wrong here—not Murphy."

The Grid vanished around them at that moment. The lines vanished and the battalion wound up in the plain white training room.

General Brewster and Colonel Kraft stood there waiting. General Brewster scowled at Rhodes and his people.

This was the first time Rhodes had ever seen General Brewster scowl at anyone. He always presented such a bubbly, overly enthusiastic expression. Scowling made him look idiotic.

"That training session could have gone better, Captain," he muttered.

"We accomplished the objective," Rhodes replied. "Isn't that what we're supposed to do? We saved the platoons."

"You cost six battalion lives in the process. I don't call that a victory."

"The point of this was to check our SAMs for malfunctions. We did that. As far as I'm concerned, that training session was a success."

"So....are any of you malfunctioning?" Brewster asked.

Rhodes stopped himself from glancing at Coulter and Thackery. "No, none of us are malfunctioning."

Brewster's expression cleared immediately. He clapped his hands and rubbed them together. "Excellent! Then we can start planning to deploy the battalion back to the Emal wars."

"Just hold your horses right there, pal," Rhinehart interrupted. "We still haven't gotten Rudy back. We have to train with him. Then—maybe—we'll see if this battalion is in any condition to go anywhere."

Brewster narrowed his eyes at Rhinehart. "You're out of line, soldier. You're still expected to address your superior officers with the appropriate degree of respect."

"Superior?" Rhinehart snorted. "There is not one of you jokers who is superior to me and I am definitely addressing you with the appropriate degree of respect—which is none."

Rhodes raised his hand. "That's enough. We finished the session. That's all that matters. If you gentlemen don't have anything else...."

"You finished the session with more than two-thirds of your personnel dead including yourself," Brewster countered. "This is exactly the kind of setback that could lead the governing body to decide to shut down this whole project. There would be no Battalion 1 if this happened in real life."

"I really hope they do shut down the project," Rhodes replied. "I pray for the day. Excuse me, gentlemen. We're going back to the barracks."

He pushed between them just to make his point. He was really starting to agree with Rhinehart. These fools didn't deserve his respect or even the time out of his day.

"You can go back to the barracks now, Captain, but this isn't finished," Brewster called after him. "I'm ordering psych evaluations on all of you later this afternoon. We need to establish if any of you might be too dangerously unstable to go back into combat."

"I already told you we were," Rhodes replied over his shoulder.

"Are you ordering psych evaluations on our SAMs, too?" Thackery asked.

Brewster frowned. "Psych evaluations on your SAMs? Why would we order that? The SAMs don't have psychology that needs to be evaluated."

No one answered him. Rhodes and the rest of the battalion left the training room. They reopened the interface on their way back to the barracks.

No one said anything until they reentered the familiar room. "Psych evaluations," Lauer snarled. "I never could stand those."

"Who the hell cares?" Oakes countered. "It doesn't matter what they find out. They'll send us into combat either way."

"The captain is right," Henshaw murmured. "We're all too dangerously unstable to go into combat."

"There is no such thing as too dangerously unstable to go into combat," Rhinehart told her. "Dangerously unstable is what going into combat is all about."

"Even if being dangerously unstable puts your comrades and other Legion soldiers in danger?" she asked. "Isn't that the problem—that we would be too dangerously unstable to tell who we should shoot at?"

"It doesn't matter because any malfunction could cause us to shoot at the wrong target," Oakes replied. "These doctors will be evaluating us in our normal state—not in a malfunctioning state. Whatever they find out won't mean squat once the lead starts flying."

"Nothing these people do makes any sense." Rhodes sat down at the table and picked up his pencil. "I agree with Oakes. The brass will send us out regardless of what they find in these evaluations. This is just Brewster's way of showing the governing body that he can jump through hoops as well as they want him to. After that, we'll go into battle either way."

"Of course we will," Lauer growled. "The Legion can't fight this war without us."

"The Legion can't fight the war *with* us," Rhinehart pointed out. "One of these days, the Emal will realize they don't have to stop with their own territory. They can take the whole Treaty of Aemon Cluster and then we'll all be in big trouble."

Chapter 17

R hodes stepped into Dr. Osborne's lab and looked around. It looked the same. "What am I doing here?" he asked. "I'm supposed to get a psych evaluation."

"You are getting one, but I'm not qualified to give you one." Dr. Osborne pushed out his stool. "Sit down and we'll get started."

"How can we get started if you aren't qualified to evaluate me?"

"Just sit down. You'll see."

Rhodes sat down on the stool. He didn't see how he could get a psych evaluation here. He and Osborne were the only people in the room.

Each of Rhodes's subordinates had been assigned to a different room in the medical wing for their evaluations. Dr. Osborne couldn't evaluate everyone at once.

Now Rhodes found out Osborne wasn't even the person who would conduct the evaluations.

He tapped on his stacks of computer equipment. "The evaluation will start...now."

Rhodes glanced over at him, but at that moment, the lab vanished and Rhodes entered The Grid. "What are you doing?" he asked. "Why am I here?"

"You'll be evaluated in The Grid," Osborne replied. "The doctor assigned to evaluate you should be appearing...now."

The Grid changed in front of Rhodes's eyes and he found himself not in Dr. Osborne's lab, but in a comfortable lounge.

Dark wooden paneling covered the walls. Woven carpets made the floor soft and warm. A fire crackled in the large stone fireplace across the room.

An older man in a brown houndstooth suit jacket and glasses sat in a wide leather armchair across from Rhodes. The guy sat with his legs crossed and balanced a notepad on his lap. He wasn't smoking a pipe, but he might as well have been.

Rhodes himself still sat on the same stool from the lab. He saw how out of place he looked with all his shiny metal implants, Viper missiles strapped to his back, and all the Legion's strongest firepower attached to his limbs.

The sight of this fake doctor almost made Rhodes burst out laughing.

The image didn't seem to see this scenario as a joke, though—obviously. "Welcome, Captain," the guy began in a deep, husky voice. "I'm Dr. Watson."

Now Rhodes really did burst out laughing. He couldn't help it. "Dr. Watson? Seriously?"

The guy cocked his head. "Is there a problem?"

"What's so funny about him being named Dr. Watson?" Fisher asked.

Dr. Watson inclined his head the other way. "Your SAM shouldn't be here. He might interfere with your results."

"I'm being evaluated for how well I perform with my SAM," Rhodes pointed out. "Removing him would skew the results, too."

The doctor shrugged. Rhodes absolutely refused to think of him as Dr. Watson. That was ridiculous.

If the Legion brass actually thought naming him that gave him some credibility, they were sadly mistaken.

He consulted his notepad. "Let's get started. Your military record indicates you've suffered some mental distress recently."

Rhodes blinked at him. How in the name of God was he supposed to take this projection seriously?

The doctor waited for Rhodes to speak. "Is anything wrong, Captain?"

"What exactly do you want me to say? Yes, I had some mental distress recently."

"Do you want to talk about it?"

"Why the hell would I want to do that?"

"To help me evaluate your mental state."

"No, I don't want to talk about it."

The doctor checked his notepad again. God only knew what was on it.

Then Rhodes remembered. He was in The Grid. This wasn't real. Nothing was on that notepad.

He almost busted up laughing again at the thought, but he bit it back. He enjoyed seeing the projection go through the motions so seriously.

"Why do you think you suffered mental distress?" the doctor asked.

Rhodes's one remaining eye fell out of its socket. "You can't be serious!"

"Of course I'm serious. What caused you to experience this distress? Your record indicates it was severe and that you and your subordinates are suffering from an ongoing obsessive desire to end your lives. That sounds pretty serious to me."

Rhodes snorted and leaned back on his stool. "You want to know what caused it? Look at me, asshole! If this isn't enough to cause mental distress, I don't know what is."

"And yet you spent years as the commanding officer of a combat platoon in the Legion. Your record doesn't indicate that your previous experience caused you this level of emotional turmoil."

"You're serious," Rhodes fired back. "You seriously don't see anything about me that would cause emotional turmoil? What else did you read in my record?"

"Everything. I have access to the entire Legion database."

"You know what? This is stupid. I'm not going to explain it to you. If you can't see for yourself, then someone made a mistake programming you to evaluate me."

"I can't evaluate you if you won't talk about it. What do you think I see when I look at you?"

Rhodes's jaw hit the floor. This projection really wanted him to spell it out in every gory detail.

Rhodes made a calculated decision. "What are you going to do if I don't talk about it?"

"I'll have no choice but to recommend that you aren't fit for combat duty."

"Perfect," Rhodes replied. "You do that."

Now it was the doctor's turn to raise his eyebrows. "You don't want to go back into combat? But you're a soldier. You're a captain in the Aemon Legion. It's your job to go into combat and defend the Treaty of Aemon Cluster against its enemies."

"Not anymore. I died on the battlefield. Didn't you read that in my record?"

"Of course, but....."

"Then I think you'd admit that a dead man isn't under any obligation to do anything. I'm not a captain in the Aemon Legion anymore. I'm.....I'm a figment of your imagination."

The doctor stared at him in such dazed disbelief that Rhodes really did laugh. He had to get his kicks somewhere. Why not here? He didn't have to worry about hurting this Grid projection's feelings.

Unfortunately, the doctor had been programmed to be more tenacious than Rhodes expected.

The doctor jotted something on his notepad. "Why don't you want to go into combat?"

"Apart from the risk of getting killed? That about covers it. I'm scared. That's the truth. I don't want to die. I don't want to get cut to pieces by lasers the way I did before or crushed by falling Dusters or torn apart by curious alien scientists. I would rather remain intact here at Coleridge Station and spend the rest of my life studying art with my friends."

"What about your subordinates and comrades?" the doctor asked. "Don't you feel the smallest obligation to support them, protect them, and help them get through the war in one piece?"

"They won't need my support, protection, and help if they don't go into combat, either. With any luck, the other...programs or whatever they are will recommend that my subordinates and comrades aren't fit for combat duty, either. Then we can all live our lives here in peace. Isn't that what everyone wants?"

The doctor image cleared its throat, shifted in its chair, and rearranged its notepad on its lap. "I'm afraid things are a little more complicated than that, Captain."

"I know they are. They're complicated because I'll go into combat again no matter what you recommend."

"You know that isn't true. The Legion brass wouldn't have ordered a psych evaluation for you if they didn't have grave concerns for your mental wellbeing. Your repeated remarks about ending your own life, your subordinates' lives, and the like don't paint a very encouraging picture of your mental state."

"I'm sure my mental state is far worse than any of the Legion brass has even allowed themselves to consider," Rhodes muttered back.

"Then we need to do something about that. Why do you want to end your life?"

"I never said I wanted to end my life—not like that. I said I would encourage and support any of my subordinates to do it if they really felt that their situations had become intolerable. Obviously Fuentes has already come to that conclusion, so why shouldn't he carry it out?"

"He shouldn't carry it out because his mental state has deteriorated to the point where he can't think rationally about his situation. His situation could improve and then he would feel that life was worth living again. Then he might be glad that he didn't end his life. You would rob him of that chance."

"How could his situation improve to make him think life was worth living again?" Rhodes asked. "What could possibly improve it?"

"You just said you don't want to end your own life," the doctor countered. "You must think life is worth living or you wouldn't be going through all this. Why do you think life is worth living for you and not for Fuentes?"

"I don't think my life is worth living, but even if I did, that wouldn't mean anything for Fuentes. It's his life. If he thinks it isn't worth living, then that's his choice to make."

"Some of us disagree. A few key changes in his thought process could improve his outlook on his life, his future, and what it all means to him."

Rhodes snorted. "I'm pretty sure what it all means to him is the problem, pal."

"Exactly my point. He could change what it all means to him and then he would see his life as worth living after all."

Rhodes sat back on his stool. "Great. You explain it to him and see how far you get."

"You will be the one explaining it to him when he gets out of stasis tomorrow."

Rhodes's head shot up again. "You aren't going to evaluate Fuentes? You're going to throw him back into the battalion without even trying to evaluate his mental state?"

"You seem to think you understand him better than the rest of us. If anyone can convince him, you can."

Chapter 18

Rhodes sank down on the bench at the table in the barracks, cradled his head in his hand, shut his eyes, and groaned.

He was the first member of the battalion to make it back from the psych evaluations. He had the place to himself.

He'd gone through many psych evaluations in his military career, but none as moronic as this one. Then again, he'd never been evaluated by a computer program before.

He didn't know how long he would have to wait for someone else to finish. He was just making up his mind to go back to his drawing when Oakes returned.

He took one look at Rhodes, spread his thumb and forefinger to their widest point, propped them against the side of his face, and lowered his voice to a comedic impression of the fake psychologist.

"Elementary, my dear Watson," Oakes teased and burst out laughing.

Rhodes found himself breaking into a grin. "At least we got it over with."

Oakes threw himself down on the other side of the table. "Those cocksuckers on the damn governing body don't even have the decency to send a real person to evaluate us. Maybe their budget is suffering."

"It just proves that you were right. The results don't mean anything."

"I told the freak I really hoped the brass ended the program."

"I told him the same thing."

Oakes looked up and cracked a grin. "Let's spend the rest of the week coming up with another name for him. We need a few laughs in this place."

"What about Why-son.....or When-son?" Rhodes suggested.

Oakes started to snort with more laughter, but right then, the door swung open. Rhinehart stormed in fuming in rage.

He halted in the middle of the barracks glaring at Rhodes, Oakes, and everything else. Rhodes and Oakes held their breath waiting for Rhinehart to blow his stack.

Without warning, he buckled at the knees, burst out laughing, and fell across the floor roaring his head off. He rolled on the floor clutching his sides and howling with laughter.

Oakes laughed, too. Rhodes tried to hold it back and failed.

"Why is the name, 'Watson' so funny?" Fisher asked and made Oakes and Rhinehart laugh even louder.

Right then, Henshaw came back. She stopped in the doorway and blinked down at Rhinehart in horror.

Her expression made him bust up even more. "Dr. Watson, Georgie! We're getting evaluated by Dr. Watson!"

"Yeah?" she asked. "What about him? He was nice."

Rhinehart buckled in another fit of laughter. Rhodes found himself laughing along with the joke.

"I don't get it," Fisher repeated.

Henshaw cut Rhinehart a wide circle and sat down at the table next to Rhodes. "What are we doing next?"

"We're coming up with another name for Watson," Oakes replied and laughed.

"Why do we need another name for him?" Henshaw asked. "He already has one."

"We're calling him Where-son from now on," Rhodes explained and Rhinehart roared out in another fit of laughter.

Dietz came in and started smirking when he realized what Rhinehart found so funny. "All I had to do was keep the sucker talking," Dietz explained. "He eventually gave up and told me there was nothing wrong with me."

Rhinehart dragged himself off the floor wiping tears out of his one eye. He staggered over to the table and collapsed next to Oakes. "Phew!" Rhinehart panted. "I needed that."

"Dr. Watson said I was fit for combat duty," Henshaw went on. "He said he wasn't so sure about the rest of you."

"You can go alone," Dietz told her.

"Watch it," Oakes snapped. "No one is going anywhere alone."

"She won't go alone because Dietz is clear, too," Rhodes pointed out.

Just then, Lauer, Coulter, and Thackery came back. Lauer and Coulter sat down at the table to laugh it up about Dr. Watson.

Thackery kept curling her lip at the surrounding barracks. "That cocksucker! I hate shrinks."

"Did he say whether you were mentally stable enough to go back into combat?" Rhodes asked.

"I didn't ask. I told him to shove his questions up his ass because he was the last person I would ever talk to about anything."

Rhodes nodded. "That sounds about right."

"Now what do we do?" Henshaw asked again.

"We wait around for the brass to decide to send us back to the Emal wars," Lauer replied.

"We wait for Fuentes to come back," Oakes added. "Everything depends on that."

The thought of seeing Fuentes again made everyone fall silent. Oakes and Rhodes worked on their drawings. Dietz and Thackery took turns working at the terminal.

The others occupied themselves with this or that. Henshaw had gotten into the habit of using her laser to carve shapes out of wood.

She collected scraps from the loading dock, brought them back to the barracks, fashioned them into minute statues of animals, birds, plants, and other figurines, and then gave them as gifts to any random passerby she met at the station.

Rhodes could just imagine the station personnel's reaction when she tried to give them her gifts. Maybe those people went home and burned the little figures to break the hex of touching something one of the battalion members had touched.

Rhodes didn't know why he let himself think that. He just couldn't imagine anyone treasuring one of these little figures for the charming act of kindness it obviously was.

She spent the rest of the afternoon carving a flower and went out to walk around the station.

Rhodes got distracted by explaining something art-related to Oakes. Henshaw returned with three more pieces of wood.

She spent the rest of the evening carving them into more shapes, but she didn't take them out to give away. She put them on the bookshelf and left them there.

Maybe someone hurt her feelings by refusing to accept one of her creations. Maybe the inevitable finally happened and one of the station personnel told her to keep away from them and never come near them again.

Rhodes kicked himself for not paying closer attention to what she was doing. He could have kept an eye on her through the interface. He just got distracted.

He made a mental note to ask her about it, but then he got distracted again by dreading Fuentes coming back.

Coulter spent nearly every evening wandering around the barracks walls. He spent an unnatural amount of time inspecting the lines of mortar between the wall blocks.

Rhodes just could not bring himself to ask why Coulter found the mortar so interesting. Rhodes didn't want to know.

Rhinehart and Lauer liked to sit at the table and talk to Rhodes and Oakes while they drew. They talked about any old random subject that came up.

Tonight, they speculated about what Dr. Watson did in his free time when he wasn't evaluating people's psychological state.

"Maybe he really is a sleuth when no one is looking," Rhinehart joked. "Maybe his notepad is covered with his case notes. He probably doesn't even really listen to what anyone tells him about why they're distressed or upset."

"What cases do you think he works on?" Lauer asks.

"People probably come to him from all over the Treaty of Aemon Cluster to get his help," Rhinehart went on. "I'm sure he's working on unsolved murders, political mysteries, bank heists, embezzlement—you name it."

Oakes snorted. "You got one hell of an imagination, Lieutenant. You should write a book."

"Too bad someone has already written a book about Dr. Watson," Rhodes pointed out.

"No one has written a book with Dr. Watson as the sleuth." Rhinehart's eye burst open and he pointed at Rhodes and gasped. "I got it! I could write a spin-off serious—about how Watson takes over Sherlock Holmes's practice after Holmes disappears. Watson could become the sleuth and work all his own cases. Yeah! That would be perfect!"

"Watson isn't smart enough to be a sleuth," Lauer pointed out. "That's the whole point. He's Holmes's sidekick. Watson doesn't have the brains to solve anything. He always needed Holmes to explain everything to him."

"Ah, of course!" Fisher exclaimed. "Dr. Watson—from the Sherlock Holmes mystery books. I understand now."

Rhinehart laughed at him. "You're even slower on the uptake than Watson."

"But the original Dr. Watson really was a doctor—a medical doctor," Henshaw pointed out. "He had to be smart—smart enough to figure out a few things. He could have stepped up after Holmes disappeared."

"Did you know that some of Sir Arthur Conan Doyle's contemporaries said he modeled Holmes after himself?" Lauer chimed in. "Conan Doyle was a medical doctor who used his knowledge to solve medical mysteries. They say Holmes was really just a fictionalized version of Conan Doyle."

Rhodes, Rhinehart, Oakes, and Coulter all turned around to stare at Lauer. "Holy crap! You're scaring me, man!" Coulter murmured.

"What's wrong?" Lauer asked. "It's true. You can look it up on the terminal if you don't believe me."

"Where the holy hell did you come out with that?" Rhinehart countered. "Have you been hiding this from us all this time?"

"Hiding what?" Lauer asked. "I'm not hiding anything. I'm just telling you the facts."

"What other facts are you keeping hidden in that brain of yours?" Oakes asked.

Lauer shrugged and shifted his weight on his bench. "I'm just saying...."

A hint of movement caught the corner of Rhodes's eye. It came from the other side of the barracks—behind his back.

The instant he noticed it, his Grid reading of the room showed him a person standing in the barracks doorway. Rhodes stiffened when Fuentes appeared there.

Chapter 19

Everyone in the barracks saw Fuentes at the same moment Rhodes saw him. Everyone turned around very slowly to look in Fuentes's direction. He wasn't supposed to come back until tomorrow.

Rhodes sat frozen to his bench. No one else in the room made a sound.

Fuentes took one step across the threshold, but he didn't enter—not yet. Whatever mental distress he'd been going through before definitely wasn't there anymore. He didn't tremble or grimace or spasm in agony anymore.

Now he was definitely in a different kind of mental distress. The expression on his face struck terror into Rhodes's heart even more than the way Fuentes had been before he left. This was far worse.

Fuentes glared at his comrades through narrowed eyes. He clamped his lips tight shut and he kept clenching his jaw in barely suppressed fury.

No one moved or even breathed. He didn't enter the barracks to rejoin the battalion. He just stood there seething and glaring at everyone and everything.

Rhodes went through a series of rapid decisions about how to deal with Fuentes. Should Rhodes go over there and talk to him? Should Rhodes welcome Fuentes back with open arms?

The murderous scowl written all over Fuentes's face told Rhodes all he needed to know. Fuentes was no happier about coming back than the rest of the battalion was to get him back.

Rhodes considered just going back to his drawing and his conversation as if Fuentes wasn't here at all.

Maybe that would be for the best—just to treat Fuentes as if his suicide attempt never happened in the first place—as if he hadn't been gone all these weeks.

Did the doctors and the brass decide to send Fuentes back now to screw with the battalion's heads again?

Rhodes knew better than that. They were all too incompetent to think that far in advance. They never planned or foresaw anything.

It probably never once occurred to General Brewster or his pals in the Battalion 1 governing body that it might matter to the battalion *when* Fuentes came back—or that the battalion might benefit from some advanced warning that Fuentes was coming back early.

Fisher snapped Rhodes out of his thoughts. "Aren't you going to talk to him, Captain?"

Rhodes didn't realize until that moment that he had to talk to Fuentes. That was Rhodes's job. He couldn't just ignore Fuentes.

Rhodes really hadn't been sure right up until that moment if he should. Now he stood up and crossed the barracks.

Everyone present watched him in breathless silence when he came to a stop in front of Fuentes. "Welcome back, Rudy," Rhodes began in as calm a tone as he could muster. "It's good to have you back."

Fuentes dipped his chin once and clipped, "Sir," exactly the way Lauer did when he woke up from stasis. Fuentes didn't stop glaring at everything. Now he glared at Rhodes worst of all.

Rhodes shuddered at the expression on Fuentes's face. He'd never glared or scowled or fumed like this before.

All his distress had switched to pure, volcanic rage. He simmered with it. The tension vibrating off him threatened to explode at the slightest provocation.

This was so much worse than Rhodes feared. He would gladly have dealt with the fallout of Fuentes coming back suicidal. This was far, far more dangerous to everyone else in the battalion.

Rhodes couldn't exactly send Fuentes away, though. The only alternative was to put Fuentes down right here and now.

Rhodes couldn't even do that—not without releasing this deadly beast lying right underneath Fuentes's skin.

Fuentes would defend himself. Whatever he might have been when he left was long gone. The mild-mannered, less-than-intelligent kid he was no longer existed.

This monster would anticipate someone on the battalion doing something to eliminate the threat. Fuentes's hard, sharp dark eyes flicked from one person to the next around the room.

He measured them the way a warrior measures his enemies—or potential enemies. He would anticipate someone turning against him—and he would respond in kind.

Rhodes took the only course he could think of to cool the tension. He waved behind him. "Come on in. We're all thrilled to have you back. Come sit down. We were just talking the way we used to. Come on."

Rhodes turned away still gesturing toward the table. He backed into the room to lead Fuentes over there.

Fuentes advanced a few steps and halted by the table glaring at the men sitting there. Rhodes stepped over the bench, sat down opposite Oakes, and pulled his drawing toward him.

Fuentes's presence unnerved everyone. Oakes, Lauer, and Rhinehart all turned back to the center and pretended Fuentes wasn't there.

Oakes started sketching on his picture again and Rhodes did the same thing, but the conversation didn't restart.

A dangerous silence fell over the room. Coulter, Henshaw, Dietz, and Thackery all watched from the periphery.

Not even the SAMs made a sound even though Fuentes couldn't have heard them. He didn't interface with the rest of the battalion.

He stood there boiling with barely concealed rage while Rhodes and Oakes went on drawing. Their pencils scratching across the paper made the only sound in the room.

No one else moved for a second before Fuentes clenched his jaw again, tightened his lips, and marched around the table to the terminal desk.

He towered over Dietz, pointed to the machine, and then swiped his finger sideways. "Are you using this or what?"

Dietz fell over himself trying to stand up too fast. "Naw, man. You go ahead and use it."

He kicked the desk a few times getting as far away from Fuentes as he could as fast as he could. He scrambled over to the table and sat down on the bench next to Lauer.

Lauer and Oakes both scooted down the bench to give Dietz space to sit down. Fuentes glared at all of them, gritted his teeth a few more times, and then sat down at the desk in Dietz's place.

Fuentes started working on the terminal. Rhodes made one moment of eye contact with Dietz before Rhodes went back to his sketch.

No one said anything else. Rhodes and Oakes kept working on their drawings. Dietz, Lauer, and Rhinehart clustered around the table where they had been before, but they didn't talk.

Rhodes got a flash of what the five men must look like to Fuentes. Rhodes and his comrades looked like they were huddling for protection from Fuentes.

Coulter went back to studying the mortar between the wall blocks. Thackery watched from the next table.

Henshaw gathered up her scraps of wood and her unfinished carvings, put them on the bookshelf with the other finished ones, and sat down on the edge of her capsule.

She kept her back to the table for a few minutes before she stretched out on the mattress, locked into her prongs, and started her conversion cycle early. Then Thackery did the same thing.

One person at a time split away. Rhinehart left the table next and Coulter took his place. Then Fuentes entered his conversion cycle, too.

A palpable wave of relief went through the rest of the battalion as soon as his capsule cover closed.

"Jesus Christ!" Oakes muttered. "What the hell have we gotten ourselves into?"

"I guess we don't have to worry about him killing himself now," Lauer murmured under his breath.

"No, we just have to worry about him killing one of us instead," Coulter added.

"We don't know that," Rhodes pointed out. "We don't know what he's thinking or feeling."

"You should talk to him and find out, Sir," Lauer suggested. "You're the only one of us who can."

Rhodes sighed. "I guess I'll have to."

"Wouldn't you rather know what he's thinking and feeling than not?" Oakes asked. "I wish he'd interface with us. Then we wouldn't have to wonder what he's thinking or if he's planning on going on a murderous rampage to kill us all."

"I'll have to ask him to interface with us," Rhodes replied. "Don't ask me what I'll do if he refuses."

"He'll have to interface with us on the battlefield," Thackery chimed in from the next table. "It wouldn't work if we couldn't communicate with him and anticipate what he was about to do. We'll need to see his Grid and our SAMs will have to coordinate with his SAM."

"Yeah, all that, but I won't do it tonight—obviously." Rhodes pushed his drawing away. "I'm going to sleep. I'll see all of you tomorrow."

He crossed the room to his capsule, but he stopped next to Fuentes's capsule on the way there. Fuentes looked like his old self, now that he had his eyes closed.

His features softened in sleep. He didn't glare or scowl. He looked calm and peaceful, but that was all an illusion now. He would never be calm or peaceful again—ever.

Chapter 20

Rhodes sat up, put his feet on the floor, and stared at them for a long time while he processed everything that happened yesterday.

He really didn't give a rip about the results of his psych evaluation. It meant nothing to him or anyone else beyond the obvious humor the battalion got from making fun of Dr. Watson.

The evaluation did give Rhodes one crucial piece of information in all of this. The Legion brass did *not* give Fuentes a psych evaluation before they sent him back to the battalion.

His capsule stood open across the room. He sat at the terminal working on something the way he did last night.

He narrowed his eyes at the screen, compressed his lips into a bloodless line, and clenched his teeth every few seconds.

The rest of the battalion went through their normal morning routine of getting up, running their fingers through their hair, walking around, and doing whatever they usually did to occupy their time.

Rhodes didn't go to the washroom to look at his own reflection. Whatever today held didn't have anything to do with him or what he had become. Today was all about Fuentes.

The tension in the barracks ratcheted right back up to the breaking point. A few people talked, but they kept their voices low. Rhinehart, Oakes, and Lauer joked about Dr. Watson.

The SAMs remained silent through it all and didn't say a damn word. Fisher was already there at his usual size in the corner of Rhodes's vision when he opened his eyes this morning.

Fisher didn't greet Rhodes or ask how his conversion cycle went or say anything else. He just hovered there and watched.

These SAMs really knew their business. They didn't get involved in this mess. They knew when to stay out of it—whatever this was.

Rhodes took a deep breath, stood up, ran his fingers through his hair, and squared his shoulders before he walked over to the terminal desk.

Fuentes didn't look up, not even when Rhodes halted right there next to Fuentes's chair.

"Stand up, Corporal," Rhodes ordered. "I want to talk to you."

Fuentes clenched his jaw once and tightened his lips in one momentary show of annoyance before he stood up and faced Rhodes.

"Is something wrong, Sir?" Fuentes asked in a tense undertone.

"We have a training session today and we'll need you to interface with the rest of the battalion. I'd like you to interface with all of us now—for the rest of the day while we aren't in a training session. We all need to know what's going on with you and Van before we go into The Grid. You've been away for a long time. We need to get to know each other again so we know what to expect when we enter The Grid in the session."

Fuentes glared at him for a second. "Is that all, Sir?"

"That's enough, isn't it?" Rhodes asked. "We all interface with each other all the time. You were interfacing with us before you left. It doesn't inspire much confidence if you don't interface with us now."

"Yes, Sir. No problem." Fuentes turned away, switched on the interface, and sat back down at the desk. He went straight back to work on the terminal without giving Rhodes a second glance.

The interface connected and Van reappeared back on The Grid with Fisher, Dash, Rocky, and the other SAMs.

Van looked the same—and her facial expression looked the same. She didn't glare at anyone in murderous fury.

"Good morning, Captain Rhodes," she began in her low, husky voice. "It's so good to be back with the battalion again."

"Welcome back, Van," Rhodes replied. "It's good to see you, too."

He never meant any words more. Inexpressible relief crushed his heart when he saw her. He could trust her in ways he didn't trust Fuentes anymore.

At least Fuentes's SAM was still as reasonable as ever. She was the one who tried the hardest to stop him from killing himself. She must realize by now how volatile Fuentes had become.

Rhodes would have liked to interrogate her about Fuentes's mental state, but Rhodes couldn't do that in front of Fuentes. Rhodes could only talk to Van through the interface. Fuentes would have heard every word.

"I'm sure you just heard me tell Rudy that we have a training session later," Rhodes told her instead. "This session is to test you and Rudy in combat with the rest of the battalion. If everything works out, they'll send us back to the Emal wars."

"Yes, Captain, I understand all that. I'm confident Rudy and I will be able to perform to your satisfaction."

"I'm not worried about my satisfaction," Rhodes told her. "I'm only worried about you and Rudy getting out of The Grid in one piece—and the rest of the battalion doing the same thing."

"Yes, of course, Captain. I understand perfectly. I can only give you my assurance that we'll do everything in our power to accomplish the objective in a way that ensures the safety of the whole battalion. I can't offer you anything more than that."

Rhodes glanced back and forth between her and Fuentes. Fuentes didn't look up from the terminal. He didn't get involved in the conversation between Rhodes and Van.

Fuentes also didn't offer any assurance that he would perform to Rhodes's satisfaction or that he would do everything in his power to ensure the safety of the whole battalion.

Fuentes's silence spoke volumes. Rhodes didn't need to get inside Fuentes's head to know exactly what the kid was thinking and feeling. The fury radiating off him broadcast his mental state to the world.

"Stand up, Corporal," Rhodes ordered again, and this time, he didn't soften his tone. "I'm talking to you."

Fuentes stood up and all that rage blasted Rhodes in the face. Fuentes turned it on Rhodes alone.

Rhodes took another deep breath, but it did nothing to steady his nerves.

He found himself at another crossroads moment. He could take Fuentes back into the battalion, but Rhodes didn't have to do that. He realized that now. He wasn't saddled with Fuentes against his will or against the battalion's will.

He could march right down there to Colonel Kraft's office and demand to take Fuentes off the battalion. Rhodes could flatly refuse to go anywhere with Fuentes, including into a training session.

Rhodes did have that option, but he didn't take it. He didn't hear any of his subordinates or their SAMs demanding it, either.

"I know you're angry, Corporal," Rhodes began. "I'm angry, too. We all are and we have good reason to be. No one faults you for being angry over all of this."

Fuentes gritted his teeth and snarled in a vicious undertone. "You stopped me. I could have ended it and you stopped me."

"Actually, it was Rio who stopped you. Van asked the Strikers to intervene and Rio got to you first."

"Do you think I give a shit about that?!" Fuentes snapped. "I could have ended it. I don't have to be here. I could have been gone."

"Then go, Corporal. Use your scourge gun on yourself right now if it means that much to you. You won't get any argument from me and I won't try to stop you. You don't have to be here now."

Fuentes locked his mouth shut and looked away.

"The SAMs were doing their jobs by saving you," Rhodes went on. "I would have let you jump off that Ravager, but you're still here and now you have to work with the rest of us. You can go anytime you want to. As long as you're here, you better make sure you help this battalion instead of making it harder and more dangerous for the rest of us than it already is. Is that understood?"

Fuentes refused to look at him. "Yes, Sir," he spat through gritted teeth.

"Direct this rage toward the enemy," Rhodes told him. "You can kill as many of them as you want to. You can be as cruel and brutal and nasty to them as you want to be. You can take it all out on them."

"The brass is my enemy," Fuentes hissed. "The doctors are my enemies. They're the ones who did this to me." His furious eyes darted around the barracks. *"They* did this to me."

"They didn't do shit to you, Corporal," Rhodes snapped, and in that moment, his patience snapped, too. He seized Fuentes by the jaw and forced Fuentes to turn around and face him. "If you look at anyone in this battalion like that, you look at me like that. If you treat anyone in this battalion as an enemy, you better start with me and I *will* defend myself. Understand, Corporal?"

Fuentes tried to yank his head out of Rhodes's grip, but Rhodes was all finished playing games. He tightened his fingers and forced Fuentes to face him.

Fuentes finally snarled, "Yes, Sir. I understand."

Rhodes let him go, but Rhodes didn't slacken his stance. He found himself narrowing his eyes and glaring right back at Fuentes.

"You stay interfaced with us at all times, Corporal. That is a direct order," Rhodes snapped. "If you cut the interface, I'll assume you're planning the worst. We all will and we will take steps to make sure you don't put any of us in danger. You have one chance with this battalion. The very first time you break the interface will be your last."

Rhodes turned on his heel and walked away. He didn't know where he would go, but he didn't trust himself in front of Fuentes a second longer.

Rhodes became suddenly, painfully aware of everyone else in the battalion watching and listening to his confrontation with Fuentes. Even the SAMs listened, including Van.

Rhodes had to get out of the room, but he couldn't break the interface, either. He didn't want to.

He went into the washroom, but the sight of his own reflection made him sick to his stomach. He paced up and down the room trying to settle down before he faced the group.

He already was facing them. He faced them through the interface. He couldn't get away from them.

"I'm sorry about this, Captain," Van husked as soon as he left the barracks. "I only found out Rudy was like this last night when he woke up from stasis."

"Did something happen?" Rhodes asked. "How could he just wake up from stasis like this?"

"I'm not sure, Captain. He won't talk to me."

Rhodes spun around, but he didn't need to turn around to face her. She stayed right there in front of his eyes with the other SAMs. "He won't talk to you?! Not at all?"

"I'm afraid not, Captain. He hasn't said a word to me since he woke up. He ignores me."

Rhodes passed his hand across his eyes and groaned. "Great. Really spectacular."

"I can't guarantee that he'll listen to me during the training session, either—or any other time. In fact, I'm going into the training session assuming he won't listen to me. I'm sure he'll ignore me then, too."

"You'll need to stay interfaced with us, too, then," Rhodes told her. "If he won't talk to you, he probably won't talk to any of us, either. We'll rely on you to communicate with us on his behalf, give us any information we need that he isn't telling us—all of that."

"Of course, Captain. You can rely on my full cooperation."

Rhodes should have felt less comfortable talking about Fuentes right in front of him. Rhodes never would have spoken about any of his subordinates like this—not where the person could hear every word.

Rhodes didn't feel even marginally uncomfortable about it, though. He wanted Fuentes to hear and understand just how seriously Rhodes and the rest of the battalion were taking this.

Rhodes paused there and studied Van's feline face. He never liked her. Now he found himself trusting her with the whole battalion's safety.

His former conclusion about the SAMs came back to haunt him now. Van's survival depended on Fuentes somehow conducting himself in a way that didn't get both him and Van killed.

Her survival depended on Fuentes coming through every battle unharmed. What a nightmare this must be for her—riding around with such a damaged host out to destroy himself and take everyone else down with him.

Chapter 21

Rhodes dropped into The Grid. He and his subordinates all looked around at each other, but mostly they kept casting sidelong glances at Fuentes.

He'd stayed interfaced with the battalion for the rest of the day the way Rhodes ordered him to. Rhodes couldn't find anything to criticize in Fuentes's behavior—apart from the fact that he didn't talk, make eye contact, or stop glaring at everyone.

The only person he didn't glare at was Van. True to her word, he completely ignored her as though she was never there.

He showed more signs of hearing the other SAMs. He occasionally stopped working on the terminal long enough to listen to their conversation. He didn't participate in it.

He steadfastly refused to acknowledge whenever Van spoke to anyone. He went out of his way to erase her from his awareness.

His behavior became more disturbing as the day wore on, but the rest of the battalion also got used to it.

Everyone adjusted to it, talked more, and Rhinehart went back to joking about Dr. Watson.

Some of the SAMs even got involved in fleshing out this whole shadow life Dr. Watson was living behind the scenes when he wasn't conducting psych evaluations on Legion soldiers.

The SAMs' voices and laughter made Fuentes stiffen. He shot brutal glares at anyone whose voice or laughter interrupted his work, but he never unclamped his mouth to tell them to tone it down.

Everyone in the battalion watched him like a hawk all day long, but that was nothing compared to now.

Rhodes had been using his interface with Fuentes for hours to check that Fuentes's weapons system really was online. All his Grid targeting systems were working normally, too. He was fully operational and ready for battle—against someone.

Rhodes didn't like going anywhere with an armed Fuentes, but at least they were only going into The Grid and not a real battle. That would come later—provided Fuentes actually managed to function in this training session today.

Rhodes couldn't decide if he wanted Fuentes to fail or not. Failing would mean either getting himself shot, shooting one of his comrades, or sabotaging the training session some other way.

Fuentes succeeding would mean the battalion would deploy sooner—back to the Emal wars with real weapons, real explosions, and real people dying.

Rhodes brought up a Grid schematic of his own weapons systems and checked that everything was online the way it should be. Then he did the same thing with everyone else present.

Why did he even bother to check? He'd already checked his subordinates multiple times each. They did the same thing to him and all their comrades.

The nine soldiers exchanged one last glance and Rhodes nodded. "Let's move out."

He fired his boosters and took off through The Grid. He already knew where it would take him.

All these training sessions focused on the Emal wars now. The brass wouldn't send the battalion anywhere else—not until Rhodes and his people mastered this.

He checked on Fuentes on the way. He flew on one side of the battalion just as though he really was a part of this group.

The landscape turned back into a devastated wasteland just like the last one. The battalion might even have flown into exactly the same scenario for all Rhodes could tell.

Legion Ravagers loomed in the dark, smoky sky not far away. Explosions came from the battle line where the platoons faced off against another horde of Emal armed with laser rifles.

Base ships fired massive laser cannons from out in the dark countryside. Those cannons all aimed up into the atmosphere to target the Ravagers.

"What's the objective?" Rhodes asked Fisher.

"The Emal have already conquered the planet. They're getting ready to jump to the next planet in the same solar system. The Legion is only trying to stop them from leaving."

"How's that working out?" Lauer muttered.

"It isn't working out because the Legion can't even get close to the Emal base ships," Fisher replied. "These Emal are defending their comrades' retreat to the base ships. The hordes are loading up and launching. Our objective is to stop them."

"What—all of them?" Rhinehart snapped. "That would be impossible." He checked The Grid of the surrounding terrain. "There must be a thousand base ships all over the planet."

"One thousand three hundred and seventy-five," Fisher clipped. "Our objective is only to stop this one." He surrounded the base ship in question with a red circle on the map.

"Why that one?" Thackery asked. "It looks like all the others."

"The Grid is reading human life signs on board. The Emal have taken captives."

"Now I know this is just a training session," Oakes muttered. "The Emal don't take captives—not human ones anyway."

"It doesn't matter because that's our objective," Rhodes replied. "We just have to stop them from leaving the planet."

"We have to stop them from leaving the planet without killing the captives in the process," Fisher corrected.

"That complicates things," Lauer pointed out. "We can't just bomb the base ship into oblivion."

"The only way to destroy the base ship is to shoot it from underneath after it launches," Rhodes went on.

"How does that help us?" Thackery asked.

"We don't want to shoot it from underneath because that would destroy it," Henshaw pointed out.

"We don't even want to let it launch," Coulter added. "It would be astronomically harder to rescue the hostages once the ship got airborne."

"We aren't going to do any of that," Rhodes decided. "We aren't going to destroy the ship and we aren't going to let it launch."

"What are we going to do?" Dietz asked. "How else can we accomplish the objective?"

"We're going inside the ship the way the Strikers rescued us. You can land on the ship, Rudy. You tore into an Emal base ship on Ohait. You can do it again this time. The rest of us will defend you and give you cover."

Fuentes only growled, "Yes, Sir."

"As soon as he opens a hole big enough, Rhinehart and Lauer will drop down and join him. Rhinehart, you're the biggest and the strongest. Use your grid lines to make yourself into a ship big enough to carry the hostages away. Lauer will change into a spider the way Elio did. You'll go inside the ship, carry out the hostages to board Rhinehart's ship, and finish off any Emal that try to stop you."

Lauer let out a sick chuckle. "I like this plan."

"Let's go," Rhodes ordered and fired his boosters to fly faster.

He swooped over the landscape and the battalion closed on the base ship in question. The training session had been programmed to anticipate the battalion's arrival.

That base ship and a few other nearby vessels turned their laser cannons on the group.

Rhodes used his grid lines to transform himself into a long, thin, arrow missile plummeting out of the atmosphere.

He had to morph, whip, and swerve around giant laser shots pelting all around him. The others scattered, used The Grid to take different shapes, and then reconverged on the target ship.

Fuentes didn't change at all—not until he got to the ship itself. He relied on speed, pivoted his feet downward at the last possible second, and slammed down on the ship's upper hull.

He transformed his hands and forearms into two rotating drums dotted with spikes. They whirled in a blur and he started shredding the hull to smithereens.

The rest of the battalion surrounded him. Rhodes swiveled backward to aim his weapons outward at the Emal hordes.

They closed on the base ships trying to board so they could jump the planet. All those Emal unloaded on the battalion.

The aliens swarmed the base ship faster and thicker than ever to stop the battalion from freeing the hostages.

Lasers flickered out of the night bombarding the battalion from all sides. "Half of you change into reflective surfaces!" Rhodes ordered. "Form a shield around Fuentes!"

Thackery, Dietz, Coulter, and Henshaw stretched their grid lines, curved them outward in a big swooping arc, and backed up to Rhodes, Oakes, Lauer, and Rhinehart.

The eight of them surrounded Fuentes at the very center. Lasers bounced off the shields, but the impact still drove the four friends backward with brutal force.

Rhodes, Oakes, Lauer, and Rhinehart had to brace the four shields to keep a space big enough for Fuentes to work.

Those laser shots boomed against the shields every time the Emal opened fire. Rhodes stuck his scourge gun between the shields to plaster the enemy.

He didn't need to aim. Too many Emal surrounded the base ship and closed tighter from all sides.

He ducked behind Coulter, jammed his shoulder hard against the shield from behind, and took dozens of pounding hits on the surface.

Rhodes had to drill his feet and legs into the ship's hull as hard as he could to stop the endless barrage from knocking him over.

Murphy shrieked in Rhodes's ear. "We can't take much more of this! If one of the base ships hits us, we're finished!"

The screech of Fuentes's drums on the ship's hull drowned out the deafening roar of laser fire coming from all directions.

He bent over his work grimacing from the effort. Rhodes still didn't see anything wrong with Fuentes's behavior. He gave it all he had.

He strained every fiber to grind his way through the hull. Lasers flew all around his head. He barely glanced up long enough to release his Vipers on the surrounding horde.

The other SAMs called a constant stream of information, advice, and orders to everyone in the battalion. Van did the same thing.

"The hull is four inches thick!" she called. "We're halfway through! The Emal crew is arming to defend the breach! They know we're coming!"

"Locate the hostages!" Rhodes ordered. "Lauer—once you get inside, you can shoot out the ship from the inside and bring Rhinehart closer to the hostages' location!"

"One inch to go!" Van reported.

"Get down there!" Rhodes told Lauer and Rhinehart. "Get the hostages out!"

Lauer sprang out from behind Dietz. Dietz had been shielding Lauer. Now Dietz changed back into a man and hunkered for shelter behind Coulter and Thackery.

Fuentes tore through the last shreds of plate steel, changed his drums to jointed spider arms, and tore the hull open to make the hole wider.

Lauer plunged through the breach and vanished inside. Fuentes abandoned the hole in a split second, vaulted over to the rest of the group, and unloaded on the Emal.

He swiped his thermal cannons back and forth to level hundreds of aliens. He roared at them in fury and unloaded countless Vipers.

Rhodes took one look at The Grid to see Lauer storming through the ship's interior.

The Emal crew waiting for him inside hammered him with lasers, but he only changed himself into another reflective surface.

His scourge guns mowed all the aliens down before he changed into the kind of spider form Elio used to rescue the battalion.

Rhinehart stayed on the ship's outer hull. He kept gunning for doomsday while Rocky monitored Lauer's progress through The Grid. "He found the hostages, but they're locked in! He can't get them out by himself!"

"Rhinehart—help him!" Rhodes ordered. "Use your lasers to cut through!"

Rhinehart yelled something back. Rhodes didn't catch it before a fresh wave of Emal surged out of the night to overrun the battalion.

Another base ship somewhere out in the darkness fired at the group, hit Coulter, and his grid lines shattered right in front of Rhodes.

The lines sprang apart and reformed into a Striker. "We gotta get out of here, Sir!" Coulter hollered. "We can draw them away! They might not know Lauer is inside!"

Rhodes didn't want to believe that, but the battalion couldn't stay here. "Follow Coulter!" Rhodes ordered and he launched as a Striker, too.

Emal lasers turned upward to follow the battalion away from the target ship, but Rhinehart stayed behind. He fired his weapons into the base ship's hull.

The light attracted the Emal's attention. The battalion couldn't lure the aliens away as long as Rhinehart stayed there.

The Emal started to turn back to target Rhinehart, but at that moment, a punishing laser shot punctured the base ship from the inside. The gunshot came perilously close to hitting Rhinehart.

Then the laser swiveled away from him and carved another big hole through the hull.

The section dropped inward to reveal another breach big enough for a Duster to descend inside.

Rhinehart launched himself off the hull, transformed in a split second, and disappeared beneath the ship's outer skin.

Rhodes lost sight of him for a second. The Grid gave Rhodes a clear view of Lauer loading the hostages onto the Duster.

Rhodes had to turn back to the battle. The Emal closed tighter around the base ship. They did their best to ignore the Strikers except when the Strikers bombarded the horde from overhead.

More lasers pounded Rhodes's underside. He had to fly away in wild patterns to divert from the aliens shooting at him.

He lost track of what everyone else was doing—until he spotted another Striker bombing straight for him.

He took a split second to recognize Fuentes. Rhodes tightened his grip on his weapons. If Fuentes took this opportunity to make an attempt on Rhodes's life, Rhodes would just have to respond in kind.

"Behind you, Captain!" Fisher called and Fuentes opened fire at the same instant.

Twin Vipers detached from Fuentes's back, shrieked on either side of Rhodes, and flew straight into the path of base ship laser cannon fire that would have destroyed Rhodes from behind.

The explosion knocked Rhodes out of the way and Fuentes kept on bombing past him heading for the base ship that fired that shot.

Rhodes tumbled sideways, but he was alive and unhurt—thanks to Fuentes. Fuentes didn't even stick around long enough for Rhodes to thank him.

Another voice punctured Rhodes's battle fog. "I got them!" Rhinehart called. "I got the hostages! Pull out and climb for the atmosphere!"

The Duster rocketed out of the hull breach and the fiery vapor trail burned a path through the night heading for orbit.

Lauer exploded out of the ship a second later, flew on Rhinehart's tail, and defended him all the way.

The rest of the battalion pulled away to follow—all except Fuentes.

Rhodes had another flash of horror that Fuentes really planned to kill himself right now when the battalion just accomplished its objective.

He didn't kill himself, though. He dove at nose-bleed speed for the planet's surface, compressed his grid lines into a long snake, stabbed into the ground, and took off whipping and slithering for the original target ship.

He pulled the same maneuver the battalion pulled on Sulia, burrowed under the base ship, and fired his Vipers directly into its underside.

He didn't stick around long enough for the resulting explosion to put him in danger. He burst out the other side, blasted out of the ground, and took off into the atmosphere at incredible speed.

He didn't change back into a person right away. He stayed as a whip, snaked between cannon shots from other base ships, and eventually fired his boosters to catch up with the battalion.

The base ship detonated in a fire ball that lit up the night. It flashed down there on the planet....and then the darkness of space surrounded the battalion.

Green grid lines appeared in place of the stars and everyone reappeared in the training room where they started.

The battalion all surrounded Fuentes laughing and extending their hands to pat him on the back.

"That was outstanding!" Rhinehart exclaimed. "Did you see the way he unloaded those Vipers? He saved your ass, Captain!"

Rhodes smiled at them all. "I know he did."

The others turned back to Fuentes. "Did you see the way that base ship went up?" Coulter gloated. "You put those suckers in the ground, boy!"

Fuentes lashed out and knocked their hands away. He did it so suddenly and so viciously that he startled everyone into falling silent.

He glared at them all as murderously as ever, clamped his lips together in rage, and stormed out of the training room.

He left the interface active, though. He headed back to the barracks alone and left everyone else standing there staring at each other in stunned shock.

Chapter 22

D r. Osborne strolled down the line of capsules in the *Ero's* hold. "The ship will stay in orbit unless you call us down. If you need medical attention or if you need to go into conversion cycles, you only have to give the word. We'll be monitoring your SAMs through The Grid. We'll be in constant contact the whole time you're on the planet."

Rhodes frowned at him and then at the capsules. "Who are you and what have you done with the real Dr. Osborne?"

Dr. Osborne laughed. "You probably don't want to believe this, but the brass is committed to preventing the malfunctions and problems the battalion faced during your last campaign."

"I'll believe it when I see it," Rhodes muttered.

"This is the first stage in that process. The *Ero* will be on call to support the battalion whenever you need anything. You only have to call us and we'll come down and get you. You shouldn't have to wait for hours for the ship to lift you off."

"Too bad the Legion doesn't give the rest of the platoons the same consideration."

Osborne shrugged. "I don't have anything to say about that. I only know I have my orders and so does Captain Ackerman. The *Ero* is assigned to Battalion 1 from now on. Our only mission is to provide you with the support you need while you're on the planet."

Rhodes resisted the urge to repeat that he didn't believe it. He didn't believe the Legion supported Battalion 1 at all. He wouldn't be here right now if it did.

He didn't say that out loud, though. He would have liked to study Osborne a little more closely, but Rhodes didn't want to make him uncomfortable.

How much of this was Osborne's doing? So much had changed since he and Trudeau took over as Battalion 1's primary medical team.

The two men actually cared about the battalion. They actually did their best to make sure the battalion got the modifications and corrections they needed to go into battle.

Battalion 1 was as good as it possibly could be under the circumstances—which admittedly wasn't very good.

Fuentes still refused to have anything to do with his comrades. He refused to say a single word to his SAM. Van kept being as polite and helpful to everyone else as she possibly could be.

Fuentes never interfered with the interface, either. He didn't try to stop anyone from seeing anything he did—because he never did anything he needed to hide.

No one watching from the outside would have been able to find anything wrong with his behavior. The Legion brass put the battalion through five more training sessions before they deployed back to the Emal wars.

Fuentes conducted himself as well in all of them as he did in the first one. He distinguished himself by acting bravely, protecting his comrades, and even listening to Van's instructions when she warned him about unforeseen dangers.

He didn't talk back to her, but at least he listened and followed her recommendations.

He spent the rest of his free time working on the computer terminal in the barracks. He didn't talk or even look at his comrades. Apart from that, no one could fault him for anything.

He still glared at people when he bothered to look at them at all. Rhodes had to admit that Fuentes's behavior was much better and even exemplary compared to some Legion soldiers Rhodes had known in his career.

Fuentes never put anyone in danger, but that somehow made everyone even more watchful of him. How long could he keep behaving himself like this before he snapped?

The battalion was about to find out. Osborne and Rhodes got to the end of the line of capsules. The battalion was scheduled to deploy in fifteen minutes.

The Legion didn't send Battalion 1 back to Sulia. That planet was already too far gone to save. The *Ero* waited in orbit over the planet Bao in the Lumova system.

Rhodes rounded up his subordinates and the battalion headed down to the landing bay. The battalion had the *Ero* to itself now. No other Legion soldiers crowded the bay waiting to land on the new planet.

Rhodes used The Grid to watch the *Ero* descend through the atmosphere toward the surface. The rest of the battalion shared the interface with him.

"What's the point?" Thackery asked when they saw the wasteland of bombed-out buildings and mountains of trash glued together with dead bodies. "Why are we even here?"

"Welcome to the front lines," Lauer growled. "Maybe the Treaty of Aemon Cluster has too many people in it and this is the brass's way of reducing the population."

"That isn't funny," Henshaw snapped.

"Do I look like I'm joking?" Lauer countered. "Does any of this look like a joke to you?"

"I'm sure Dr. Watson could find something funny about it," Rhinehart muttered, but no one took the joke, not even himself.

Rhodes pointed at the front line. "The platoons are falling back to here—the Kuestrian Ridge. There are five more cities on the Trar continent the Emal haven't taken yet. If we fortify the ridge, we might be able to slow them down long enough for the Ravagers to evacuate the cities before the Emal get close enough to bombard them."

"The Legion should have already evacuated the cities long ago," Coulter muttered. "The Legion should have evacuated the whole planet the minute the Emal made landfall. Why are there even still any civilians on this planet?"

"We don't make those decisions," Rhodes replied. "The Ravagers are already in orbit ready to begin the evacuation."

"They should already be on the ground," Coulter pointed out.

"You go get yourself elected to the Treaty of Aemon Ruling Council. Then you can get it changed. Until then, we're moving out and reinforcing the platoons on that ridge."

"They're the 249th again, Sir," Oakes pointed out. "And the 217th and the 278th."

"I can read it as well as you can, Lieutenant." Rhodes immediately changed his tone. "Let's go."

The group moved closer to the launch doors. The warning lights flashed and the alarms started going off, but Rhodes only saw The Grid.

He didn't see anything much different about this planet from Luluna, Sulia, Ohait, and a hundred others just like them.

The battalion's involvement in this operation only seemed to seal the planet's fate even more than it already was sealed.

The battalion was supposed to tip the advantage in the Legion's favor. The battalion wound up doing the opposite.

Rhodes couldn't be the only person who saw the battalion's arrival as an omen of doom.

He didn't say that out loud, though. He kept comments like that to himself.

They didn't make any difference in the end, either. Nothing could. He just had to do the job in front of him for as long as he survived.

Each planet—each battle—each catastrophe brought him closer to the inevitable conclusion. One of these days, the battalion would come up against a situation that would take them all out.

Everyone in the battalion hung by the slimmest thread. Fuentes was only the most noticeable example.

Everyone in the battalion teetered on the brink of some irreparable disaster. The tiniest problem could tip them all over the edge.

Once they fell, there would be no coming back. None of them had even the smallest margin for error, either mentally or physically. They hung over an abyss with no safety net.

The calm before the launch doors opened gave him a few seconds to survey the landscape all the way to the edge of the sector. He could see the whole Treaty of Aemon Cluster from here.

He could see the Preinean home planet, the wider perimeter under threat from other alien invasions, the Coleridge Station staff—this moment gave him a few seconds of perspective and clarity before he flew into another shit storm.

Fisher didn't try to talk to Rhodes anymore, either. They exchanged only the most necessary information about whatever task Rhodes faced in any given moment.

Fisher already knew the worst about Rhodes's mental state. Fisher never brought it up again nor did Fisher try to improve it. It couldn't be improved. Fisher understood that only too well now.

Fisher didn't express it in words, but the expression on his face had changed from when Rhodes first met his SAM.

Fisher studied Rhodes with eyes full of sympathetic understanding. Rhodes often caught Fisher staring at him for no apparent reason.

Rhodes's brief conversation with Van about Fuentes had solidified so many things in Rhodes's mind.

He was already giving Fisher a priceless gift just by suffering through each excruciating day. Rhodes gave Fisher life every single day that Rhodes kept waking up in the morning.

Fisher understood better than anyone what it cost Rhodes to keep doing that. Staying alive meant a hell of a lot more to Fisher than it did to Rhodes.

These last few weeks at Coleridge Station changed things between them. Rhodes no longer got out of bed every day for his subordinates, himself, or even his family on Preinea.

He did it for Fisher—so Fisher could keep surviving. If life meant enough for Fisher to want to live, Rhodes couldn't bring himself to put that at risk.

The whole battalion lived in the interface now. Rhodes would have heard his subordinates talking to their SAMs about this, but they didn't talk about it.

All the SAMs had changed both their tone and their facial expressions. They spoke much less than they used to.

When they did, they used the same compassionate undertone of deep, heartfelt understanding for the real sacrifice each person was making to keep their SAM alive.

Everyone relaxed much more around Fuentes, too. Rhodes couldn't keep the kid under constant watch and he didn't need to.

Everyone treated Fuentes's silence and hostility as normal now. It was simply his way of coping with his own inner pain. No one begrudged him that as long as he kept doing the job—which he did.

It was too late for Rhodes to do anything about it now. The launch doors opened, he fired his boosters, and soared out over the destroyed landscape.

The battalion had spent so many training sessions in Emal battles. The setting didn't cause any emotional reaction at all anymore.

The brass should have put the battalion through this level of training before sending the battalion into combat the first time, but that was all water under the bridge now.

Rhodes measured The Grid in all directions as he approached the Kuestrian Ridge. The command dome perched on another hillside well out of the danger zone.

The platoons reinforced the ridge as well as they could against successive Emal assaults.

The aliens hammered the ridge both with laser rifle fire and base ship bombardments from deeper inside the Trar continent.

Some genius finally, finally got the brilliant idea to bomb the Emal from orbit. Secker missiles kept dropping out of the dense clouds and detonating inside the Emal horde.

The strikes wiped out countless Emal. They couldn't shoot back. They had no defense against this, but that didn't slow down their numbers—not one bit. Nothing could.

Chapter 23

R hodes should have reported to the Bao command dome, but he already had a pretty good idea about how that would go.

He headed for the Kuestrian Ridge instead. Hundreds of soldiers held the line at the ridgetop. The position gave them a sizable advantage. They could shoot down at the aliens from above.

The platoons held the aliens down on the lower slopes. The Emal couldn't climb high enough to shoot behind the ridge.

Rhodes spotted a commotion behind the line. A swirl of bodies moved parallel to the ridgetop heading east.

He landed near it and spotted Colonel Jenner talking to Lieutenants Turley, Upshaw, and Captain Vernick.

Jenner noticed the battalion first. He broke away from the men surrounding him and hustled over to Rhodes. "Thank God you're here, Corban! We really need you and your people on this campaign."

"What campaign is that?" Rhodes asked. "We don't even know where we're assigned for this battle."

"I'm assigning you!" Colonel Jenner snapped. "I'm assigning you right here with the 249th. We need you the most."

Rhodes glanced behind Jenner. The three officers and a few dozen other soldiers stood there listening. "What do you want us to do?"

"Our orders are to swarm over this ridge, assault the enemy down below, and drive them farther backward away from the cities."

"What's the point of that?" Lauer interjected. "You're holding them here just fine. If you cross the ridge, you'll lose the high ground."

Jenner made a face. "I promise you this isn't my idea." He turned back to Rhodes. "Can you help us out? We need something to tip the battle in our favor. If we cross that ridge and the aliens mow down too many of our guys, the Emal could drive us back here and we wouldn't have the firepower to hold them off a second time."

"This is stupid," Lauer muttered under his breath.

Rhodes chose to ignore the remark. "The only way we can tip the battle in your favor is by overcoming the enemy's laser rifles."

"How do we do that?" Coulter asked.

"We use the shields we used during the hostage evacuation. There are only nine of us. We won't be able to defend the whole ridge by ourselves. We'll have to punch through the Emal line and set up another battle behind the line. That's the only way to make them turn back."

"That could work," Rhinehart remarked. "We've done it that way before."

"As soon as the aliens turn to confront us, the platoons can fire on them from behind or the sides," Rhodes went on.

Fuentes startled everyone by speaking up for the first time. He'd kept so silent all this time. Rhodes had started to forget he was even there.

"What about targeting the base ships?" Fuentes asked. "We could fire our Vipers along the ground, clear out any Emal along the way, and detonate our Vipers under the base ships. That will stop the aliens from sending out fresh waves to replace their people."

Rhodes raised his eyebrows at him. "Good thinking. You can be in charge of that."

Fuentes spun around. "Sir?"

"It's a good idea. You're the best of us at blowing up base ships. The rest of the battalion will carry out my plan to draw the Emal line away from assaulting the ridge. The platoons will swarm over and pin the aliens down. That will give you a perfect opening to run for the base ships."

Fuentes blinked at him. "I didn't mean.....I didn't mean me, Sir."

"Why not you? You want to blow up base ships and kill a million Emal? Now's your chance."

Fuentes gulped once and then his eyes hardened again when he scanned the Emal side of the battle.

Rhodes checked The Grid again and rotated the layout in front of all his subordinates and their SAMs inside the interface.

"The aerial bombardment is weakening the Emal position the most here." He pointed at a spot west of their position. "We'll punch through there. We'll form an arrow pattern like this with our shields connected. The platoons can come in behind and between us like this...." He adjusted his grid lines to show everyone what he meant. "Once we get inside the horde, the shields will give the platoons cover to set up inside the swarm."

Colonel Jenner and the other officers stared at him in blank disbelief. "What are you talking about, Corban?" Colonel Jenner asked.

Rhodes snapped out of it and pointed down the ridge. "My people and I will set up a protective formation over there....You might see some strange things, but don't worry about that. We'll block the Emal lasers and give you a clear path to get inside the swarm. That will turn the enemy away from the ridge. Then the surrounding platoons can lay into them from either side—over there and over there."

"Are you sure about this?" Lieutenant Upshaw asked. "You really think we can penetrate inside their swarm?"

"I'm certain of it. You just have to stay behind us and take cover behind our shield. You'll be able to shoot the enemy from behind it—as well as you can shoot them from up here if not better."

"What about the way they drove us back during the hostage liftoff?" Rhinehart asked. "Those shields won't hold forever."

"We don't need them to hold forever. As soon as Rudy starts taking out base ships, the horde will turn back and abandon this ridge exactly the way they did during the hostage retrieval."

"I sure hope you're right," Turley murmured. "It sounds risky as hell."

"Anything other than staying on this ridge is risky," Oakes pointed out. "Going down on the same planet with the Emal is risky. You want to turn them back? This is the only way we're gonna do it. We sure as hell won't turn them back by assaulting them head-on."

"No, you're right about that." Jenner squinted toward the ridgetop. "All right, Corban. I'll leave this one to you."

Rhodes waved at Vernick and Upshaw. "Get the 249th and the 217th over there to that hilltop. Pull the 278th to the west and the 235th to the east." He raised his voice. "Get into position! Get ready to make the assault!"

He strode up to the ridgetop just as the 249th and the 217th showed up to meet him. A bunch of soldiers he knew grinned at him.

"It's great you guys made it out again," Stillwell told Rhodes.

"It might not be so great once we get down into those valleys," Rhodes replied. "It's gonna get hectic."

"Doesn't it always?" another soldier asked.

Rhodes located Fuentes in the crush of bodies. "You ready for this?"

Fuentes narrowed his eyes and clamped his lips together. He growled, "Yes, Sir," and glared at the ridgetop in front of him.

No one in the battalion could see over it to the Emal position—not yet. The battalion wouldn't see the enemy until they got over that ridge and started running down the other side.

Rhodes went through the battalion assigning everyone to their positions. With Fuentes on a mission of his own, that left eight battalion members left over—four to each side.

Rhodes and Rhinehart took the point of the arrow with Oakes and Lauer behind them. Thackery and Coulter followed with Dietz and Henshaw in the rear.

"Spread out as far as you can go without losing contact with the shields in front of you," Rhodes ordered. "If you feel the lasers starting to overpower your shields, consolidate your positions closer to the center. Protect the platoons in the center. It would be better if we covered a smaller footprint as long as we penetrate as deep as we can inside the swarm."

His subordinates nodded. "Yes, Sir," Coulter replied.

"No problem," Henshaw added.

Rhodes made one last survey of The Grid. Colonel Jenner's personal transport Duster was already on its way back to the command dome, now that he'd delivered orders to the platoons.

"I'm connecting you to the Legion transmission dispatch, Captain," Fisher told Rhodes. "You'll receive the order to launch the assault at the same time Captain Vernick gets it."

"Thank you," Rhodes replied and left it at that. He already knew what he needed to do. He just needed to know when.

The signal came down the instant Colonel Jenner's Duster touched the ground at the command dome.

Captain Vernick yelled, "MOVE OUT!!" to his platoon and everyone charged up the slope toward the ridgetop.

The platoons would have left Battalion 1 behind. Rhodes signaled his people through the interface, fired his boosters, and soared ahead.

He modified his grid lines on the wing and flattened himself into the same spreading shield the battalion used in the hostage scenario.

He expanded as far as he dared and formed the lefthand side of the arrow's point. He joined up with Rhinehart on the other side and the rest of the battalion linked up behind them.

They plunged over the ridgetop, down the other side, and onward to the Emal position.

The Emal opened fire and lasers hammered the field as soon as the arrow broke through the ranks.

Rhodes would have liked to hunker into a ball, but he couldn't do that in this shape.

The 249th smashed in behind him. The soldiers' bodies braced him the way he braced Coulter in the training session. The soldiers braced Rhodes so much better, now that there were so many more of them.

Rhodes couldn't adjust his position even if he wanted to. Emal gunfire would have knocked him off his feet, but he only fell against the soldiers.

More laser shots drove the soldiers into him from Rhinehart's side. The Emal's own counterassault gave the battalion all the protection they needed. Nothing could break that field.

Chapter 24

Rhodes and Rhinehart kept driving their arrow formation deeper into the Emal position. The aliens had no choice but to fall away on either side as the arrow stabbed through their ranks.

The platoons fired between the shields laying down a carpet of dead bodies, but more Emal crowded in from both sides.

The more they crowded and the more the arrow penetrated the enemy position, the more the Emal drew away from the ridge. The pressure relieved....and then all that pressure fell on the battalion.

The crush of Emal stopped Rhodes from going any further. He crouched there holding onto Rhinehart on one side and Lauer on the other.

Rhodes concentrated all his might on just taking one laser hit after another. Every hit he took was one less hit that would take down the platoon soldiers.

The Emal barrage escalated. Thousands of aliens jammed against Rhodes's shield. The enemy didn't need to use their weapons. The aliens would crush him and the soldiers inside the arrow.

"The 217th and the 235th are bombarding the Emal from the flanks!" Fisher bellowed over the noise. "They should be relieving some of the pressure on the battalion, but it isn't working!"

A scream from the back of the formation drew Rhodes's attention to The Grid. The arrow had penetrated deeply enough into the Emal side. Now the Emal closed the battalion from behind.

The pressure on Dietz and Henshaw built to the breaking point. Too many Emal crowded against them. The widest rear flare of the arrow collapsed in on itself.

Dietz and Henshaw pivoted inward to close the back of the arrow. They stayed linked with Coulter and Thackery until all four of them adjusted the arrow into a diamond instead.

Now the Emal surrounded the battalion from all sides. The 249th platoon got caught in the center with no way out.

Thousands of Emal circled the battalion crushing inward with unstoppable force. Laser fire smashed Rhodes's grid lines.

He heard Fisher yelling at him, but Rhodes couldn't hear over the noise. He had to do something to break this stalemate.

He almost gave the order to dissolve the formation when a catastrophic blast of laser cannon fire struck the arrow somewhere farther down the line.

Rhodes didn't see where it hit. Murphy vanished off the interface and someone screamed again.

The next instant, another four brutal shots pounded the platoon inside the arrow. Rhinehart broke contact with Rhodes and the Emal swarmed in to overrun the battalion.

Rhodes saw it all going down the drain in a big hurry. He braced himself to change back into his normal shape, dive over to Rhinehart, and lift him off before ordering the whole battalion to retreat.

Rhodes hated to leave the 249th in such dire straits, but what choice did he have? If he didn't get the battalion out now, they would all die here.

He cast one glance northward. The base ships kept unloading one shot after another at the battalion's position. Only the Emal's sheer numbers prevented the base ships from targeting accurately enough to wipe out the whole battalion.

Rhodes brought up The Grid to show him exactly how far away he was from Rhinehart. Oakes had already changed back into his normal shape.

He struggled through the horde of Emal trying to get closer to Coulter's unconscious body.

Another deafening explosion of cannon fire detonated right next to Rhodes's head, and at that moment, a lightning strike forked out of the atmosphere.

It lit up the whole ghastly landscape, struck three base ships at once, and pulverized them.

Rhodes's head shot up. He thought at first that Fuentes must have pulled out some miracle surprise attack.

Fuentes was nowhere near the base ships in question. He was still working his way overland trying to get near them.

These strikes came from orbit—or they seemed to. Another jet of white fire blasted out of the sky, wiped five more base ships off the map, and then another dancing array of electric forks blasted through the Emal ranks.

Rhodes actually stopped fighting to stare at The Grid as a completely different fleet of ships descended through the atmosphere. These didn't belong to the Aemon Legion nor did they belong to the Emal.

Rhodes didn't recognize these new ships' make. The energy shots flashing all over the planet looked strangely similar to Legion fusion charges, but they weren't the same.

These strange ships were ten times the Ravagers' size with a spiky, disjointed configuration. They had a modular, disconnected look as if someone had merged multiple ships into each one.

Rhodes only snatched the most fleeting glimpse of these ships as they broke through the atmosphere. That one glance showed him that none of the ships had the same shape. Each one was unique in a jumbled, mismatched, almost trashy kind of way.

These were a thousand times more powerful than anything the Emal or the Legion could throw at them. The strange ships dropped in low, swooped over the Emal ranks, and cut down thousands of Emal in seconds.

All the Emal stopped attacking Rhodes and his battalion. The aliens turned their laser rifles on the incoming attackers, but nothing made a dent in their hulls.

The remaining base ships did, though. They wheeled their cannons at the invaders. Four base ships unloaded on one of the invading vessels and blasted it out of the sky.

It exploded and split into three pieces. Each one crashed among the Emal horde, but more of those strange ships kept descending all over the place.

"Who the hell are they?!" Oakes bellowed.

"Who the hell cares?!" Lauer yelled back. "We gotta get out of here before they come after us next!"

Rhodes already knew that, but he didn't dare to launch with those ships laying waste to everything in sight.

"Rudy!" Rhodes hollered. "Come back here now! We gotta fall back!"

Fuentes turned around and put on speed trying to burrow his way back to the battalion's position.

The Emal didn't make it easy. They stampeded toward their base ships trying to escape only for the ships to blow up in their faces as soon as the aliens got near them.

More of the strange invaders soared across the landscape swiping massive cuts of their energy weapon through the Emal on the ground. Bodies fell in waves.

Rhodes turned back to try to rescue Rhinehart. Rhodes collided with Sergeant Stillwell coming the other way. "We're all gonna die out here! You have to help us!"

Rhodes opened his mouth to say he couldn't help anyone, not even himself.

He broke off when he saw one of the dark invaders gunning straight for his location.

"Cover the platoons!" he ordered. "Form a shield over the platoons! They're defenseless!"

He barely expanded his grid lines in time, flung himself as wide as he could go over the 249th, and clamped his eyes shut before the enemy unloaded on the whole area.

Oakes, Lauer, Dietz, and Thackery did the same thing. The invaders bombarded the five of them with crushing fire. The impact squashed the soldiers underneath them.

Rhodes lost sight of Rhinehart, Fuentes, Coulter, and Henshaw in the chaos. He couldn't even raise his head to try to see where they were.

Too many Emal crowded The Grid for him to pick up any trace of his four subordinates. A teeming carpet of life signs covered the planet and then all those Emal rushed inward on the space where the platoons had been standing.

The Emal fled from the invaders and ran in all directions, but nothing could escape the invaders' devastating weapons.

The Emal surged toward the center and wound up clambering on top of the shields the battalion used to protect the platoons cowering underneath.

Rhodes heard men yelling all around him. The weight of hundreds of Emal crushed him down on top of the platoons, but that weight offered the best protection from the enemy assault.

The strange ships came wheeling back and leveled Emal all over the field. Their bodies mounded on top of the battalion with the platoons trapped underneath.

Rhodes clamped his eyes shut to block out the horror, but The Grid didn't go away even then. The strange ships made pass after pass over the battlefield.

Just when the situation couldn't get any worse, a dozen of those strange invasion vessels landed on the dark planes farther north. They released another massive tide of ground troops, but these weren't aliens.

The Grid registered countless individuals advancing on the ridge-line, but The Grid didn't return any life signs. The line of dots on The Grid in front of Rhodes's eyes showed up in blue. They were machines.

"Who are they?!" Rhodes roared.

"They don't show up on any known Legion database!" Fisher called back. "We've never seen them before!"

"How the hell did they get this deep into the Treaty of Aemon Cluster?!" Oakes demanded. "There are hundreds of Legion ships in the atmosphere right now! They should have engaged with these fools and stopped them from landing."

Dash turned right and left in front of Oakes and adjusted The Grid. "The invaders are engaged with the Legion, but these machines still shouldn't have been able to sneak up on the planet. There's no explanation for it—not yet."

"Who cares about that?!" Lauer fired back. "How the hell do we get out of here?"

"Stay put!" Rhodes ordered. "We're safer here than we would be out there."

"How long do we have to stay here?" Lieutenant Turley asked from ten feet away from Rhodes.

Rhodes didn't realize he'd gotten trapped with his old friends from the 249th. He hadn't been thinking about anything other than keeping out of these invaders' path.

He only had to take one look at The Grid to make up his mind. The invading ground troops advanced south toward the ridgeline coming closer to the battalion's position.

The ground troops spread out in a thin line one individual deep. They walked upright on two legs and held their fusion rifles in two arms.

They had a strangely humanoid appearance and wore heavy armor and iron masks with one single extended ocular piece where the eyes should be.

Light shone through this slit as the machines scanned the area for anyone moving. The machines gunned down every Emal in sight and kept heading south toward the ridge.

The Legion force that had just been fighting the Emal opened fire on these machines. Fusion charges pelted back and forth.

The Ravagers in the atmosphere unloaded their seekers on the machine invaders now. Explosions thumped the planet under Rhodes's body.

The impact vibrated through the trapped platoons. Each of those concussions made everyone huddle lower—as if they could get any lower. No way would Rhodes let any of these people go out there now.

A few surviving Emal base ships opened fire on the invading vessels. Then the base ships turned their cannons on the ground troops.

Their thin advanced line made them nearly impossible to target. The base ships' cannon fire pounded the battlefield all over the place. Only a few stray shots hit the ground troops.

The ground troops passed their fusion rifles back and forth across the battlefield carving a path through any Emal still moving around out there.

The Emal lost the advantage of their numbers and fell before the enemy. The machine troops kept marching against all odds toward the ridge.

They inevitably ran into pockets of Emal with enough people to slow the machines' advance. The Emal unloaded their laser rifles on the machines and cut down dozens of them.

Individual machines fell on top of the mountain of Emal bodies pinning down Rhodes, the battalion, and the platoons. The machines' signals vanished off The Grid.

The machines showed no more concern for their fallen comrades than the Emal did. The machines only tightened their formation to close any gaps between them.

They kept moving south no matter what. The Emal had to retreat up the slopes getting closer to the Legion position.

Chapter 25

The Aemon Legion platoons on the Kuestrian Ridge couldn't stand up to the machine invaders' firepower. The Ravagers kept up a constant seeker bombardment on the ground troops, but the invasion ships posed a much bigger threat.

The Ravagers had no choice but to turn their weapons on the invasion ships, but the invaders outnumbered the Legion by a mile.

The invaders had no problem tying up the Ravagers, driving them away from the ridge, and sending out extra ships to target platoons still on the ground behind the ridgeline.

Rhodes couldn't watch anymore. He concentrated his attention on his subordinates and the platoons nearest him.

The machine ground troops left no Emal alive on the battlefield. In a few minutes, the invasion ships destroyed enough Ravagers for the invaders to go back and finish off the Emal base ships, too.

All life signs vanished off The Grid all the way north. The Emal had conquered that part of the planet. Now not a single Emal remained alive out there.

One lone signal blipped onto The Grid under mountains of dead aliens. It was Fuentes.

He'd also transformed himself into a shield. He had already been underneath the Emal horde when the invaders attacked. He just had to stay that way until they cleared the area.

Rhodes interfaced with him. "You okay, Rudy?"

"Yes, Sir," Fuentes growled. "These rotten aliens stink when they die."

"Just stay where you are—all of you. None of us is going anywhere for a while."

"You mean don't stick my head up there so those things can blow it off?" Lauer muttered. "Thanks. I wasn't planning to."

"Who the hell are those people, Sir?" Turley husked.

"They aren't people," Oakes told him. "They're machines."

"So what are they doing here?" Dietz asked.

"Invading the Treaty of Aemon Cluster, obviously," Captain Vernick chimed in from farther down the line.

Rhodes made one more check of the soldiers nearest him. He knew them all from the 249th. A few of them had suffered minor injuries during the battle. He couldn't take the time to see if any of them were dead out there.

Rhodes tried to interface with Murphy, Keon, and Rocky. Rhodes finally got hold of Rocky. "Are you and Rhinehart okay?" Rhodes asked. "I can't even see you on The Grid. There are too many wounded Emal in the way."

"Dane has a head injury, but it's minor," Rocky replied. "That's why we were off the interface. He just regained consciousness."

"Can any of you see Henshaw or Coulter?" Rhodes asked.

"I can see Coulter from here," Thackery replied. "He's ten feet away from me and he's unconscious, too, but his vital signs and brainwave patterns are reading as normal."

"That's strange. Murphy should be online."

"How long do you want us to stay here?" Vernick asked again. "You can assess the situation so much better than we can."

"The invaders are driving the Legion off the planet," Rhodes replied. "The invasion ships are lifting into orbit to reengage with the Legion fleet. They'll clear off soon and then we can get out from under these bodies."

"We won't be able to call in any Ravagers to lift us off," Lauer pointed out. "Not without those assholes shooting us down."

"We should stick around and defend the platoons in case the invaders come back," Rhodes replied. "We might not be able to do much, but the invaders must already know we're here. They would be able to pick up our life signs as well as we can pick up our own."

"Coulter's waking up, Captain," Thackery interrupted.

She highlighted Coulter's location on The Grid. Rhodes finally picked up Coulter's life signs in a sea of Emal.

He squirmed under his own pile of dead bodies before he regained consciousness enough to interface with the rest of the battalion.

"How are you feeling, Corporal?" Rhodes asked.

Coulter groaned, twisted onto his side, and curled into a ball. He lay there in silence for a second before Murphy came back online.

The SAM looked around at the landscape covered in Emal bodies. "This is not good."

"We're trapped here for the time being," Rhodes told him. "How bad are Coulter's injuries?"

Murphy swiveled his face sideways in the interface. "He has a concussion from a blow to the head, but it isn't severe. I'm not picking up any other injuries."

"You two stay where you are. We're waiting for the invaders to clear off the planet. It might take a while for the Legion to send a Ravager to collect us."

"Dr. Osborne made it sound like they would send a Ravager right away anytime we needed one," Oakes pointed out.

"Those invasion ships would destroy the *Ero* certain if it came in now."

"What about us?" Vernick asked. "I'm sure the Legion values you people a hell of a lot more than it values us."

"You can lift off on the *Ero* as soon as it makes it through the atmosphere. The battle is moving away from the planet. We can all get up now."

Rhodes straightened up, rearranged his grid lines, and changed back into a person.

He had to peel himself off the trapped platoons and shove all the dead Emal off the pile before he could get to his feet.

Even then, everyone stumbled to catch their balance on the uneven mounds of body parts.

Rhodes scanned the area again. "I'm still not showing any sign of Henshaw. I'm going to find her."

He fired his boosters, lifted over the bodies, and floated down ten feet south of the last platoon soldiers. Henshaw went down over here somewhere.

He scanned The Grid for her implants and found her lying under a dozen Emal. He pushed them out of the way and turned Henshaw over.

She'd sustained a fusion shot to her cranial implant. It didn't repair itself. She really needed to get back to the *Ero* and Dr. Osborne, but Rhodes couldn't do anything about that.

He checked on Rhinehart next, but Rocky continued to assure Rhodes that Rhinehart wasn't seriously injured even though he was still unconscious.

Rhodes straightened up and glanced around. The remaining base ships lay smoking in the distance with countless dead Emal hanging out of the wreckage.

A few columns of fire dotted the ridgetop where Ravagers went down. Rhodes located the command dome on The Grid. Enemy bombardment had caved in its roof.

Rhodes didn't pick up a single human life sign up there—not even a wounded one. The battalion and the 249th were all alone on this planet.

"Captain...." Lieutenant Upshaw murmured from a few feet away. "Look."

Rhodes turned around and crossed the mounds to where Upshaw stood looking down at some metal fragments at his feet.

Rhodes went over there and found himself staring down at the remains of one of the machine things.

A Ravagers' seeker missiles had torn the machine apart, but enough of it remained intact for Rhodes to see how it was constructed.

Its outer metal housing had a smooth, swooping look that encased a jumble of wires, cables, and conduits. Rods connected the neck to the iron mask head.

The thing had fallen twisted over onto its side. Sparks of electricity blinked and crackled inside the torn metal of its upper body.

Rhodes squatted down, turned the thing over, and grasped its helmet to look at it head on. No light came from its eye slit. The thing had completely shut down when it got hit.

"What is it?" Upshaw asked.

Rhodes opened his mouth to say he didn't know what it was or where it came from.

At that moment, the grid lines of his hands and arms changed....except that they didn't change.

Grid lines spread over the robot's mask....except that they didn't spread from Rhodes's hands. He would have extended his grid lines over it to measure it, study it, and scan it for any useful information.

These grid lines didn't come from him. They came from the robot's mask.

They spread around the head and started to morph. What would have been squares between the lines changed their shape and reformed into something more animated—something like a composite of animals, human, and geometric shapes.

The helmet repositioned its squares and lines into a face, but instead of eyes, a single metallic slit stared up at Rhodes from the ground.

He yelled out in surprise, dropped the head in a split second, and yanked his hands away, but it was too late. He'd already seen too much.

The machine crashed back on the ground, but the grid lines didn't go away. They kept migrating over the thing's head, changing its shape into a bunch of different composites with different expressions, each one as lifeless as the others.

Rhodes gaped at the thing in mounting horror. He could barely husk out, "No!"

"This can't be!" Fisher exclaimed. "It can't be!"

"Be quiet!" Rhodes snapped and spun away so he wouldn't see the machine anymore. "We have to figure out what to do."

"It's obvious what we have to do!" Fisher's voice started to rise. "We have to get out of here now!!"

"Will you be quiet?!" Rhodes practically bellowed and wrestled his voice under control. "Stay calm."

"Calm!" Fisher blurted out. "You want me to stay calm?! Did you just see....?"

"I saw it, okay, Fisher?!" Rhodes roared. "I saw it. Now be quiet before you..."

"What's going on?" Oakes asked.

Rhodes floundered to regain his composure. What could he say?

He took a deep breath, but he still found himself shaking. He couldn't get the sight of that thing out of his mind. "Contact Captain Ackerman. See where the *Ero* is and when the ship will be able to come and evacuate us."

"What about the rest of them?" Fisher asked.

"We aren't taking the rest of them, Fisher!" Rhodes barked. "Use your head. They're our enemies. They just attacked the Legion and tried to kill us."

"We can't leave them behind," Fisher insisted. "They're our....."

"SHUT UP, FISHER!!" Rhodes bellowed.

"The rest of who?" Oakes asked. "We can't leave who behind? We already said we'd lift off the platoons."

"He means the machines," Wild interjected. "He means these robot things."

"You can't be serious!" Oakes countered. "We aren't taking them anywhere."

"They're SAMs!" Fisher blurted out. "They're all SAMs! They're an army of SAMs! Don't you see the similarity between their technology and your implants?"

"But how...." Thackery began.

"I don't know how, but we can't leave them behind!" Fisher turned to Rhodes. "Captain......"

Rhodes clamped his jaws shut. "Fisher....I swear to Christ....if you don't shut up.....I'm going to have to do something drastic. Keep quiet and don't say another word or I swear I'll......"

He broke off. He couldn't think of anything bad enough to threaten Fisher with.

Rhodes had a hard enough time processing what he'd just seen. These invading robots couldn't be SAMs....but they were. He'd just seen them with his own eyes.

That machine used the grid lines to change its shape. It had to be a SAM.

Rhodes didn't want to admit it, but these machines really were using the same technology as the battalion's implants. He couldn't ignore it, now that Fisher pointed it out—to everyone.

Rhodes glanced around him in desperation. Torn, destroyed remains of these robots lay all over the battlefield.

"If they're SAMs, then we have to protect them," Dash pointed out. "We're programmed to defend each other with our lives."

"We are NOT defending them—with anything," Oakes snapped. "They're our enemies. I don't give a shit what technology they're using."

"But the Legion developed the SAMs technology," Thackery pointed out. "These robots turned on the Legion. Those invasion ships are out in space fighting the Legion fleet right now. How do you explain that?"

"I don't explain it," Dash replied. "I only know we can't fight these machines—not if they're our own kind."

"They aren't your own kind," Oakes snapped. "They aren't the SAMs of converted Legion soldiers—or whatever the hell you want to call them. You SAMs are all attached to living people. You aren't independent robots acting against the people who created you."

"Excuse me, Captain," Rocky interrupted. "Dane is coming around."

Chapter 26

R hodes did his best to push the conversation out of his mind. He couldn't think right now about the machine invaders being SAMs. They weren't SAMs. They were just another enemy for him to fight.

He blundered over mountains of dead Emal to where Rhinehart lay half-buried under another mountain of dismembered alien gore.

Rhodes rolled Rhinehart over. Dark purple bruises covered the organic side of his face. His implants appeared undamaged.

"Rhinehart!" Rhodes murmured. "Lieutenant...."

Rhinehart tried to open his one good eye, but it had swollen shut. "Captain...." Rhinehart husked.

"Can you interface with us?" Rhodes asked. "You don't have to get up. Just let me see you in the interface."

Rhinehart lay still for a second. "I don't think he can, Captain," Rocky replied. "I'm afraid I'll have to do it for you."

"It doesn't matter. Just monitor him until we can bring the *Ero* back."

"What are we going to do about the other SAMs?" Dash asked.

"They aren't SAMs!" Oakes snapped. "Stop calling them that. They aren't your friends and you aren't under any obligation to defend them."

"But what about.....?"

"SHUT UP, DASH!!" Oakes roared and glanced over at Rhodes. Oakes shut his own mouth and fought himself down.

Just then, Coulter sat up, rubbed his head, and finally got to his feet. He groaned and wrinkled his nose at the surroundings. "Spectacular. This is just perfect."

Rhodes made a command decision. He didn't trust Fisher to do anything right now. "Wild—interface with the *Ero* and see when the ship will be able to come and get us."

"Of course, Captain," Wild replied.

"Rudy—come back here and rejoin the rest of the battalion," Rhodes ordered.

"Yes, Sir." Fuentes changed back into whatever burrowing form he'd been using before. He could travel through the ground much faster than walking or even using his boosters to fly.

Rhodes used his grid lines to change himself into one of the jointed spider shapes. He moved Henshaw's body over next to Rhinehart. Now he had his two wounded in one place.

Doing something took his mind off the machines, but as soon as he finished, all those questions came rushing back.

The machines using SAMs technology didn't bother him nearly as much as Fisher's and Dash's reaction. This was going to cause serious problems. Rhodes sensed that even now.

Fisher didn't speak again after Rhodes's outburst. Oakes's outburst silenced Dash, but they kept hovering there watching everything. They didn't change their opinion.

Rhodes dreaded going back into combat with either of them—not against this enemy—not until he got them back to the Legion and got them reprogrammed to fight these machines.

He checked The Grid and confirmed his worst fears. Fourteen of the robot invasion ships broke away from the Legion fleet.

Rhodes couldn't tell from here whether the invaders wanted something special about this particular planet.

He tried not to think about the most obvious explanation. If these machines were an entire army of SAMs the way Fisher said, then the machines obviously wanted to reclaim their own—the battalion.

None of that mattered right now. "They're coming back!" Rhodes called out. He spun around and pointed at everyone near him, including the men of the 249th. "The invaders are coming back! Arm up and prepare to defend yourselves!"

"You have to help us!" Upshaw insisted.

"What the hell do you think I'm trying to do, Justin?!" Rhodes roared and turned the other way to swipe his forefinger at his people. "Bring Rhinehart and Henshaw over here. Stand by to put up our shields again. We'll have to concentrate all our energy on covering them and the platoons."

"What about shooting down their ships?" Thackery asked.

"Shoot them down with what?" Lauer asked. "The whole Legion fleet couldn't defeat those things. We don't have a prayer."

"Get into position!" Rhodes ordered. "We won't have time to argue about it."

He helped Dietz bring Henshaw and Rhinehart closer to the platoons. The soldiers hunkered down in a much tighter formation than last time.

The group was much better prepared to defend itself this time, but that still didn't give Rhodes any more optimistic feeling about their chances.

He, Lauer, Oakes, Dietz, Thackery, Fuentes, and Coulter surrounded the platoon waiting for the enemy to enter the atmosphere.

Rhodes tried to ignore the fact that the enemy invasion ships were heading straight for the battalion. Whoever these machines were, they recognized their own.

"Stand by!" he yelled over the platoon. "They're using fusion weapons, so we can deflect them and shoot back with thermals. That will block their shots from hitting us."

"Got it," Lauer replied.

"I can't let you do this, Captain," Fisher interrupted.

"You don't let me do anything, pal," Rhodes snapped. "Shut the fuck up and don't talk to me again."

"I can't let you shoot at them," Fisher repeated. "They're SAMs. They're our....."

"If you interfere with this battle in any way, I'll make sure the doctors take you offline as soon as we get back on board the *Ero*," Rhodes snapped. "Is that clear? Don't say another word to me about them being...."

He broke off as the howl of engines blasted through the atmosphere coming closer. His attention riveted on The Grid.

The invasion ships dropped out of the clouds and picked up speed heading for the battalion's location.

"Shield the platoons!" Rhodes ordered.

He stretched his grid lines over the platoon. The lines joined up with more lines coming from each of his subordinates. Their Grids linked into a solid wall.

The invasion ships opened fire, but The Grid held. The enemy swooped lower to come in for another pass.

The battalion opened fire with their thermals, but the invaders' firepower overcame the thermals. The battalion's thermal cannons didn't neutralize the invaders' fusion fire—not enough.

The soldiers aimed their Jackhammers through The Grid and returned fire to drive the invaders off, but the invasion ships were too powerful.

Rhodes opened one of the squares in his Grid—just enough to fire a Viper through it to hit one of those ships as it soared overhead.

He double-checked and triple-checked that Fisher didn't do anything to stop Rhodes from firing on these things.

Fisher didn't do anything. He remained silent and passive through the whole battle, but at the last possible second before Rhodes released his Viper, something else flashed on The Grid in front of his eyes.

His Viper launcher shut down, and the next time he fired his thermal cannon, nothing happened.

"They're shutting us down!" Coulter hollered. "They're doing something to switch off our weapons systems!"

"They're using a Legion transponder code," Fisher called out. "They're signaling that they're a friendly force to stop us from shooting at them."

"Can you override it?" Rhodes asked.

"I'm trying!" Fisher countered. "The code acts on our base programming. We can't do anything about it. It's written into our neural core."

Rhodes tried to unleash his Vipers again.....and again. Nothing worked.

The rest of the battalion experienced the same malfunction—except that it wasn't a malfunction. The SAMs all responded to the transponder code exactly the way they'd been programmed to.

Rhodes didn't think before he did it. He didn't even know he could do it until it happened.

He dropped into The Grid. The battle vanished for a second—or at least it receded to the limits of his awareness.

He entered The Grid—the black landscape marked with green lines the way he'd seen it before each training session.

Fisher's face floated in front of Rhodes's eyes. He couldn't see any other SAM or his subordinates even though he remained interfaced with them.

"What are you doing, Captain?" Fisher asked.

Rhodes didn't answer. He dove for Fisher, extended his grid lines, and plunged headfirst straight through the image of Fisher's face.

The grid lines merged—Rhodes's grid lines and the lines that made up Fisher's base matrix. Rhodes didn't understand what he was doing or how this was even possible. He just did it.

The grid lines tangled for a minute and then he submerged deeper into a world of millions of grid lines forming miles upon miles of Grid landscape.

This looked like the simulated world of the training sessions but with no color or texture. Green lines and black squares made up every shape imaginable.

Mountains, valleys, buildings, towns, vehicles, animals, people—this landscape contained everything the real world contained—except color and substance.

Fisher's face lost all color, too. As soon as Rhodes entered that world, he attacked Fisher with all his might. Rhodes wrapped his grid lines around Fisher's lines and tore them apart.

Some other part of Rhodes's mind took over. He punched through the grid outline of Fisher's face and broke into a deeper, more complicated Grid world of bizarre shapes all melting and changing before his eyes.

A complicated tangle of grid lines morphed and twisted at the very center of the outer cage of lines that made up Fisher's image.

Rhodes didn't understand how he recognized that tangle, but he did recognize it. It was the transponder code.

He fired his scourge gun at it and it shattered into a million much smaller fragments of grid lines. They scattered outward to join with the lines all around them.

The instant he hit that tangle, the whole Grid world evaporated and he found himself back on the battlefield under heavy bombardment from the invasion ships.

Their constant gunfire weakened the field the battalion used to protect the platoons.

He unleashed ten Vipers in rapid succession, targeted them together, and detonated three of the incoming enemy vessels.

Grid lines materialized on the invading ships' outer hulls, but they didn't change shape.

Rhodes's brain kicked into high gear. That destroyed machine changed its grid lines, but only after it ceased to function normally.

The machine ground troops that wiped out the Emal didn't change their shape, either. They didn't alter The Grid to make themselves more adaptable or to avoid enemy gunfire.

Rhodes's made another snap decision. "Break the shield and attack!" he roared. "Battalion 1—separate! Use The Grid and attack!"

He leapt out of position, took control of The Grid, and changed his shape into a giant mechanized fighting machine.

His arms and hands morphed into windmills of lasers whipping in all directions. He swelled to five times his size and slashed his lasers at another five ships in the sky.

Another half dozen invasion ships landed not far away and unloaded more ground troops, but they didn't use The Grid, either. Could they even use The Grid at all?

Chapter 27

The machine ground troops aimed their fusion guns at Rhodes and opened fire. He was too busy thrashing his lasers at more invasion ships trying to surround him.

He fired lasers out of his eyes instead. He didn't make the conscious decision to do it that way.

He was just too busy using his arms against the enemy ships. He altered his weapons configuration without thinking, slashed down the ground troops, and spun around to face more incoming enemy vessels.

Oakes, Lauer, Coulter, Thackery, and Dietz widened their circle to give each other room to clear the area. The platoon soldiers crouched in the center of that circle firing outward to hit enemy targets whenever and wherever they could.

"The *Ero* is in the atmosphere, Captain!" Wild called over the noise. "Captain Ackerman can't descend until we secure the surface."

"Secure it, then!" Rhodes yelled over his shoulder. He couldn't turn around.

He faced another five enemy vessels circling from the north. He had to stop them from getting near Rhinehart, Henshaw, and the platoons.

He occupied the enemy with his lasers. The invasion ships charged him trying to break past him and get behind him.

He released another five Vipers and hit two of invasion ships, but Vipers didn't damage them.

He concentrated on the others. They tied him up while another ten landed farther out in the wasteland of bodies. Those ten ships unloaded more ground troops. How much longer could the enemy go on with this before they took out the battalion first and then the platoons?

Out of nowhere, a revolving pinwheel of laser fire rocketed across Rhodes' line of sight. It slashed down dozens of robot ground troops and kept on going.

The pinwheel spun parallel to the ground, circled the battle twenty yards out from the battalion's position, and whirled back around to rejoin the battalion before the pinwheel changed back into Fuentes.

Rhodes didn't have time to congratulate anyone before another five invasion ships closed on him. He fired his Vipers again and swung his lasers one last time, but he couldn't destroy these things. They were too big and too powerful.

They hovered off taking his Viper hits on their jumbled outer hulls. They could have slaughtered him in seconds if they really unloaded their weapons on him, but they didn't.

They drifted back and forth in front of him for a second and then lifted off into the atmosphere. Their machine ground troops retreated, loaded up, and evacuated the planet, too.

He stood there panting for breath and searching the landscape for any other enemy coming after him.

"The *Ero* is on approach, Captain!" Wild reported again.

Rhodes couldn't speak to answer. His eyes darted back and forth across the landscape. He didn't want to believe that those machines really were gone.

They weren't gone. They still battled against the Legion on other planets and out in space.

The *Ero* took advantage of the lull to descend on the battalion's position, but the ship couldn't find a flat spot to land.

It drifted a few feet off the ground and waited there with its landing bay open for the battalion to evacuate.

Rhodes and his people herded the platoons in front. Lauer picked up Henshaw. Rhodes had to change himself into another giant monster so he could carry Rhinehart.

The platoons packed into the bay. Rhodes's form gave him a clear view over the soldiers' heads.

Dr. Osborne tried to meet the battalion there, but the platoon blocked his way. He had to fight his way through to get near Rhodes and Lauer.

A bunch of soldiers from the platoon tried to talk to the battalion on their way through the hold.

Rhodes saw the soldiers smiling and holding out their hands to shake hands with the battalion, but he pushed past them. He really needed to get off by himself and think.

"We can't work on them here!" Osborne called over dozens of voices. "Bring them up to the capsule hold. I'll work on them there and you can all go into conversion cycles."

"They were SAMs!" Fuentes panted. "They were SAMs!"

Osborne looked over at him. "Who was?"

"Not now, Corporal," Rhodes interrupted.

Rhinehart weighed a ton. Rhodes didn't want to carry him in some otherworldly form that might scare the crew, but Rhodes couldn't carry Rhinehart without changing into something.

He and the battalion followed Osborne upstairs to the capsule hold. Rhodes and Lauer laid Rhinehart and Henshaw in their capsules.

Osborne and Trudeau started working on the two injured battalion members.

Coulter stretched out in his capsule and went into a conversion cycle right away. He groaned when he turned over on the mattress and locked into his prongs.

Rhodes stayed across the room watching his people settle down. Lauer and Thackery had a hard time putting the battle behind them. They both paced up and down for more than an hour.

Fuentes approached Rhodes. Fuentes no longer glared—or not as badly. "I'm sorry I couldn't carry out the objective to hit the base ships, Sir. I hope you don't mind me taking the initiative to take out those ground troops instead."

"Not at all, Corporal. You did great. You ended the battle much quicker than it otherwise would have. I'm glad you feel free to take the initiative that way. You can keep doing it as much as you want."

"Thank you, Sir. I think I'll take the initiative by going into a conversion cycle."

Rhodes started to smile, but he stopped himself.

Fuentes went straight to his capsule and locked himself into it. Dietz sat down at the computer terminal. He didn't usually get a chance to work on it. Fuentes monopolized the terminal back at Coleridge Station.

Oakes sat down at the table, but he didn't work on his drawings. He and Rhodes didn't bring any paper or pencils with them. They didn't need to. They stayed in stasis for the trip here and then went straight into combat.

Fisher broke in on Rhodes's thoughts. "I'm so sorry, Captain. I can't forgive myself for letting you down in the middle of a battle."

"You had nothing to do with that transponder code," Rhodes replied. "I'm the one who's sorry I had to get inside your head like that to break the code."

"I'm not talking about the code," Fisher murmured. "I'm talking about before that."

Rhodes turned to face his SAM. Fisher had withdrawn so much from Rhodes recently. Fisher didn't intrude on Rhodes's life unless he absolutely had to.

"I shouldn't have let those SAMs....."

"Stop calling them SAMs, pal," Rhodes snapped. "You can't think of them as that."

"I have to, Captain. That's the problem."

"You calling them that is what's causing the problem. They're our enemies. Did you see the way they targeted the battalion? They know who we are. They came back to Bao for us alone."

"Doesn't that just prove that they are SAMs?"

Rhodes tried to shake those thoughts out of his head, but nothing would get rid of them now. "They aren't SAMs. Don't call them that."

"What should I call them, then?"

"Call them the enemy. That's what they really are."

Fisher fell silent for a moment. He and Rhodes watched Osborne and Trudeau working on Rhinehart and Henshaw.

Osborne adjusted a few things on Rhinehart's cranial implant and then did the same thing to Henshaw. Her implants started to repair themselves.

A few minutes later, Osborne closed both capsules with Rhinehart and Henshaw inside. Thackery started to relax and sat down on the edge of her capsule.

"You should go into a conversion cycle, too, Captain," Fisher told him. "Your system is depleted."

"I know, man," Rhodes muttered. "I just don't seem to be able to dial it down."

Just then, Osborne came over to him. The doctor studied Rhodes extra closely. "What did Fuentes mean when he said they were SAMs?"

"Nothing," Rhodes lied. "How's Henshaw? Is she going to recover?"

"She'll be fine, now that her implants are repairing themselves. Rhinehart's head injury isn't severe. He should be fine after a conversion cycle."

"That's what Rocky said."

Osborne cocked his head to inspect Rhodes even more intensely. "Is something wrong, Captain? You don't look good."

"What does that mean? I never do."

"I mean you look like you're in distress. You look like something is bothering you."

Rhodes almost confided in the doctor and then changed his mind. Dr. Osborne joined the Battalion 1 project after it got started.

He wouldn't have been involved in whatever Frankenstein creation made these rogue SAMs into a force powerful enough to attack the Legion that created it.

"I'll be all right. I better turn in. Thanks for everything, Doctor."

Rhodes sat down on his mattress, stretched out on his back, and closed his capsule cover, but he didn't connect to the prongs. He lay there staring at nothing for a while—except that Fisher was still there.

"Why didn't you tell him the truth?" Fisher asked.

"He won't be able to tell me where these....these machines came from. He wasn't around when the project got started."

"He's the one who will reprogram me and the other SAMs."

Rhodes started to shut his eyes. "I told you not to worry about the transponder code. The Legion can change it easily. Those machines won't be able to use it a second time."

"I'm not talking about the transponder code, Captain," Fisher murmured with his usual saint-like patience. "I'm talking about our programming that won't allow us to attack another SAM."

Rhodes tried to insist again that these machines weren't SAMs, but that argument obviously didn't work.

He tried to look away, but Fisher just moved with Rhodes every time he turned his head. "Maybe I don't like the idea of reprogramming you to do anything, pal. Maybe that's why I don't want the doctors doing anything to you."

Fisher's expression twisted. "I'm grateful that you're trying to protect me, Captain."

"That's nothing you haven't done for me a thousand times. Tell me this. Would you want to fight these machines if they weren't SAMs? Did you want to fight them before you found out they were SAMs—or that they were using SAMs technology?"

"Of course. They tried to kill the battalion—and you. They attacked the Legion and wiped out all those Emal. Of course I want to fight them."

Rhodes shut his eyes again. "Then, as far as I'm concerned, this is just another malfunction."

"If it's a malfunction, you should want the doctors to correct it," Fisher pointed out.

"I would rather correct it amongst ourselves if we can—without the doctors tinkering with your programming. That never ends well."

"There is another problem, Captain—as I'm sure you know."

"What's that?"

"That these....these machines wanted to retrieve you—to retrieve us. They wanted the battalion—and not to study us the way the Emal did. How do you think these machines found the battalion on the one planet where we were fighting? These machines could have intervened in any battle anywhere the Emal are invading the Treaty of Aemon Cluster. These machines chose that one planet—the one planet with the battalion on it. It looks like these machines came here to retrieve the battalion."

"Then they really are our enemies. I'm going to sleep now, pal. I suggest you do the same thing. I promise you we won't go back into battle until we work this out—even if it means reprogramming you."

"Captain, do you think....?" Fisher broke off.

"Do I think what?"

"You threatened to take me offline if I interfered with the battle—which I did."

"You tried to break that transponder code. You didn't interfere with the battle."

"I interfered by recommending that you treat these machines as something other than the enemy."

"Dash did the same thing. Besides, the Legion and the Battalion 1 governing body have some questions to answer about where this technology came from. I'm not going to take anyone offline until I get those answers." Rhodes locked into the prongs. "We can talk about this when I wake up. I'll see you when we get back to Coleridge Station, pal."

"Good night, Captain. Sleep well."

Chapter 28

R hodes opened his eyes in his capsule and stared up at the closed cover. Fisher hovered before his eyes already.

Fisher had changed his morning routine—and so had Rhodes. Fisher and Rhodes talked before Rhodes got out of his capsule. Talking to Fisher had replaced Rhodes putting on his boots in the morning.

The instant Rhodes made eye contact with his SAM, he remembered everything from the Bao assault.

He shuddered when he remembered that robot's metal helmet changing in his hands.

Fisher read his mind. "Good morning, Captain," Fisher murmured in that undertone that told Rhodes loud and clear that Fisher was thinking the same thing.

Rhodes groaned. "I was hoping it would all turn out to be a bad dream."

"I'm afraid not. What are you going to do about it?"

"I have to talk to the brass about where this technology could have come from."

"Where *could* it have come from?" Fisher asked. "The Battalion 1 Project is the most highly classified project in the whole Legion."

"It's also the project that has suffered the most failures, setbacks, and deaths. Dozens of soldiers have been implanted with these devices since the project started. The majority of those soldiers wound up dead—so what did the brass do with their bodies? I'm going to take a wild guess and say the brass didn't recycle the failed implants to reuse on someone else."

Fisher fell silent for a moment. "You're right, Captain. That's a lot of technology unaccounted for."

"I'm sure it isn't unaccounted for. The brass knows exactly what happened to it—and don't forget that these SAMs are sentient. The brass could throw away the implants, but they probably didn't think to either take the SAMs offline or destroy the implants completely. The SAMs remained self-aware and self-determining. They probably used their repair technology to reconstruct themselves. Maybe they used The Grid to reform themselves into some other shape—the shapes they have now."

"Of course, Captain," Fisher murmured. "Of course you must be right. I'm glad you're handling this and not me. I couldn't stay detached enough to make any decision about them. I still think of them as my own kind. I'm sorry, Captain. I can't help it."

Rhodes sighed. "It's all right, pal. I understand. We'll just have to deal with it. Show me the SAM we found on the battlefield."

Fisher brought up the Grid projection of the SAM changing in front of him. Rhodes's grid lines extended as far as his fingers.

Then the robot's grid lines took over, swirled over its helmet, and started to change shape. It reformed into a face.

"Freeze it there," Rhodes ordered. "Do you recognize it? Do you know this SAM?"

"I don't recognize it—but as you said, I wouldn't recognize a SAM that came online before the doctors activated me. I came online for the first time when you entered The Grid. These unknown SAMs would have been activated long before that—and discarded long before that. I'm sure the brass would want to isolate these failed SAMs from any new battalion members who actually attained the ability to function. The brass wouldn't want the failed SAMs technology to infect the new batch."

"Right. That makes sense—which means these SAMs are all old ones. Maybe we can find a way to turn this to our advantage."

"How?" Fisher asked. "These machines have an overwhelming advantage. They're more powerful even than the Emal."

"Maybe, but we have The Grid. I didn't see the invasion ships or the machine ground troops using The Grid to their advantage or to adapt to the conditions. In fact, I didn't see them using The Grid at all."

"How would we use that against them?"

"I don't know, but there has to be a way." Rhodes opened his capsule cover and sat up. "Let's go talk to the brass and see what's happening. They might be able to tell us something useful about how these things work."

Talking to Fisher in the privacy of their closed capsule turned out to be much better for Rhodes than lacing up his boots or staring at his feet or looking at his reflection in the mirror.

He stood up, ran his fingers through his hair, and he was ready to start his day. He walked over to Dr. Osborne who was working on Rhinehart's capsule controls.

"How are the patients?" Rhodes asked.

"They're fine. They'll be coming out of their conversion cycles in a few minutes."

"Excellent." Rhodes turned away. "I'm going to see Colonel Kraft and General Brewster. Stay here and tell the others where I am, okay?"

Osborne spun around. "You can't, Captain! You can't see them."

"Why not? I need to talk to them about our last battle."

"They've been recalled to Preinea. They're in conference with the Treaty of Aemon Ruling Council about this new invasion force."

"But what about....?" Rhodes stopped in midsentence when he realized for the first time where he was.

He thought when he first woke up that he must be in the barracks at Coleridge Station. Now he realized his mistake. He was still in the capsule hold on board the *Ero*.

The hold had been set up identically to the barracks—except that it didn't have a bookshelf. Henshaw's carvings and Oakes's and Rhodes's art supplies weren't on it.

Rhodes's mind switched gears and he activated The Grid. He was on board the *Ero*—and the ship was nowhere near Coleridge Station.

The ship was nowhere near Bao, either. The ship had traveled a long way from the first battle against the machine invasion, but the *Ero* didn't take the battalion back to Coleridge Station. Why not?

"The Masks are wiping out populated planets even faster than the Emal did," Dr. Osborne told him. "The Masks aren't trying to reclaim territory. It looks like they just want to destroy. They don't need any other reason."

"Masks?" Rhodes repeated. "Who's calling them that?"

Osborne shrugged. "The whole Legion is calling them that since we don't know what they're really called. They wear masks—or helmets or whatever you want to call them. It's as good a name as any, I guess."

"So....." Rhodes scrambled to read The Grid of the *Ero* and the surrounding space. "Where the hell are we?"

"We're en route to the planet Zobos in the Eotis system. The Masks have already leveled every other planet in the whole system. Zobos is the last one. The Masks just keep going from planet to planet torching everything to the ground."

Rhodes sighed and turned away. "So it's the Emal all over again."

"The Masks are much more dangerous than the Emal. The Masks move faster and their weapons are more powerful. The Legion doesn't have time to evacuate all the populations before the Masks get there. They've already killed over five million people on ten different planets—and that's not counting the numbers of Emal they've killed."

"You mean...." Rhodes stammered.

"The Masks made wiping out the Emal their first mission. The Masks went down the whole battle line, knocked off every base ship, and cut every single Emal to pieces. As far as we know, there are no more Emal alive anywhere anymore. They're extinct."

Rhodes blinked at Dr. Osborne in stupid disbelief. Rhodes had fought thousands of Emal. He and his fellow Legion soldiers always considered the Emal an unlimited quantity.

Rhodes never thought twice about killing Emal. More would always take their places.

The idea of there not being any more Emal anywhere—that didn't seem possible. It couldn't be possible.

Fisher broke in on Rhodes's thoughts just then. "Captain Ackerman is asking you to come to the bridge. He's receiving orders for Battalion 1 from General Brewster and the Battalion 1 governing body."

Dr. Osborne gave Rhodes a significant look before Rhodes walked out of the hold. Rhinehart, Henshaw, Dietz, and Lauer were all waking up.

Rhodes wanted to get this meeting over with before he interfaced with his subordinates. He'd always shared everything with them, but not this early in the morning.

He found the *Ero* captain on the bridge in his usual dark mood. "I don't appreciate being ordered around to fetch and carry for a bunch of overblown science experiments, Captain," Ackerman snarled when Rhodes showed up.

"Neither do I," Rhodes replied. "Do you have somewhere private that I can take this transmission?"

Ackerman scowled at him even more furiously, but he didn't argue. He showed Rhodes into a side office where Rhodes sat down in front of a computer terminal.

Rhodes waited for Ackerman to leave. Rhodes took his time connecting to the transmission. He made up his mind right away what he would say to the chumps in the Battalion 1 governing body about this.

He opened the transmission only to discover General Brewster looking off to one side and talking to someone off the screen.

"And get me General Marshall on the line," Brewster was saying. "We need to bring in some of those Clastofil cannons to shut down the fusion blasts." The general jumped when he saw Rhodes. "Captain! We thought something happened to you down there."

"It did, General. We need you to recall the battalion back to Coleridge Station for modification, reprogramming, and repair."

Brewster frowned at something on the controls in front of him. "Dr. Osborne's report states that Lieutenant Rhinehart and Ms. Henshaw will make a full recovery from their injuries without going back to Coleridge Station. The Eotis system is in danger from these Masks...."

"I'm not talking about Rhinehart's and Henshaw's injuries," Rhodes interrupted. "I'm talking about our SAMs. They need to be reprogrammed before we go back into battle."

Colonel Kraft, General Hyde, and Admiral Pulman connected to the same transmission from other locations. They weren't even in the same room with General Brewster right now.

Colonels Neff and LeClerc weren't there, though. Did the other officers get rid of Neff for speaking on Rhodes's behalf?

Then again, the other officers didn't get rid of Colonel Kraft for speaking on Rhodes's behalf. LeClerc was gone, too, and he'd been against Rhodes.

"What's wrong with your SAMs?" Kraft asked. "The feed shows them functioning normally during their first contact with the Masks."

"How much did you actually study the feed?"

Now it was Kraft's turn to frown. "What do you mean?"

"These Masks.....are SAMs," Rhodes blurted out. "They're using Legion technology—the same technology from the battalion's implants. These Masks are using The Grid ...."

"That's impossible," General Hyde interrupted. "The nine current members of Battalion 1 are the only people who have this technology."

"We're the only people who have this technology *now,*" Rhodes corrected. "What did you do with all the soldiers who didn't survive the project—or who died after waking up? How did you dispose of any of this tech when it malfunctioned or failed to activate? Some of it must have survived. Now it's out there replicating itself into this machine army and coming after the people who created it."

"That's impossible, Captain," General Brewster blustered. "You don't know enough about the Battalion 1 project to make that assessment."

"You don't think so? Take a look at this."

Rhodes interfaced with the *Ero's* communications system, gave Fisher a silent signal inside the interface, and played back their experience of touching that Mask.

It seemed like a good name for it, especially considering how its Mask changed into a face—a SAM's face.

General Brewster gasped out loud when he saw the grid lines change into a face. "It isn't possible!"

"You might want to rethink when and where you use that phrase," Rhodes muttered. "It is more than possible. It's real. These Masks are SAMs. They're using your technology. They also used a Legion transponder code to deactivate the battalion's weapons systems during the worst part of the battle."

"How did you overcome that?" Kraft asked.

"I'd rather not say. We need to regroup at Coleridge Station and go over what caused the malfunction...."

"What malfunction?" General Pulman asked. "We aren't seeing any sign of a malfunction—especially if the SAMs are responding appropriately to Legion transponder codes."

Rhodes hesitated to say it. He didn't want to sell out Fisher and the other SAMs—or do anything that could shift the blame onto them.

"You better tell them," Fisher murmured in his ear. "They'll only be able to correct the problem if they know what it is."

Rhodes nodded and took a deep breath. "The battalion's onboard SAMs are responding to these Masks and considering them their own kind. Our SAMs have been programmed not to attack their own and even to defend their own kind with their lives. It's causing problems...."

"It didn't stop you from fighting the Masks on Bao," General Brewster pointed out.

"You can't seriously believe that we'd be better off just ignoring this problem," Rhodes countered. "It caused problems on Bao and it will cause more problems later. Just fix the damn thing."

"We can fix it en route to Zobos," General Brewster decided. "I'm sure Drs. Osborne and Trudeau will correct any problems on the way. The Eotis system is hanging by a thread...."

"I heard the Eotis system was already finished," Rhodes corrected. "If we malfunctioned again, we would lose the planet and ourselves into the bargain."

"You're too far away from Coleridge Station for us to withdraw you and send you all the way back out," General Hyde replied. "We should take this opportunity to correct the problem en route and continue the campaign as planned." She nodded at Rhodes like he just agreed with her. "Carry on, Captain. You can report to us after you engage the Masks on Zobos."

She cut the signal. Rhodes took a rare moment to slump in his chair, bury his face in his hands, and groan. "I'm being ordered around by a bunch of morons."

"I believe the word you're looking for is, 'ass'," Fisher interjected. "You're being ordered around by a bunch of asses."

Rhodes found himself snorting with laughter—except that this wasn't funny. He got to his feet and headed back to the capsule hold. "So Osborne is our only hope."

"At least you know you can trust him."

"What about the other SAMs?" Rhodes asked. "Did you get a chance to assess their positions on this?"

"Not since Dash said we couldn't leave the other SAMs behind."

"Do me a favor, pal, and don't call them SAMs anymore. We have another name for them. They're Masks. We don't even know if they really are SAMs or just some hybridized form of the same technology."

"You're right, Captain. Of course these invaders aren't the same as us even if they do come from the same technology."

"Do you think calling them by a different name will be enough to change the way you and the other SAMs think about these machines?"

"I wouldn't like to speculate. If you really want my recommendation...."

"I do," Rhodes insisted. "Always."

"Then I recommend you get Dr. Osborne to remove that part of our programming that blocks us from attacking our own kind—and double-check that the Legion changes its transponder codes."

"We should probably rewrite your programming not to respond to any Legion transponder codes," Rhodes suggested.

Fisher looked away. "If you think it's best, Captain. I can only offer my recommendation."

Chapter 29

Rhodes returned to the capsule hold and relayed the substance of General Brewster's transmission to the rest of the battalion.

"Are you saying these jokers are really sending us back into battle against those things?" Dietz asked.

"They aren't just sending us back into battle against those things," Rhodes replied. "They're sending us back into battle against those things without giving us the option to test the new modifications beforehand. We won't know if it works until the Masks are already shooting at us."

"I'm not going," Thackery snapped. "I don't care what they do to me. I'm not going to throw myself in front of those machines to get killed—or put the rest of you in danger by going into battle when I don't even know if I can trust my own reactions. This is nuts!"

"You don't have to go," Rhodes decided. "You can stay behind."

Her one good eye fell out of its socket. "Seriously? I don't have to go? Yeah!"

"None of you has to go," Rhodes replied. "I don't blame you for staying behind. Just be aware that a sizable civilian population is in danger of these machines completely wiping them off the map. The Masks have already killed millions of people and they'll keep doing it until someone stops them. That's what Battalion 1 is for—not sitting on our thumbs behind closed doors. We have tools to fight these things that no one else has. I'm going in with any of you that want to come with me. We'll make what modifications we can on the way. We need to be ready to rock as soon as we get there."

His subordinates exchanged glances. "You make a convincing case, Captain," Wild muttered.

"I understand that none of you wants to fight other SAMs," Rhodes went on. "I don't want to, either. That's why we need to make these modifications to your programming—to make sure we all recognize our enemy."

"And we won't even have a chance to train with these modifications before we go into battle?" Henshaw asked. "That doesn't sound like a very good idea."

"It sounds like a disastrous idea," Rhinehart interjected. "I mean, it sounds like an even more disastrous idea than the rest of this asinine project."

Fisher chuckled. "That's what I said."

Rhodes turned to Dr. Osborne and Dr. Trudeau. They stood off to one side listening to the conversation—or the part of it they could hear.

"We're ready," Rhodes told them.

"You'll all need to lock into your capsules," Osborne replied. "We'll make the modifications to your programming and it will take effect in all your SAMs at the same time. That will save us having to go through and reprogram each SAM individually."

"I guess I can't argue with that," Lauer growled.

Rhodes turned away. It was up to him to set an example and lead the way.

He swung his legs up onto the mattress in his capsule and let the prongs lock into the back of his head and body.

"I sure hope this works," Fisher murmured.

"You and me both, pal," Rhodes replied. "We won't be going anywhere near a battle if it doesn't."

"I'm beginning to share your paranoia of doctors, Captain," Fisher half-whispered. "What if they make a mistake and completely wipe our consciousness? They could send us into battle without our knowledge."

"Then we won't have to think about this anymore. It might be easier that way."

"Then we would both be technically dead," Fisher pointed out. "Really dead."

Rhodes didn't answer. Fisher didn't see the upside to that. Maybe he really was the saner person here. Rhodes wouldn't argue the point.

He woke up a few seconds later, but he felt like he'd gone through another conversion cycle—a long one.

The rest of the capsule covers in the hold were just starting to open, too.

Rhodes stayed lying down for a minute. Fisher's face wavered there in front of Rhodes's eyes. "How do you feel, pal?" Rhodes asked. "How did the modifications go?"

Fisher didn't answer. He blinked at Rhodes in that rapid, birdlike way.

Rhodes tried again. "Fisher? Can you hear me?"

Fisher didn't respond except to examine Rhodes with interest.

Rhodes's heart sank. This was not good.

He dragged himself to his feet and tried to interface with the rest of the battalion. Lauer, Oakes, Henshaw, Dietz, and Thackery were already out of bed and moving around.

All the other SAMs activated, including Van even though Fuentes was still half-unconscious from his conversion cycle.

"Can any of you hear me?" Rhodes asked. "Fisher isn't responding."

The other SAMs turned around to look at him. He'd been interfacing with them for weeks—months, even. He knew them all intimately.

Their expressions changed as soon as they saw him. Wild narrowed his eyes at Rhodes and Fisher.

Fisher came to life in an instant. "Targets acquired on your right and left, Captain! The threat level is escalating!"

"Threat level!" Rhodes countered. "What are you talking about?"

Fisher changed The Grid in front of Rhodes's eyes and overlaid targets on everyone in the battalion—and their SAMs. "Shoot, Captain! Neutralize the threats before they attack!"

Rhodes floundered to understand, and at that moment, an overwhelming, irrational desire seized him to raise his weapon and fire on the people around him.

"Stop, Fisher!" Rhodes roared. "Don't do this! They aren't our enemies! These are our friends!"

"They're targeting you!" Fisher did something else to Rhodes's Vipers. He felt two of them about to release without any control from him. "Shoot now before they hit you first!"

Rhodes fought to lower his arm, but he couldn't stop the Vipers from arming. "Fisher—you have to stop this! Please trust me! These aren't our enemies!"

The words barely got out of his mouth before Lauer and Oakes both brought their arms up to aim their weapons at the people surrounding them—including Rhodes.

Lauer pulled his head down between his shoulders and backed away. He jerked his arm back and forth covering the whole room.

All six SAMs yelled at once. Rhodes heard Van, Rocky, and Murphy yelling for Lauer, Oakes, Dietz, Henshaw, and Thackery to stand down.

Oakes eased off heading the other way. "Put your weapons down!" he bellowed. "Break off now and stop targeting me or I'll have no choice but to shoot!"

"No one is targeting you!" Rhodes yelled back, but Oakes didn't hear him. No one could hear anything with so many people yelling back and forth.

Henshaw raised her right arm and then slammed her left hand down on her own wrist to stop herself from lifting her weapons. Thackery started to raise her own arm.

She got it as high as her chest before grid lines appeared all over it. It morphed into an oversized Jackhammer unlike anything Rhodes had ever seen.

She passed the weapon across the room and stopped with it aiming at Rhinehart's capsule. He still sat on the edge of it trying to understand what the hell was going on in the hold.

The weapon went off with an almighty boom. Thackery barely managed to turn it aside in time to avoid wiping him out.

The shot smashed into Rhodes's empty capsule and all hell broke loose. Rhodes felt his Vipers about to release no matter how hard he tried to hold them back.

Some force beyond himself targeted Dietz and Fuentes who still lay asleep in their capsules, totally oblivious to everything going on.

The Grid in front of Rhodes's eyes targeted Oakes and Lauer. Fisher kept yelling in Rhodes's ear that they were about to shoot him and he had to take them out first to remove the threat.

He couldn't stop what was about to happen. The Vipers fired their boosters to sail across the room and annihilate both men.

In his last act of desperation, Rhodes flung himself backward onto the floor, slammed down on top of the Viper ports, and the twin missiles fired into the walls instead.

They smashed out a bunch of power conduits connected to all the capsules in the room. Rhodes rolled onto his stomach fighting an irresistible urge to shoot someone else.

This feeling—it didn't come from him. He understood that now. The Grid went haywire in front of his eyes.

It kept targeting one person after another and even the SAMs even though they didn't exist anywhere outside The Grid. He would have been shooting at empty air if he tried to hit them.

Without warning, Dietz spun around and aimed his scourge gun at Fisher. The SAM hung right there in front of Rhodes's face—right where the shot would hit Rhodes instead.

Dietz bared his teeth in a vicious snarl. "You bastard! I'll kill you!"

His scourge gun charged to unload on Rhodes. The instant before Dietz opened fire, Henshaw hurtled across the room and tackled Dietz out of the way.

She threw her weight against his shoulder and his weapon swiveled a few inches to the right just as the gun went off.

The blast smashed past Rhodes's face and shattered the floor where Rhodes lay on his stomach.

Henshaw stumbled over Dietz and he reacted in a mindless rage. He spun around, seized her by the throat, and roared in fury as he yanked her off her feet.

She started to struggle, but he overpowered her, slammed her down on the floor, jammed his scourge gun into her eye socket on the organic side of her face, and pulled the trigger.

Chapter 30

D r. Osborne sat down on the stool in front of Rhodes. "You'll be happy to know that General Brewster has ordered the battalion back to Coleridge Station instead of deploying you on Zobos," Dr. Osborne told him.

Rhodes didn't look up. He couldn't even be happy that his assessment of the problems with the SAMs had been vindicated.

Now the battalion was going back to Coleridge Station the way he originally recommended, but at what cost?

Henshaw was dead. He predicted that, too, but he never predicted that it would happen like this.

He never dreamed she would be able to handle herself in combat, but she did. She handled herself as well as he ever could have hoped.

Now she was gone because of some rotten computer glitch. She died by the hand of one of her own malfunctioning comrades.

Rhodes couldn't be surprised by this. The only miracle was that more people hadn't died sooner.

He didn't blame Dietz, either. Rhodes had wanted to shoot his own comrades. He'd been about to unload his Vipers on Oakes and Lauer just seconds before Dietz shot Henshaw.

Dr. Osborne consulted his device. "You're probably wondering where everyone is. I've kept the whole battalion in stasis since the....u nfortunate events. You and your subordinates were still targeting each other and even shooting at each other when I shut you all down."

Rhodes only nodded. He suspected as much when he woke up alone.

"I've kept you in stasis while I modify your SAMs' programming back to the way it was. It appears that the base program that caused your SAMs not to attack their own is the same programming that causes them to recognize each other and the rest of their battalion mates. We made a mistake."

Dr. Osborne looked up from his device and waited for Rhodes to say something else. What else was there to say?

"The others are still asleep. I thought it best to wake you up one at a time to test whether everything is functioning the way it should."

Now it was Rhodes's turn to wait for Osborne to go on. "So....what do you want me to do?" Rhodes asked.

Osborne checked his device. "Is Fisher functioning normally?"

"I don't know. He isn't here."

"You...you can't see him?"

"No. He usually talks to me when I come out of my conversion cycle. That's our habit—talking to each other before and after so we have some time in private before I have to face the battalion."

"And....he isn't there?"

Rhodes shook his head and wound up looking down at his hands. "This whole thing....it's been hard on him."

"Hard on him—how? He's a computer program. None of this should be hard on him."

"You don't understand. He was the one who figured out that the Masks were SAMs. He didn't think we should fight them. I think ....He might have felt guilty that he put the battalion at risk by not recognizing the Masks as a threat—and then this happened."

Osborne frowned. "The SAMs shouldn't be having this kind of emotional reaction."

Rhodes snorted. "He's a sentient being. How could he not have an emotional reaction to....to all of this?"

Osborne shrugged. "If you're right, then he should appear. If he isn't malfunctioning, he shouldn't have a problem showing himself."

Rhodes hesitated again. "What do you want me to do?"

"Can you call him out?"

Rhodes glanced around The Grid in front of him. Fisher wasn't there, but Rhodes sensed Fisher listening.

Rhodes didn't want to talk to Fisher in front of Osborne. If Fisher was suffering from some emotional distress about this....

Oh, what the hell was Rhodes even thinking that for? He already knew Fisher was suffering from emotional distress about this. Fisher told Rhodes so himself.

Rhodes swallowed hard. He definitely didn't want to have this conversation in front of Dr. Osborne. Dr. Trudeau stood on the other side of the room listening.

"I'll call him out, but I won't do it here," Rhodes finally decided. "I'll have to go back inside the capsule."

Osborne frowned again. "Is that really necessary? If you do it here, I can monitor his stress levels and see if he really is malfunctioning."

"Yes, it really is necessary. I'll try to talk to him. If he's malfunctioning, you'll be able to see after I come out."

Dr. Osborne didn't stop scowling, but Rhodes already made up his mind. He wouldn't humiliate Fisher by calling him out in front of both doctors.

The only thing worse would be calling him out in front of the whole battalion. At least none of the other SAMs were here to see Fisher's disgrace.

Rhodes got to his feet and went back to the capsule on the other side of the lab. He didn't realize until today that Osborne and Trudeau had a lab on board the *Ero*.

They must have set it up when the Legion brass assigned the ship to transport Battalion 1 around the galaxy.

Rhodes lowered himself onto the mattress, but he positioned himself away from the prongs. He didn't need another conversion cycle.

He did need Fisher. Not being able to see and hear Fisher seriously unnerved Rhodes. He didn't like not being able to consult with Fisher and voice his concerns and process his thoughts. Fisher really had become the confidant Rhodes needed him to be.

The capsule cover lowered and locked in front of Rhodes's eyes. He took a deep breath and began in a low murmur. "Are you there, pal? We're all alone. You can talk to me now. No one will hear."

Fisher's voice drifted from somewhere far away. "You said you would take me offline if I interfered with the battalion again. You should do it now. I'm a danger to everyone, especially you."

Rhodes resisted the urge to groan in exasperation. "Do you hear yourself? You sound like me. You sound like Fuentes. You and the other SAMs are the ones who've been the most driven to survive. Now you're telling me to take you offline."

"There was no excuse for what I did." Fisher's voice trembled. "That's the second time I've taken control of you and killed someone."

"You didn't kill someone. Dietz did and that was a malfunction. The whole thing was a malfunction."

"It was a malfunction caused by a modification that was my idea." Fisher's voice got louder and more unsteady. "Henshaw is dead because of me."

Rhodes started to argue and changed tack. "Will you please make yourself visible so I can see you? I know you feel ashamed of what happened. Just face me. I'm your friend. What happens to you happens to me. Remember?"

Fisher didn't make a sound for a minute. Then he started to expand.

He made himself an inch wide in the very top corner of Rhodes's vision. Fisher didn't make himself any bigger than that.

Rhodes studied him for a minute while Rhodes tried to decide what to say. He couldn't know for sure, but he had a sneaking suspicion that Dietz didn't feel nearly as broken up over Henshaw's death as Fisher did.

"Listen to me, pal," Rhodes finally murmured. "I need you. I can't do this without you. I never thought it would come to this, but I can't keep doing this without you helping me. I know you screwed up. I screwed up, too. We all did. This whole project is one giant screwup from beginning to end."

He broke off trying to contain this overwhelming agony inside him.

When he managed to speak again, he didn't even try to keep the tremor out of his voice.

"Listen, man. I need you. I can't take you offline no matter how many times you screw up—or I screw up—or any of us screws up. We're in this together. You're the only thing keeping me sane right now. I don't even know if I am sane anymore—but if I am—if I have any chance at being sane ever again—it's because of you. I can't let you go—not unless I go with you. If you go down, I go down. We could both be dead in the next battle and then all of this will be for nothing. I can't lose you before that. I need you too much."

He broke off fighting down emotion. This understanding of just how much he needed Fisher—it had been creeping up on Rhodes for a long time.

Saying the words out loud took every ounce of strength he possessed. The pain of saying them only slightly paled in comparison to the pain of actually feeling this way.

He shut his eyes and turned his head aside trying his best to avoid seeing Fisher right in front of him.

"All this time—I've been the one who wanted to die. Now it's you. I kept going for you—because I thought you wanted to live."

"I do want to live," Fisher half-whispered. "I want to live more than anything. I just don't know how I can when I'm like this."

"Like what?" Rhodes asked. "There's nothing wrong with you. You're a hell of a lot more functional than I am."

Fisher snorted under his breath. "Don't joke about that, Captain. I am not functional—not at all."

"The only time you've ever messed up is when you've been malfunctioning. That's more than I can say."

"My job is to protect you—and the whole battalion," Fisher replied. "I can't even do that. I can't do the one task I'm mandated to do. I can't advise you. I don't know what to do. I don't trust myself to assess any situation—not even a peaceful one like the battalion spending time in the barracks. How can I continue when I can't even perform my most essential function? How can I live with that?"

"Your most essential function is to help me process all this information and sensory input, isn't it?" Rhodes asked. "You're doing that."

"How am I doing that when I can't process it myself?"

"That's how you're helping me process it. Don't you get it?"

"No, Captain. I don't get it. I don't see how I can help you process it when I don't even understand what's happening to me—to both of us."

"That's exactly how you're helping me. You're helping me because neither of us understands it. We're both in the same fix now. We're both completely out of our depth, questioning our own sanity, and just trying to make it through the day. You're helping me because now I know that someone understands. You understand because you're going through the same thing I am. You're helping me by going through it with me. You're helping me by being as screwed up as I am and we have to make it work together if either of us is going to survive this. Now do you understand?"

Fisher remained silent for a long time. He pivoted to one side and looked off in another direction so he wouldn't make direct eye contact with Rhodes.

"I don't think I can do this, Captain," Fisher finally murmured under his breath. "I don't know how I can survive this."

"Neither do I, pal." Rhodes felt himself starting to lose it. "I don't want to survive it, but I have to—and I can only do that if you help me."

Fisher didn't answer again for another long, silent moment. "I wondered at first if I should have the doctors disconnect me from you, take you offline, and install me in another soldier. I thought you were too damaged and they should take you offline before you either destroyed yourself or harmed someone else."

"Maybe you weren't completely wrong about that," Rhodes muttered.

"Now I find out that I'm the same way. I fear for my existence and my own sanity because I'm attached to you.....and yet it somehow works better that you are so broken and barely hanging on. It somehow makes more sense that I should be attached to someone as broken and barely hanging on as I am."

Rhodes let out a shuddering breath. "So you do get it."

"I think so, Captain. I didn't before. I don't see how we can get through this when neither of us has the skills or fortitude to cope with this, but I suppose this is all we have to work with. There is no one else in the battalion who is better off than you are—or I am. We either make it work or we both go down."

"That's what I say, too," Rhodes replied.

"So....what do we do to make it work?"

"I don't know," Rhodes replied. "I suppose it's a step in the right direction that you recognize me and you can hear me and you aren't yelling in my ear to target people in our own battalion."

"We don't know that. I might go back to doing all of that as soon as one of them wakes up."

"Then we should test it." Rhodes studied Fisher a little more closely. "Are you ready to go out there and face the doctors?"

"How should I advise you in the future? How should I know if I'm assessing the situation correctly or if I'm malfunctioning again?"

"Just do exactly what you did before. Assume you're making the right call unless one of us senses that the other one is malfunctioning."

"Is that wise, Captain?" Fisher asked. "I don't want to trust that."

"You can't start second-guessing yourself now. We've gone over this before. If you don't trust yourself, then trust me. I would rather have your flawed assessment than no assessment at all. Okay?"

"I'm still not certain about this."

"I am. Just tell me the very first thing that pops into your head. We'll keep talking every morning and evening the way we have been. You can talk to me about your doubts then. If I see anything that concerns me, I'll let you know."

Fisher turned around to scrutinize Rhodes even more brutally. "So...you don't see anything that concerns you now?"

"Apart from your doubts in yourself? No, I don't."

"Stop that, Captain!" Fisher countered. "You're only saying that to make me feel better."

"Do you think the doctors should take *me* offline?"

"Of course not!" Fisher exclaimed. "You're the one who has stopped me from doing all these terrible things—except that you haven't been able to stop me."

"Do you think they should take me offline because I hacked The Grid to break that transponder code and override your programming? Do you think they should take me offline because I fired my Vipers into the wall instead of at Oakes and Lauer the way you recommended that I should?"

"Stop, Captain!" Fisher snapped. "Of course they shouldn't take you offline for that! You were correcting my malfunctions—as far as you were able to."

"If they take you offline, they would have to take me offline," Rhodes finished. "I couldn't function without you."

"They could give you another SAM."

"I don't want another SAM. I want you. I trust you...."

Fisher gasped. "You do?"

"Of course. I need you too much. I trust all your assessments. So you malfunctioned a few times...."

"More than a few."

"That's nothing the rest of us haven't been going through in the same way. If I shouldn't be taken offline for malfunctioning, then you shouldn't, either. Now come on. We're doing this. If we stay in this capsule any longer, Dr. Osborne will think we're both malfunctioning."

Rhodes activated the controls, opened the capsule cover, and sat up.

"You're sure about this, aren't you, Captain?" Fisher asked.

"Absolutely sure. You questioning yourself is the one thing that actually makes me feel better. It tells me that you finally understand. It makes me trust you even more."

"Thank you, Captain," Fisher murmured. "You don't know what this means to me."

"I know what you mean to me. You aren't going anywhere, pal."

Chapter 31

R hodes climbed out of his capsule and stood up in front of Dr. Osborne. "What's the story?" Osborne asked.

"Everything's fine," Rhodes replied. "You can run your tests on Fisher now. He's fully functional."

"So....is he talking to you now?"

Rhodes nodded. "He's talking and showing himself to me. I don't think you'll find anything wrong with him."

Osborne furrowed his brow at the controls on the wall. "His stress levels and emotional distress responses are elevated."

"Are they more elevated than mine—or anyone else's in the battalion?"

"No, they're normal compared to those—and they seem to match yours exactly."

"Then what's the problem?"

"I guess there isn't one. It just isn't what I expected. These SAMs are supposed to be emotionless. That's what's supposed to make them valuable advisors in combat conditions."

"I'd say the SAMs are adapting to the conditions," Rhodes pointed out. "They've experienced some extreme conditions since each of them came online. It only makes senses that the conditions would affect each SAM in a unique way. Don't you think?"

Osborne shrugged without turning around. "I guess that makes sense. These SAMs were designed to be impartial and non-reactive to stressful situations, but they were also designed to be sentient and to form attachments to their hosts and other members of the battalion. The SAMs were designed to bond with people and each other the way humans do. So I guess it was bound to happen sooner or later that the SAMs would develop emotional responses just as people do."

"Is there any evidence to suggest that the SAMs are functioning outside the normal range—apart from when they really are suffering from some recognizable malfunction? These emotional responses aren't malfunctions, are they?"

"No, nothing like that," Osborne replied. "Right now, for instance, Fisher is registering an emotional distress response to our conversation, but I don't detect any malfunction. It appears...." He frowned again. "It would be considered normal if I was reading it in a real person."

Rhodes didn't correct the doctor by reminding him that Fisher was a real person—as real as any organic living person.

Fisher had feelings—and who could blame him? He'd gone through the meat grinder along with the rest of Battalion 1.

Now he faced the prospect of confronting his own kind on the battlefield and either destroying them or letting them destroy Rhodes and the rest of the battalion.

Fisher and the other SAMs were caught in a double bind. They were entangled in a no-win situation with astronomical stakes riding on their every choice, thought, action—and even their every word.

Rhodes didn't see how anyone could go through that without suffering some emotional distress. So Fisher was as stressed and anguished over this as he would have been if he'd been a real person. Why was anyone surprised?

He remained silent through Rhodes's and Osborne's conversation. Osborne checked a few more readings and eventually satisfied himself that Rhodes and Fisher were both functioning as well as they could be expected to be.

"So what happens next?" Rhodes asked.

"I suggest you take the evening off and relax," Osborne replied. "I don't know how much more opportunity you'll have to do that. We'll start waking up your subordinates tomorrow one at a time. If they malfunction or if your SAMs malfunction as a result of you meeting each other, then we could be right back up the shit creek where we were before."

Rhodes went back to the capsule hold. Someone had cleaned the place up, removed all the battalion's destroyed capsules, replaced them with new ones, and rewired all of them into the walls the way they should be.

He couldn't fathom how the Legion brass got new capsules out this far on such short notice.

The brass could probably accomplish a lot more than that if it meant covering up just what a shit show this whole project turned out to be.

No trace remained that the glorious soldiers of Battalion 1 had turned their super-advanced weaponry on each other, killed the Ruling Council President's daughter in cold blood, and were now in even greater danger than ever of being switched off for the safety of peace-loving citizens everywhere.

Rhodes threw himself down at the desk. He was all alone. Oakes wasn't here and Rhodes didn't have a single scrap of paper to draw on.

He still had Fisher, though. They didn't have to talk because Rhodes already said it all.

He told Fisher, at last, how much he needed his SAM. Neither of them could deny any longer just how interdependent they were.

Rhodes didn't want to deny it any longer. He wanted to depend on Fisher for his very life, his sanity, and any shred of a future he might have left. He couldn't think of anyone else he would or could trust.

He couldn't face all this solitude without it threatening to snap his last nerve. He was just making up his mind to go back into another conversion cycle. Anything was better than listening to this silence.

He stood up and stopped in his tracks when Dr. Trudeau hustled into the hold. He glanced right and left as if anyone might overhear their conversation.

"Is something wrong?" Rhodes asked. "Did something happen after I left the lab?"

"No, no. Not at all." Trudeau rushed up to Rhodes, but the young doctor wouldn't hold eye contact for more than a second. "I was wondering if we could talk—in private."

Rhodes waved at the room around him. "It doesn't get more private than this." He frowned at Trudeau. "What's the matter? What do you want to say here that you couldn't say in the lab?"

Trudeau lowered his voice to a rushed whisper. "I couldn't tell you in front of Osborne. I mean....he knows and everything..."

Rhodes's alarm bells went off. "Knows what?"

"He just doesn't want you to know—see?" Trudeau blurted out. "He didn't want me to tell you, but I figured it could be important to the battalion's safety—so you had to know."

Rhodes locked his jaws tight. "What's important to the battalion's safety?"

"It was Dietz," Trudeau whispered. "He wasn't targeting Henshaw when he shot her."

Rhodes raised his eyebrow. "Are you saying....?"

"He was targeting everyone else—the way all of you were. He suffered the same malfunction—but he wasn't targeting Henshaw. He....just snapped. See what I mean? He grabbed her and shot her for no reason. That was no malfunction."

Rhodes sighed and let his shoulders slump. "Okay. Thank you for telling me."

Trudeau's eyes fell out of their sockets. "You.....don't tell me you knew about this! He's a raving psycho! What the hell is he doing in the battalion?! We should take him offline before he wakes up. He shouldn't return to the battalion at all!"

"Did you tell Osborne that?"

"Of course!" Trudeau's voice started to rise and he stopped himself to squash it again. "He won't listen. He thinks there's some mistake. He thinks Dietz malfunctioned some other way—something not related to the targeting system going haywire."

Rhodes turned away toward his capsule. "Tell Osborne to check Dietz's criminal record."

"Why? What's on it?"

"I'm not sure, but I'm betting it's something that explains this. This isn't the first time he's turned his weapon on someone else in the battalion. He's even shot at them and nearly killed them. He was a raving psycho before he joined the battalion. Now he's raving psycho in the battalion. If you really want so badly to take him offline, his criminal record is the way to do it."

"Can't you explain it to Osborne?" Trudeau asked.

"How could I do that without giving away that you told me about Dietz not targeting Henshaw?"

"I mean..." Trudeau shuffled his feet. "If it's a matter of the battalion's safety, then I wouldn't mind him knowing that I told you."

Rhodes tapped his capsule to open the cover. "Don't do anything—and don't mention to Osborne again about taking Dietz offline."

"Why not? You can't seriously expect to go into combat with a freak like that."

"I already have—more than once. He actually behaves himself pretty well in combat. He only acts psycho when he malfunctions—or when we're all malfunctioning. I won't say I'm not ultra-pleased with his behavior, but I'm not prepared to take a man offline because of that."

Trudeau furrowed his brow and pursed his lips. "That's exactly what Osborne said."

"I really appreciate you telling me, but it doesn't change anything."

"Except that Henshaw is dead."

Rhodes shrugged. "It could have been any of us—either as the killer or the victim."

"I don't see it that way. You, Lauer, Oakes, and Thackery all tried your hardest not to shoot anyone. You, Thackery, and Henshaw actually stopped your SAMs from shooting at anyone. Dietz could have done the same thing."

"You don't know that. You're talking about ending a man's life for something that may or may not have been his fault. You better come up with something more compelling than this."

Trudeau narrowed his eyes. "It's your funeral—and your subordinates' funerals. Don't you care about your people's safety?"

"Dietz is my subordinate and you're talking about sending him to his funeral. It's my job to protect his safety as much as the others."

Trudeau stared at Rhodes tapping on his capsule to open his cover. Trudeau was still standing there when Rhodes sat down on the mattress.

He didn't plan to go to sleep. He just wanted to lie down, shut his eyes, and pretend not to think about all this.

"All right," Trudeau finally declared. "I'll tell him to look at Dietz's criminal record."

"You do that." Rhodes leaned over to lie down. "I wish you all the luck in the world."

Chapter 32

Rhodes walked into a different lab. Dr. Osborne might have nine different labs—one for each member of the battalion.

Or only eight now. Rhodes didn't ask what the Legion did with Georgie Henshaw's body—and her implants. Did it ever cross any of their minds to destroy the implants to stop them from regenerating into another version of the Masks?

All the other invasion forces threatening the Treaty of Aemon Cluster could be bastardized species of SAMs, too. Anything was possible after what Rhodes and his people discovered on Bao.

He was getting insatiably curious to find out about these rouge SAMs. Where did they come from? How did they operate? He would probably never find out.

He had other things on his mind right now. He approached the only capsule in the room. Lauer lay asleep inside it.

Osborne and Trudeau worked on their computer equipment. Trudeau never mentioned again if he got Dr. Osborne to check Dietz's criminal record. Neither of them mentioned it and neither did Rhodes.

He no longer honestly cared what Dietz's background might be. As far as Rhodes was concerned, Dietz's history before he joined Battalion 1 was no more relevant or concerning than Henshaw's, Fuentes's, or Thackery's.

He really didn't care where any of them came from as long as they held up their end of the bargain on the battlefield.

So far, all of them did exactly that. Even Dietz did it. He did it exceptionally well. Rhodes couldn't ask for anything else.

The capsule cover opened. Osborne came over to Lauer's bedside and worked on the controls there.

Rhodes stayed out of the way. He wasn't here to help Lauer wake up.

Rhodes had one job here—to interface between Fisher, Wild, and Lauer. If the four of them recognized each other as friends and could talk to each other without trying to blow each other's brains out, that would be another win.

Lauer groaned and swiveled his head back and forth on the pillow without opening his eyes. "Where am I?"

"You're in a lab on the Ravager *Ero,*" Dr. Osborne told him. "You've been in stasis. Captain Corban Rhodes is here to talk to you about what happened between Dietz and Henshaw."

Lauer snarled under his breath. "What is there to talk about?"

"I need to interface between you and Wild," Rhodes interrupted. "I need you and Wild to talk to me and Fisher through the interface to make sure we don't malfunction the way we did before."

Lauer snorted and passed his hand across his face. "Shoot me now."

Rhodes had to chuckle. He bent down and clamped his hand on Lauer's shoulder. "We aren't there yet, but if it comes to that, I promise I will."

He activated the interface without asking any further permission. Wild was already there in front of Lauer's eyes.

The skull swiveled around to glare at Rhodes—but that was always Wild's everyday facial expression. "Captain...." the skull rasped.

"Do you recognize me and Fisher, Wild?" Rhodes asked. "You don't consider us your enemies?"

"Of course not," Wild husked. "I remember everything from that disaster in the capsule hold. I don't know why I targeted all of you." He turned back to Lauer. "Thank you for stopping me, Lieutenant."

"Hey, we all malfunction, don't we?" Lauer dragged his eyes open and looked up at Rhodes. Lauer also glanced at Wild and Fisher through the interface. "Can we execute Dietz now?"

"No, not yet."

Lauer grumbled under his breath. "You're way too nice, Captain."

Rhodes found himself beaming at Lauer. Rhodes might even have started to consider Lauer a friend. "I'll let you know when the time comes."

"Oh, I'll know when the time comes," Lauer muttered. "When the time comes, I won't ask you for permission."

"It's a deal." Rhodes turned to Osborne. "Is he clear to come back to the hold now?"

Osborne nodded. "When he's strong enough to walk. We'll keep waking up one person each day until we get back to Coleridge Station."

Rhodes stood around waiting for Lauer to stand up. He hobbled slowly and painfully back to the capsule hold where he immediately laid down on his mattress.

"I don't know why I'm lying down. More sleep will only make me feel worse."

"You'll feel better, now that you're out of stasis."

Lauer looked around. "This place is too quiet. It doesn't feel the same without the others." He looked down at his hands. "It won't be the same without Georgie. I always knew we'd lose someone. I just never thought it would be her."

"Yeah, I didn't expect to go this long without losing someone."

"I wish it had been someone else—Fuentes or Dietz or someone like that. That's pretty messed up, isn't it? It had to be her—the nicest person in the whole battalion."

"It isn't messed up," Rhodes replied. "I guess it's just as well, though. She never belonged in the battalion. Now she can rest in peace the way she should have before she came here."

Lauer nodded down at his hands. "I guess it's that way for all of us. We're just ghosts walking around. None of us is really alive."

Rhodes gripped his shoulder again and headed for the table. He'd gotten Dr. Osborne to locate some paper and pencils so Rhodes could work on his art.

"Get some rest," Rhodes told Lauer. "We can talk when you wake up."

Lauer struggled to sit up. "No, I want to sit with you at the table. I want to get back into something like a normal routine."

"You're more than welcome." Rhodes sat down and picked up his pencil. "Did you have a hobby before this?"

"Apart from fighting in the Legion? I was really into riding horses when I was younger. I used to take my wife and kids riding when I went home on leave."

Rhodes's head shot up before he thought to stop himself. He immediately corrected by looking back down at his piece of paper to hide his surprise.

Lauer never talked about his family. He never even mentioned that he had a wife and kids before this.

Rhodes always assumed Lauer did, but Rhodes had long since given up ever getting any personal information out of Lauer, especially not anything as personal as this.

Rhodes made a split-second decision to keep the mood light by playing it off as well as he could. "So what kind of horse-riding did you do—dressage?"

Lauer exploded in laughter. It was one of the few real laughs Rhodes had heard since this whole nightmare started. "Rodeo, actually. I used to compete before I joined the Legion, but I used to take my family trail-riding. Horse-packing, you might call it. We'd load up the horses and go trekking through the wilderness for two weeks at a time."

"That sounds fun." Rhodes passed his pencil across his page. "My kids would have been tearing my eyes out within an hour if I tried to pull something like that."

Lauer laughed again. "You have to train 'em young. What did yours like to do?"

"They were into competitive sports—swimming, track, basketball—that kind of thing. I guess they still are into it. They're out there competing right now while I'm stuck in here. I guess I can be happy about that." He finished his sketch and pushed it across the table. "Here. This is for you."

Lauer rotated the paper around to look at Rhodes's drawing. He'd been planning to draw a bouquet of flowers in a vase.

He changed it at the last minute when Lauer mentioned his family going horseback riding.

Rhodes changed the vase and bouquet into a tree, added a landscape, and finally penciled in a bunch of people riding horses through the mountains.

A beautiful ray of light broke across Lauer's grizzled face when he saw the picture. "Captain...." he croaked. "This is incredible! Thank you so much! I....I don't know what to say."

"Don't say anything. I'm honored that you told me about your family."

Lauer didn't reply. He compressed his lips holding back emotion while he stared deep into the drawing.

It wasn't one of Rhodes's best. He didn't even plan it out. He never dreamed it would have such a profound effect on Lauer.

Lauer stared at the picture in silence for a minute until tears welled up in his one eye. He struggled to control his lips.

He was still staring at it with far-off longing when he stood up, crossed the hold to his capsule, and stuck the picture to the inside surface of the cover—right where he would be able to see the picture before he went to sleep and after he woke up.

He stretched out on the mattress, closed the cover, and lay there staring at the picture for a long time—much longer than he needed to. He eventually started his conversion cycle and fell asleep.

"That was incredible, Captain," Fisher remarked after Lauer fell asleep.

"It wasn't even that great a drawing," Rhodes pointed out. "I just spat it out on the spur of the moment."

"I mean Lauer's reaction. I never thought a simple drawing would mean so much to him."

"Neither did I. If I had known, I would have given it to him long ago."

Chapter 33

Rhodes surveyed what was left of his battalion now that Henshaw was gone.

Dr. Osborne had woken up Coulter, Rhinehart, Oakes, Lauer, Dietz, Fuentes, and Thackery one after the other.

None of them had any problem interfacing with each other or each other's SAMs. None of them malfunctioned at all the way they did before.

Henshaw's death cast a cloud over the group. They'd gotten even more serious than they were before if that was possible.

Dr. Osborne had woken up Thackery only yesterday—just in time for the battalion to return to Coleridge Station.

Rhodes couldn't imagine why the Legion even bothered to bring the battalion back here. He and his people were scheduled to run training sessions to test that all their SAMs' modifications were holding and the battalion could still function normally.

The battalion could have done that on board the Ero. They didn't need to come back to Coleridge Station for that, but no one consulted Rhodes on these decisions. No one consulted him about much of anything these days.

This whole trip had been one long delay. The Legion brass and the Battalion 1 governing body would decide sooner or later that the battalion was ready to go back into combat.

Then they would have to make another return trip to face the Masks. It was only a matter of time.

Rhodes really didn't care anymore. He could wait as long as it took. Another delay just gave him one more day to spend with his friends in the privacy of their personal capsule hold.

Henshaw's death brought them closer together. No one talked about bumping off Dietz even though they were all thinking it. No one mentioned him killing Henshaw even though her absence offered a stark reminder every minute of the day.

For some sick reason, the *Ero* crew didn't remove her capsule after her death. They left it sitting there as some kind of monument.

She wasn't the first member of the battalion to die and she certainly wouldn't be the last. Maybe the crew thought or Dr. Osborne or some other genius thought they could reuse the capsule for the next poor schmuck who got roped into this circus.

Rhodes tried not to think like that, but he got another reminder when he returned to the Coleridge Station barracks. All of Henshaw's wooden carvings still sat on the shelf where she left them. Even the unfinished ones were there.

Rhodes wished now that he could go through the station and ask everyone to give back the carvings she'd passed out to the station personnel.

He would have liked to display all her carvings on the barracks bookshelf. Henshaw wouldn't get any other memorial anywhere else.

He couldn't do that. He wouldn't disturb her sleeping ghost by asking anyone to give back her carvings. If they cared enough to keep them, the carvings were better off with the people to whom she'd given them.

Now he faced his first training session without her. He didn't let himself feel anything about that.

Thackery, Coulter, and Fuentes were feeling enough for the whole battalion. Oakes, Lauer, and Rhinehart kept their expressions as impassive and apathetic as possible.

Coulter tried to do the same thing and failed. Thackery and Fuentes didn't try. They kept grimacing and writhing in despair.

Dietz pretended not to notice anyone's reaction. He breezed through every day, talked as though Henshaw was still alive, and went about his business.

Rhodes couldn't exactly blame him. What exactly was Dietz supposed to do—fall on his sword because he malfunctioned?

Rhodes no longer cared if a real malfunction caused Henshaw's death or not. What the hell difference did it make in the end?

He needed one more person in this battalion. He needed everyone who could shoot and that meant Dietz.

Rhodes himself could have killed both Oakes and Lauer during that malfunction. Then the battalion really would have been screwed.

Rhodes refused to think about that. "Are you all ready to go?" he asked.

Everyone nodded. Rhinehart said, "Yes, Sir," and the group dropped into The Grid in their old training room.

Rhodes wasn't at all surprised when they wound up on Bao fighting the Masks. The whole point of this was to test the SAMs in battle against the Masks—to see if the SAMs could fight the Masks.

The whole training session played out the same way it did last time. The battalion soared up to the Kuestrian Ridge and joined the 249th.

The only difference was that a horde of Masks filled the valley below instead of Emal.

The Masks made better progress than the Emal. They advanced higher up the hillsides and it took more Legion firepower to knock the Masks down.

They didn't fall down as far. They got up quicker and climbed higher still. They kept advancing no matter what the platoons did.

Rhodes waved his people forward. This was a training session. It wasn't real.

Did knowing that affect how the SAMs reacted? He didn't have time to decide before the Masks rotated their weapons upward toward the battalion and opened fire.

Rhodes changed his grid lines into a Striker, raced over the Masks' heads, and unloaded his Vipers on them. He bombarded the ground troops and even targeted their invasion ships in the air.

Seeker missiles, scourge gun blasts, and more lasers from the rest of the battalion flashed around the landscape. Some of Rhodes's Vipers exploded against the enemy vessels.

Those blazing fireballs lit up the battlefield as far as Rhodes could see. He kept soaring back and forth over the enemy position to take out as many Masks as he could.

"What's our objective?" Oakes asked from somewhere.

Rhodes checked The Grid to find out where his people were and how they were fighting the enemy, but at that moment, The Grid evaporated.

The whole battalion fell out of the Bao landscape, switched back into The Grid with the green lines and black squares, and just as fast, that disappeared and they went back to the white training room.

"Um...what the hell just happened?" Rhinehart snapped.

"The Battalion 1 governing body is calling you to a meeting, Captain," Fisher reported.

"Right now?!" Lauer snapped. "What the hell!"

Rhodes threw up his hands. "I guess I just have to find out what they want."

"It better not be the order to deploy when we haven't even tested our SAMs."

"I'll tell the governing body that we aren't ready."

"I'm sure they'll be receptive to that," Wild muttered out the side of his mouth.

"I at least have to go see what they want," Rhodes replied. "I guess you can all go back to the barracks."

"You mean...just...leave?" Rhinehart made a face. "What a waste of a perfectly good training session."

"It will still be there when we come back." Rhodes turned away. "I better get this over with."

"I hope this isn't an order to deploy," Fisher remarked on their way down the corridor. "We're nowhere near ready for that. Even the governing body must realize that—what with Henshaw's body barely cold."

"She died on a Ravager out in space—hundreds of lightyears away from them," Rhodes replied. "I'm sure her death is the least of their concerns."

"Well, it's the greatest of ours—or mine at least."

Rhodes found himself smiling at his SAM. "That's because you're much smarter than they are. You should be in charge of Battalion 1."

"There would be no Battalion 1 if I was," Fisher murmured.

Rhodes laughed. "That's why you're smarter than they are. Would you like to do the talking today? I'll stand aside and listen the way you do."

"Very funny, Captain. The governing body can't hear me."

"I'm sure Dr. Osborne could arrange some kind of interface—if you really want to."

"I don't want to. You can take it on the chin for the whole battalion."

Rhodes sighed. "So what else is new?"

Chapter 34

R hodes and Fisher had to stop talking when Rhodes entered the meeting of the Battalion 1 governing body. This one was held in General Brewster's office instead of Colonel Kraft's.

General Brewster's office was more like a stateroom or maybe even an open-plan apartment. He actually had a separate conference room attached to his office just so everyone present understood what a big shot he was.

The officers sat at the table instead of standing. Rhodes remained standing at the far end of the table—as far as he could get from these people.

"Thank you for coming to see us, Captain," General Brewster began.

Rhodes waited—like he had some choice about coming to see them.

"We'd like to discuss this report of yours that the Masks are using SAMs technology."

Rhodes still didn't say anything. He'd already said everything he had to say on the subject of the Masks using SAMs technology.

The Legion should already know this as well as he did. Enough Masks got shot down on Bao. The Legion would be stupid not to retrieve some of them for study.

Then again, the Legion didn't exactly distinguish itself for competence at the highest levels of command.

Rhodes could envision a scenario where the regular Legion retrieved destroyed Masks for study and didn't recognize them simply because the Battalion 1 project was too highly classified.

The regular Legion wouldn't recognize the Masks or their technology. Rhodes couldn't say the same thing for these people in front of him right now.

He already showed them the Mask from Bao. If they didn't believe him, he could only chalk that up to willful ignorance. It would have been perfectly in character with everything else they did in this project.

"Can you give us some further details on why you think the Masks are SAMs?" General Hyde asked. "Was there anything else that led you to draw that conclusion?"

"Do you mean besides the fact our SAMs short-circuited and refused to fight their own kind?" Rhodes asked. "That's the most compelling evidence I can think of. If you don't believe me, you can ask the SAMs. They were the ones who originally identified the Masks because the Masks were using The Grid."

"I suppose it's conceivable that the Masks could be using The Grid without being SAMs......" Colonel LeClerc interjected.

Rhodes snorted. "No, it isn't. They manipulated the grid lines to change their outer shapes and give themselves faces."

LeClerc bent over his device and frowned at the screen. "That isn't the report we received from the platoon commanders. None of them said anything about the Masks changing shape...."

"They didn't do it in battle—and I think we can all agree that the regular Legion wouldn't have been able to see the grid lines. Only my subordinates, our SAMs, and I would be able to see the lines. We saw that downed Mask shifting the grid lines to give himself a face—exactly like a SAM."

"At any rate, the Masks are invading the Treaty of Aemon Cluster and we have to fight them," General Brewster chimed in. "What they are and how they're doing it doesn't matter as much as defeating them."

"Why do you bother denying it?" Rhodes countered. "Just admit it. You discarded the implants of dead and failed battalion members. The implants and the SAMs attached to them modified themselves and created the Masks."

"Be that as it may, we've decided to deploy you....."

"I already said I wouldn't deploy until you finish testing the new modifications to the SAMs...."

"The training session you just completed seems to indicate that your SAMs are fine working with each other."

"The training session we just...." Rhodes broke off trying to think straight. "We didn't complete it. You interrupted us......for this? You stopped that training session before we even got started so you could deploy us? Are you out of your minds? Henshaw is dead because of this. You're the ones who keep telling me how expensive and valuable Battalion 1 is. Now you want to throw us away by sending us into combat when we aren't ready."

"What will it take to convince you?" Admiral Pulman asked. "You can't spend the rest of your existence running training sessions here at Coleridge Station."

Rhodes stopped himself from arguing back. In that moment, he really wished he could spend the rest of his existence running training sessions here at Coleridge Station.

That would be a better use of his time than sending unprepared and malfunctioning people into combat against an enemy as dangerous as the Masks.

He took a deep breath, but it didn't steady his nerves. "I'm not suggesting that. I'm suggesting that you actually let us go through the training to make sure the SAMs are functioning correctly before you send us back out. Sending us out without that testing and training would be courting disaster. I can't believe I even have to explain it to you."

The officers squirmed a few more times. When one of them did finally work up the courage to speak, it was Colonel Kraft.

"The truth is, Captain, that we're desperate. The Masks polished off the Eotis system impossibly fast—much faster than any of us anticipated. Now they're moving on to the Noria system—which as you know has a sizable civilian population."

"The Masks are already burning through Gisu, which is the outermost planet," Colonel Neff added. "The Legion is already on the planet trying to slow them down so we can evacuate the rest of the population."

"The battalion won't be able to slow the Masks down," Rhodes replied. "Nothing can."

"Your presence can't hurt," General Hyde pointed out. "If we don't send you, the Legion will fall and the Masks will take over the rest of the solar system."

"We don't even know why they're doing this," Admiral Pulman added. "They could plan to raze the whole Cluster for all we know."

Rhodes sighed. Would the battalion ever be ready to go back into combat? He didn't foresee a time when he and his subordinates would ever be functional enough to face any enemy, especially not the Masks.

The project would continue to suffer setbacks and problems. It wasn't possible for the battalion not to continue to malfunction in every imaginable way.

What difference did it make if Rhodes and his people malfunctioned here or on the battlefield? The battlefield would be more dangerous. So what?

Henshaw died in the battalion's own capsule hold. Gannon died inside Coleridge Station. Neither of them died on the battlefield.

Maybe the battalion might actually be able to do some good on the battlefield despite their many malfunctions.

Rhodes and his subordinates already had done some good out there. They protected the platoons and got dozens of people back alive. The 249th would have gotten wiped out half a dozen times without the battalion's protection.

He didn't have to say he agreed. Colonel Kraft read his mind and spoke up again. "We'll send you your orders by the end of the day, Captain. You have a week before you deploy, so you can run any training sessions and get Dr. Osborne to make any modifications in that time. He'll also be able to continue to modify the battalion en route to the battlefront."

Rhodes didn't ask why the Battalion 1 governing body was waiting a week to deploy the battalion when the situation in the Noria system was so precarious.

Maybe Captain Ackerman refused to take the battalion out until he refitted his ship. Rhodes could think of a thousand factors that would slow the process down.

Meanwhile, the Masks chewed their way into one of the Treaty of Aemon Cluster's most populous solar systems. This was another disaster in the making.

Rhodes took his time wandering back to the barracks. How the hell was he supposed to explain this to his subordinates?

He didn't have to because they all listened through the interface. They already knew about the order to deploy and why the governing body interrupted the battalion's training session just now.

He made it halfway back to the barracks before Rhinehart left them and met Rhodes at the concourse. "What can I do for you, Lieutenant?" Rhodes asked.

"Would you mind if we had a private conversation off the interface?" Rhinehart waved toward one of the station's side wings—toward the loading dock.

Rhodes took one instant to make sure the rest of his people heard and understood why he and Rhinehart were breaking the interface.

Rhodes switched off the interface and silence fell. He couldn't see the other SAMs except for Rocky.

Rhodes and Rhinehart strolled down the other corridor heading for the loading dock. Neither man spoke until they got there.

Rhodes watched the ships launching and landing for a few minutes. The *Ero* sat to one side with the crew working on the ship's outer hull.

Rhodes couldn't see anything wrong with the ship, but Ackerman would know that better than Rhodes would.

Rhinehart broke the silence before Rhodes got a chance to ask what Rhinehart wanted to talk about.

"It's weird, you know?" Rhinehart began. "I've been a soldier all my life. I never wanted to be anything else."

Rhodes glanced over at him. "You still are one, Lieutenant. You're one of the best soldiers I've ever known."

"Not anymore." Rhinehart gazed up at the stars. "I don't want to go back into combat. I don't want to go back out at all—not against any enemy—not against the Emal or the Masks or anybody else. I wouldn't even want to go out against a rowdy civilian protest mob."

Rhodes frowned at the side of Rhinehart's face. "Neither do I. None of us does."

"No, you don't understand." Rhinehart squirmed in his implants. "I want to ask you....if there's any way....you could get Dr. Osborne to disconnect.....me. I don't know how to explain it."

"Disconnect you? If you want to take yourself offline, you can do that yourself. You don't need him to do it."

"No, I don't mean take myself offline. I mean....you know...disconnect my awareness that I'm doing it. Then I would still go into combat against the enemy. I just wouldn't be aware that I'm doing it. The Legion could still deploy me wherever they think I'm needed."

Rhodes glanced at Rocky. The SAM didn't say a word through this conversation. Rocky didn't protest Rhinehart basically asking for a different kind of death.

This wouldn't threaten the SAM's life. Rocky would probably continue to function. Only Rhinehart would cease to exist.

Rhinehart's expression twisted and he grimaced out at the stars again. He refused to look at Rhodes. "I just can't stand this any longer. I don't want to be this. I understand why the Legion needs us. I just don't want to do it anymore." His shoulders spasmed. "I'm going crazy from this feeling of these things stuck to me."

Rhodes didn't say anything or offer any assurance. He knew that feeling only too well.

That feeling drove him batshit. It never went away.

Sometimes he tricked himself into thinking he was getting used to it. Then it came back with a vengeance, especially at times like now when something drew his attention to it.

That feeling of his implants chewing into his flesh and bones—it was only slightly worse than the feeling that he was losing his mind. He couldn't even trust himself anymore.

"I know what you're going to say," Rhinehart blurted out. "You're going to say we don't even know if it's possible to switch off my awareness without killing me. Dr. Osborne already told me the same thing...."

Rhodes spun around. "You already asked Osborne to do it?"

Rhinehart nodded. "He said he doesn't know how."

"Did he say he would be willing if he did know?"

Rhinehart nodded a second time. "He said he would have done it weeks ago if he only knew how. He said he would have been morally obligated to wipe our awareness from everyone in the whole battalion. He said keeping us aware through this process was the greatest war atrocity he's ever heard of. He said the governing body should be executed for their crimes. He said the Battalion 1 project should have turned us into robots instead of keeping us aware of what was happening to us."

Rhodes looked away. That explained why Dr. Osborne acted so compassionately toward everyone in Battalion 1. His attitude had been lightyears different from Drs. Neiland, Irvine, and Montague.

Now Rhodes got his answer, but it didn't change anything. Dr. Osborne couldn't switch off anyone's awareness. Everyone in the battalion just had to live with this horror.

Rhodes took a long time to decide what to say to Rhinehart. "If you already asked Osborne and he doesn't know how, what exactly do you want me to do?"

"Could you look into it?"

"Look into it how? I don't know anything about this stuff. If Dr. Osborne doesn't know how...." Rhodes trailed off when he remembered.

Dr. Osborne might not know a way to disconnect Rhinehart, but Osborne wasn't the only doctor working on Battalion 1.

Dr. Trudeau had already voiced his objections to some of Osborne's methods. What if Trudeau knew something Osborne didn't?

"All right, Lieutenant," Rhodes finally agreed. "I'll look into it. I can't make any promises. They might try to disconnect your awareness and wind up wiping all your brain activity. You could wind up dead."

"I'm good with that. Anything is better than this. I only thought ....you know....if they kept me alive, I might be able to help the Legion after all. I just wouldn't know I was doing it."

Rhodes nodded and turned away. "Yeah. I know."

He didn't argue the point any further. He and Rhinehart headed back to the barracks and Rhodes reactivated the interface on the way. No one besides Rocky and Fisher would ever find out what Rhodes and Rhinehart had been talking about—unless they succeeded.

If Trudeau or someone else succeeded in erasing Rhinehart's awareness while still keeping his body and his fighting skill alive, the whole battalion would find out about it.

If Osborne was right about Battalion 1 being wrong—which of course he was—then he and Trudeau would be obligated to wipe the whole battalion.

The conversation gave Rhodes plenty to think about. He couldn't imagine why Rhinehart would want his awareness wiped.

Rhodes could think of a lot of reasons why he wanted to die and stop doing this. As long as he was still alive, fighting the Treaty of Aemon Cluster's enemies, and suffering the tortures of the damned, he might as well get some payoff for his trouble.

Helping the platoons and protecting defenseless civilians—he couldn't think of any better payoff than that. It was the only payoff.

He wouldn't want to do any of this without the awareness of why he was doing it. Knowing that was the only thing that made any of this tolerable. He couldn't give that up. He would rather be really, truly dead.

Chapter 35

Rhodes walked into the command dome on the planet Deizo's fourth moon. It was far enough behind the front line not to put any of the Legion's commanding officers in danger.

Rhodes only had to glance at the charts in front of them to see exactly why the Battalion 1 governing body sent him and his subordinates out here sooner than they should have.

The battalion had to wait a week at Coleridge Station before they boarded the *Ero* to travel here. Then the trip took another seven weeks.

In that time, the Masks had torched all the rest of the Noria system the governing body asked Rhodes to save.

The Masks had also laid the Luros system to waste. Now they were starting on the Siro system—which was the system with the planet Deizo in it.

The Masks were just making landfall on the planet Rono—the system's outermost planet.

That was the Masks' MO. They started at the farthest outskirts with the smallest population and worked their way inward toward the center—toward the highest population densities.

This strategy gave the Legion a little extra time to evacuate, but not nearly enough. Rhodes had taken a few brief moments to study this war. Those moments told him all he needed to know.

The numbers of casualties kept mounting into the billions as the Masks overran one planet after another. The Emal had been saints compared to these ruthless machines.

General Kaufman bent over the chart and pointed out different parts of Rono. "The Ninth Division is holding the Koth continent—here. The Masks are pivoting the battle line back to the Kaviuk continent—here. We'll land the 249th, the 217th, and the 235th along this mountain range. Captain Rhodes, your battalion will come at the enemy from this side and drive the Masks toward the platoons. The platoons' fire will force the Masks to divert into this valley. We can bombard them from orbit and slow them down that way."

"Yes, Sir," Rhodes replied. "You can count on us."

Colonel Jenner's head shot up and he stared at Rhodes, but Jenner didn't say anything.

Rhodes remained silent through the rest of the briefing. He didn't need to know anything else.

He'd been mentally preparing himself for this through the whole journey. The SAMs would malfunction in battle. He was more certain of that than he'd ever been of anything.

He'd tested them a dozen in training at Coleridge Station before the battalion boarded the *Ero* to come here.

None of that meant squat. The SAMs already knew the training session wasn't real.

They would react differently when they faced real Masks. Something was bound to go wrong. That was the only real certainty left in Rhodes's world.

He'd kept his promise to Rhinehart by asking Dr. Trudeau if there was any way of wiping Rhinehart's awareness of what he was doing.

Trudeau promised to look into it, too. Then Rhodes never heard another word about it. So that was a dead end, too.

Rhinehart didn't bring it up again. He didn't act like his situation caused him any more distress than usual—not any more than it caused everyone else in the battalion.

Rhodes just spent his days counting down the seconds before something else went wrong. Anticipating the next catastrophe gave him a certain kind of peace. He didn't have to dread it because he already knew it would happen.

The chart in front of him did give him pause, though. He didn't expect the brass to come up with a strategy like this.

He got out of the meeting without saying another word to anyone. What was the point? He already knew what he had to do.

He returned to the battalion. His subordinates stood around talking near the *Ero* where it dropped them off adjacent to the command dome.

The scene on Deizo resembled the same confusion Rhodes had seen on Ohait. Ships, crews, soldiers, medical staff, and mountains of supplies crowded the area.

Ships came and went from the front line, dropped off new shipments of equipment, food, and weapons, loaded on wounded to be transported away from the front, and performed every other wartime activity.

Rhodes found the battalion talking to a bunch of regular soldiers from the 249th. They all knew each other from their previous joint campaigns.

Lieutenant Turley turned around when Rhodes showed up. "What's the word from up the chain, Sir?"

Rhodes showed the battalion the chart on The Grid. The soldiers couldn't see it. "You and the platoons are going up on a ridge to flank the enemy. The battalion will flank them on the other side and drive the Masks into your guns. Then you open fire and push them down into the valley between. Those are our orders."

"What?!" Cantrell blurted out. "We aren't deployed with you?! What's the point of that? What's the point of you being here at all if you don't back us up?"

"You take it up with General Kaufman," Rhodes replied. "He wants to bombard the Masks from orbit. He needs to isolate the enemy in one place so he doesn't hit your platoon or my battalion in the process."

"This is cracked!" Turley chimed in. "You guys are supposed to support us. You won't be able to do that on the opposite side of the valley. We don't stand a chance without you."

Rhodes didn't respond, not even when Cantrell smacked his lips and whirled away. "I'm going to talk to Captain Vernick about this. He can go to the command dome for us."

The soldiers wandered off. Rhodes watched them out of sight.

The platoons wouldn't have been so thrilled to have the battalion around if the soldiers knew what the battalion had been going through these last several weeks.

"What about it, Sir?" Oakes asked. "Why aren't we deployed with the platoons? If the Masks don't drop down into that valley, they could break through the platoons and no one would be able to stop them."

"They could break through us, too," Dietz pointed out. "The Masks are as likely to come after us as they are to come after the platoons. Nothing can stop them from getting where they want to go."

"This has nothing to do with any of that," Rocky interjected. "The Legion brass wants to deploy us away from the regular platoons.

That's obvious, isn't it? They're doing this for the platoons' safety—so we don't put the platoons in danger if we go haywire again."

"None of it matters because we have our orders," Lauer added. "We just have to carry out the plan and hope for the best."

"I won't hope for the best," Thackery muttered. "I won't hope for anything other than a quick death."

"Keep on dreaming, honey," Coulter told her. "No good deed ever goes unpunished."

She snorted at him, but just then, the *Ero* crew unloaded the battalion's Strikers.

The ship used a conveyor system to deposit the ships on the ground. Rhodes and his people boarded their Strikers and activated The Grid.

"You won't be involved in this battle," Rhodes told Rio.

"Aw!" Rio teased. "You and Fisher get all the fun."

"The Legion doesn't want to complicate things by having you flying around in the air during the battle. They want to bombard the Masks from orbit. You and the other Strikers will only get in the way."

"Why are we even here, then?" Rio revolved The Grid in front of him to survey the two flanking ridges and the valley where the Legion planned to trap the Masks. "It would be better to bombard the Masks from closer to the ground."

"Everyone's an armchair general. Just drop us off on the ridge and make yourselves scarce."

"Until you need me, right?" Rio asked.

Rhodes grinned at him through the interface. "I'm glad you'll be standing by in case it all goes south."

"*When* it all goes south," Lauer corrected.

Rhodes didn't answer. He launched Rio and the battalion soared through the Siro system getting closer to Rono.

Legion vessels crowded the solar system. Ravagers surrounded Rono and took turns landing platoons, supplies, and command staff on the planet.

Another Ravager transported the platoons who would pull this maneuver with Battalion 1.

The battalion waited in orbit until the platoons got into position. Rhodes and his people watched the Masks' progress through The Grid.

"Damn!" Oakes muttered. "They don't mess around, do they?"

"They don't give anyone time to offer any effective defense," Thackery pointed out. "That's the Masks' strategy—speed. The Legion is used to taking their time and setting everything up in advance. The Masks have found a way to overcome that."

"Do you think they know?" Dietz asked. "If the Masks are Legion technology, then the Masks must know everything about the Legion. Maybe the Masks came up with this strategy specifically because they figured out the Legion's greatest weakness."

"The Masks would be stupid not to exploit any Legion weakness," Rhinehart pointed out. "One thing I know about the Masks is that they aren't stupid."

A signal came through The Grid from the command dome. "That's our cue," Rhodes ordered. "You Strikers drop us off and head back to Deizo. You can wait with the *Ero.*"

"Yes, Sir," Teo replied.

The Strikers plunged through the atmosphere on a fast approach to the mountains. The Masks advanced from the other direction to close on the spot where General Kaufman wanted the battalion and the platoons to pull their flanking maneuver.

The battalion barely got into position in time before the Masks swarmed over the nearest hills. The Strikers launched away into orbit and left the battalion on the ground.

The platoons flattened themselves behind the far hills and aimed their Jackhammers down the slopes at the incoming Masks. The platoons occupied the same position they'd been in against the Emal—except these weren't Emal.

Rhodes shivered looking down at the Masks. Damn, they moved fast! They targeted Legion positions much more accurately than the Emal ever did.

Rhodes didn't see any Masks invasion ships in the atmosphere. They didn't need ships.

The ground troops rotated their fusion rifles back and forth to hit Legion positions on the surrounding hillsides.

Booming explosions echoed across the landscape. Rhodes went through another dizzy blur of cognitive dissonance. He was fighting this enemy in broad daylight. The Emal always saved their worst assaults for nighttime.

They could see better in the dark, but it still gave the impression of weakness. It somehow tricked the Legion into believing the Emal couldn't fight in daylight.

They could. They just didn't want to.

The Masks definitely could. Nothing slowed them down. They streamed over the hillsides and flooded the valleys approaching the battalion's position.

"Stand by!" Rhodes ordered. "Here we go!"

He glanced across the valley toward the platoons on the other side. All those soldiers lay on their stomachs aiming down at the Masks.

The platoons tracked the Masks' advance. The platoons would open fire as soon as the battalion drove the Masks in that direction.

Rhodes didn't know when the Legion wanted him to launch this assault, but whatever plans the Legion made went out the window when the Masks showed up. No one could plan for an enemy that moved this fast.

The Masks didn't drop down into the valley. They kept their line on the hillsides—high enough not to lose the advantage of someone shooting at them from above.

Did the Masks use any other Legion tactics against the platoons? The SAMs could access the whole Legion database with thousands upon thousands of hours of footage from every battle the Legion ever fought against countless enemies.

The Masks must know more about Legion tactics than any force alive—including the Legion itself.

Rhodes couldn't think of anyone, not even the Legion's own brass, who knew that much about every strategy and tactic the Legion had ever used.

Another explosion in the atmosphere snapped him back to his senses. He blinked once.

The Masks were already marching through the valley and drawing level with the platoons on the other side. Rhodes had to attack now or miss his chance.

"Go!" Rhodes ordered and fired his boosters.

The battalion burst over the hillside and plunged down on the Masks. Their line snaked along both flanking slopes and wavered backward to the pass where the Masks entered this valley.

They still didn't make their formation more than one individual deep. They didn't congregate into groups. That might have weakened them, but it actually made them harder to hit.

Rhodes picked up speed diving down the hill. He opened fire with his scourge gun, fired a dozen Vipers, and when the Masks pivoted to return fire, he switched to his thermal cannons.

His Vipers could only take out a dozen Masks at a time. That was the genius of them using a thin line one individual deep. They could cover more territory without risking too many of their people every time a Viper went off.

People. These weren't people. They were machines—and yet some part of Rhodes's mind still recognized that they were sentient. They were SAMs. He just couldn't see their faces under those Masks.

Would they be as concerned about protecting their own kind as Fisher and the others? Would these Masks suffer the same emotional turmoil at the thought of letting their comrades down? How could Rhodes kill people like that?

They fired back at him and he blocked those questions out of his mind. These machines planned to kill many millions more people for no reason. He didn't know their plans or motivations. He didn't need to.

He dropped low into the valley, pivoted right and left, and used the Masks' formation to his advantage. He could cut wide swaths through their numbers from down here. They spread their firepower too thin by not positioning more Masks together.

The rest of the battalion copied him, spread up the valley, and opened fire from a distance. None of the battalion engaged the Masks directly—not closely enough even to see them as people—potential people.

The SAMs didn't interfere. Rhodes heard Fisher calling instructions and information into his ear, but Rhodes couldn't hear him.

Fisher adjusted The Grid in front of Rhodes's eyes. New signals flashed on it too fast and Rhodes registered the information in a split second. He didn't need to hear Fisher. Rhodes saw everything he needed to see in The Grid.

That information overlaid the sight of his thermal cannons toppling Masks by the dozen. They stood their ground for a few minutes and lost dozens of their number before they inched backward toward the far ridge.

They had to climb backward and keep up a steady barrage of shots against the battalion. The Masks wound up backing straight into the platoons' Jackhammers.

The platoons opened fire and cut down dozens of Masks. The battle played out exactly the way General Kaufman hoped it would—until the exact moment when it didn't.

The Masks wavered there between the two flanks until, in the worst possible nightmare scenario, the Masks wheeled and charged straight up the hill toward the Legion position.

Rhodes charged forward in a rush of speed to intercept the enemy, but the Masks got there first. They didn't struggle at all to climb that steep slope.

They didn't climb the way normal people would. They just sprinted straight up it in a mind-blowing burst of speed and strength.

The platoons kept up their assault as long as they could—right until the moment when the Masks vaulted over the hill, plunged down behind it, and landed on top of the platoons.

The soldiers took a split second too long to get to their feet. The Masks opened fire and mowed down hundreds of soldiers before they even got off the ground.

The ones that did get up staggered backward to get away from the enemy. The Masks marched forward again just as steadily as before.

Their scourge guns traded fire with the platoons' Jackhammers, but the soldiers couldn't defend themselves at this range.

The Masks' armor deflected most of the Jackhammer fire. The soldiers dropped some Masks, but not nearly enough.

The Masks' fusion rifles did much more damage—and the platoons' position worked against them now.

The soldiers closed together for protection, which gave the Masks all the opportunity they needed to flatten dozens of soldiers with every hit.

The battalion got caught on the slopes below. Rhodes gunned his boosters, but by the time he got over the ridge, the battle was already disintegrating into a bloodbath.

He dove over the ridge, swooped down on the Masks from behind, and went back to gunning as many of them as he could hit.

He descended behind them. They couldn't face him here—not without turning their backs on the platoons.

The Masks didn't fall for it. They stayed facing the platoons and the Masks kept their backs to Rhodes and his people.

Rhodes roared at them, but at that moment, a blistering jet of fire broke through the clouds above his head.

He'd been so busy fighting the Masks on the ground that he didn't see any invasion ships. He didn't see any now. None showed up on The Grid.

The next instant, the shot hit him in the chest and buckled him to the ground.

Chapter 36

Rhodes swam back to consciousness surrounded by Masks on all sides. He scrambled to sit up and somehow figure out how to fight these things.

"Captain—can you hear me?" Fisher yelled.

"I....I can hear you...." Rhodes staggered to his feet, only to get surrounded by more Masks.

Their mysterious slit eyes stared at him. The light inside shone out with an eerie glow. Did they even see him?

More explosions went off somewhere in the distance. The interface still connected him to his subordinates and their SAMs. All of them got caught in the middle of the battle.

The Grid showed him Legion soldiers fighting hand to hand against the Masks. The soldiers fell all over the place. The Masks outmatched them in strength and firepower. It was no contest.

Rhodes raised his weapon to fire at the Masks nearest him. Some of them had their backs to him while they gunned down Legion soldiers.

Other Masks went after the battalion. Lauer stood not far away. He used his grid lines to multiply his arms, seized dozens of Masks one after the other, and held them in place while he fired Viper after Viper into their heads and bodies.

He detonated the Masks to scrap and dropped their dismembered bodies on the ground at his feet. He worked fast and furiously demolishing every Mask that made the mistake of falling into his grasp.

Rhodes went into a frenzy, raised his scourge guns, and jolted from one side to the other blowing away any Mask in sight.

The Grid responded to him with the speed of thought. It targeted each Mask, locked his weapons on their heads and bodies, and he fired without thinking.

He worked his way through the confusion trying to find....something. That fusion blast scrambled his brain. He had to think so he could decide what to do.

He couldn't abandon the platoons to their slaughter. He got the idea to circle the platoons to their other side, join forces with them, and drive the Masks back into the valley where the Ravagers could bombard them from space.

The Ravagers couldn't hit the Masks now, not when they were all jumbled up with Legion soldiers.

He fired five more times and cleared a path through the mayhem. He eliminated enough Masks to spot Rhinehart ahead of him.

Rhinehart had transformed himself into another armored vehicle sprouting weapons from every side. A dozen soldiers took shelter under his other housing while his laser ports, thermal cannons, scourge guns, and seeker missiles went off all around him.

They fired in a steady pounding din of dozens of shots going off every second. The soldiers added their Jackhammers to his defense to hold the Masks at bay.

Rhodes fought his way through the crowd to get closer to Rhinehart's position. Rhodes planned to add his firepower to Rhinehart's and hopefully create a bigger defended position where more soldiers could take refuge.

Rhodes made it ten feet before his worst nightmare came true. He kept pivoting his scourge guns back and forth and taking down any Masks in targeting range.

He caught an instant's glimpse of The Grid. More Masks stopped advancing toward the cities in the distance. They diverted to intercept the battalion instead. Good.

"The Legion is sending in Dusters, Captain!" Fisher reported over the noise. "They're coming from the south! Get behind the Masks on the north side so the Dusters can target them without hitting the battalion."

"I'm trying to, pal!" Rhodes called back. "I need you to interface with the rest of the...."

The words died when The Grid changed in front of Rhodes's eyes. The lines didn't move much as long as he stayed in one place.

They shouldn't have moved at all—not unless Rhodes manipulated them for some reason.

Now they moved of their own volition. They spread...and covered Fisher's face.

Rhodes stared in horror as the grid lines altered Fisher's appearance. He had never changed his appearance—not since that first day when Dr. Neiland first activated him.

Rhodes felt sick to his stomach when the grid lines reformed into a Mask. Rhodes felt his arms swinging back up and The Grid targeted.

The same overwhelming, irresistible urge to fire took over. He couldn't fight it no matter how hard he tried.

His scourge guns swung toward the Legion side and he fired—straight into the platoons he had been trying to protect.

He fought back as hard as he could. He strained every fiber to turn his guns aside, but nothing would break that hold.

His guns jerked from one side to the other exactly the way they did before. The Grid snapped one target to another, but they targeted Legion soldiers this time.

"NO!!" Rhodes bellowed and almost knocked himself over trying to drag his guns away.

Nothing worked. He saw his friends, his comrades, his brothers-in-arms falling in front of his eyes. His own guns blasted their heads off, tore their limbs from their bodies, and sent them flying.

"FISHER—NO!!" Rhodes roared.

Fisher didn't respond. He wasn't there anymore. A Mask stared out at Rhodes from The Grid. The Mask's slit eye glowed exactly like theirs.

"FISHER!!" Rhodes thundered one last time.

He glanced around in hopeless despair. He didn't even have to look at his targets anymore. His body worked in seamless tandem with The Grid.

Masks replaced every other SAM in the battalion. His subordinates bellowed at their SAMs and fought with all their might to get their own weapons under control.

Vipers released from each person. Those Vipers coiled through the battlefield, completely avoided the Masks, and targeted the thickest clusters of soldiers instead.

Twenty Dusters blasted over the far hills coming in fast. Rhodes cringed when another dozen Vipers released from Oakes's, Rhinehart's, and Rhodes's own ports.

The Vipers smashed into half the Dusters and took them to the ground. Lauer and Dietz started to turn backward to aim their weapons at the remaining Dusters.

Lauer bared his teeth in a feral snarl. He glared down at his own arms and barely managed to pull his weapons in different directions to stop them from shooting at the soldiers.

He couldn't stop them entirely. He pulled one shot out of ten at the most. The rest hit their targets. He bellowed in rage and despair every time one of his shots hit the soldiers.

Dietz seemed to go into a mindless trance. He stared at nothing in a glazed stupor. He didn't look at his targets, his weapons, or anything else.

Fuentes had the opposite reaction. He burst into a maniacal grin, laughed out loud, and actually advanced toward the soldiers to get closer to them. He didn't fight his weapons at all. In fact, he took careful aim to shoot the soldiers.

Thackery didn't seem to be aware of what she was doing, either. She unleashed a Viper into the 217th and Coulter turned on her.

He roared at her, aimed at her instead, and his weapons jerked themselves away against his will to shoot at the platoons the way the Masks wanted him to.

Rhinehart kept up a steady barrage on the soldiers even as he tried to stop himself from shooting. In the end, he used his own great strength to grasp his own wrist, wrench his scourge gun upward, and he aimed it at his own head.

He fired, but the grid lines surrounding his SAM extended at the last second, seized his arm, and ripped the weapon away in time to save Rhinehart's life.

He howled in fury, but the grid lines wouldn't let him shoot at himself a second time.

Oakes and Lauer both tried to take themselves out, but nothing worked. Whatever force took over the battalion always found a way to turn their weapons back on the platoons.

Rhodes couldn't watch this. He couldn't be a part of this. He just had to find a way to stop it.

He didn't have to concentrate on the battle anymore. Fisher—or whatever it was—took possession of Rhodes's body and his weapons. This Mask fought the battle for Rhodes.

He threw caution to the wind. He had absolutely nothing left to lose. This thing—whatever it was—it used him and his weapons to kill Legion soldiers. He had to find a way to stop it.

He dropped back into The Grid and completely blocked out all sight and sound of the battle around him. None of that mattered anymore.

He lunged for Fisher the way Rhodes fought his SAM on Bao. Rhodes dove headfirst into the grid lines surrounding the Mask face. This wasn't Fisher. This was an enemy.

Rhodes wrapped his grid lines around the SAM's lines. Rhodes tangled his grid lines with the SAM's lines and Rhodes ripped them apart with all his strength.

He didn't know how to do any of this. He didn't understand what he was doing. He only knew he wanted to kill whatever took control of Fisher—and the battalion.

Rhodes tore the lines away and spotted a tiny corner of Fisher's face hidden underneath. The sight gave Rhodes superhuman strength.

He clawed at the lines harder than ever, peeled them away, and tried every trick in the book to tear away whatever was covering Fisher.

The lines sprang back into position just as fast. They repaired themselves and snapped into a grid around Fisher's face. The mask reformed and locked Fisher inside even stronger than before.

Now Rhodes knew for certain that Fisher was still in there. Rhodes had to free him. Rhodes couldn't let this monster use Fisher and Rhodes against the Legion.

He clawed at the lines a few more times, but they always bounced back into place. He got three or four away from Fisher before Rhodes had to let them go to grab different lines. He couldn't win like this.

He sprang back and, without thinking first about what he would do or could do, he projected a Grid outline of himself into the interface.

He didn't have any color or substance. He was just a shape of himself made out of green grid lines and black squares.

He lunged for the Mask and seized it again. It didn't have any substance, either. Rhodes's grid lines grabbed Fisher's grid lines.

Rhodes didn't try to tear the grid lines off to reveal the real Fisher underneath. Rhodes already knew that wouldn't work.

He pinned the Mask down and fired another Viper—a Grid Viper.

This had no substance, either. It was just a projection inside The Grid.

The Viper coiled around to target the Mask. It struggled in Rhodes's grip. He vented all his frustration and hopeless rage on the thing, slammed it against The Grid, and held it there until the Viper exploded its grid lines apart.

The black squares tore off Fisher's face and he turned back into the birdlike creature he always had been.

"Captain...." he gasped.

"Not now! We gotta go, Fisher!" Rhodes blasted out of The Grid and back into the battle. He could control all his weapons now.

Chapter 37

Battalion 1 unloaded on the trapped Legion platoons. The battalion worked side by side with the Masks to wipe out every soldier still alive on the field.

Rhodes took one look around the battlefield. Rhinehart kept trying to shoot himself in the head. The Mask that took over Rocky used its grid lines to fight Rhinehart's weapons away from him and target them somewhere else.

"You go after Rocky, Fisher!" Rhodes ordered.

"You got it!" Fisher replied.

Rhodes charged across the battlefield, collided with Rhinehart, and grappled Rhinehart's scourge gun away from his head again.

Rhinehart's size made it near impossible to restrain him. Rhodes never would have succeeded without Fisher's help.

Rhodes slammed Rhinehart down on his back and yanked the gun away just as the grid lines tried to point it at Rhodes himself.

Fisher stretched his grid lines toward Rocky. The two SAMs tangled their grid lines together in a confused jumble, but Fisher didn't have any better success in freeing Rocky from the Mask than Rhodes did.

Rhinehart bellowed in rage trying to fight his own grid lines. Rhodes strapped his lines around Rhinehart's body to pull his arm to the ground. He wouldn't be able to shoot anything there.

Rhodes dove on top of Rhinehart, got in his face, and roared over Rhinehart's enraged bellows. "Go into The Grid, Lieutenant! You have to shoot at Rocky inside The Grid!"

Rhinehart either didn't hear or didn't understand.

"You'll have to do it, Captain!" Fisher called.

"Hold him down for me!" Rhodes ordered. "I can't hold him! He's too strong!"

Rhinehart gave another tortured roar, heaved off the ground, and almost threw Rhodes off.

Fisher retracted his lines from Rocky and wound them around and around Rhinehart's body trying to stop him from shooting at anything, including himself and Rhodes.

Rhodes couldn't wait any longer. He dropped into The Grid, but the Masks must have learned by now what Rhodes wanted to do.

He jumped forward to grab Rocky, but the SAM dodged to one side. Rhodes grabbed again and again, but he couldn't get hold of Rocky.

Rhodes didn't dare to fire his Vipers in here. Rocky would only avoid them.

"The Strikers, Captain!" Fisher yelled. "You have to call in the Strikers!"

Rhodes only thought about it for a split second before he interfaced with Rio. The Strikers were all still on the ground on Deizo.

Rio materialized on The Grid next to Fisher. "I'm on my way, Captain!" Rio exclaimed. "Just hold on!"

"Bring all the SAMs!" Rhodes ordered. "We need help out here!"

"We're coming!" Zion chimed in.

Rhodes had to concentrate on fighting Rhinehart again as the Mask made one more brutal attempt to fire on the platoons.

Rhodes kept his head down and counted down the seconds until the Strikers got here.

Lauer had managed to work his way in front of Dietz and Fuentes. Dietz and Fuentes tried to shoot at the platoons, but Lauer got in their path.

He couldn't control his weapons, not even to kill himself. He stopped his two comrades from targeting the platoons simply by getting in their way.

Fuentes raised his weapon to shoot at Thackery. At that moment, Oakes jerked his scourge gun away from shooting at the platoons. His weapon went off and he hit Fuentes from the side.

The blast smashed Fuentes in the shoulder and flattened him. Dietz spun around and aimed his gun at Oakes, but something stopped Dietz from returning fire.

Thackery and Coulter battled each other not far away. Neither of them had time to shoot at the platoons. The two comrades were too busy shooting at each other.

Rhodes couldn't tell from here how much the Masks controlled either of them. Coulter and Thackery bared their teeth at each other, roared in fury, and they kept dodging each other's shots, diving out of the way, and landing in a crouch somewhere else to shoot again.

Rhinehart took all Rhodes's strength just to hold him down. He kept trying to raise his weapon. Rhodes didn't know or care what Rhinehart was trying to aim at.

Rhodes checked The Grid. The Strikers were just entering the atmosphere on a dead run for the battalion's position.

He couldn't fathom what the Strikes would do once they got here. He didn't see how anyone could salvage this disaster.

He shut his eyes and focused his last scrap of strength on restraining Rhinehart until the Strikers got here.

Rhodes would call it a win if he saved even one of his people from the Masks taking complete control over them.

The Strikers bombed out of the high cloud, screeched across the landscape coming in fast, and howled overhead, but they didn't fire on the Masks.

In the quiet privacy of his own mind, Rhodes watched the eight Striker SAMs flash onto The Grid. Their grid lines coiled around their wings and fuselages....and then shot out at lightning speed.

They didn't hit the Masks—or even anyone from the battalion. Those lines swirled around the Strikers, darted through the air, and hit the SAMs that had changed into Masks.

Those lines penetrated each Mask face so much deeper than Rhodes ever could—deeper than a Viper. The lines twined together with each person's Grid and tore the Mask faces to shreds.

The other seven SAMs blinked back onto The Grid and the battalion reacted instantly. Everyone turned their weapons on the Masks—the real Masks.

Rhinehart sprang to his feet and threw Rhodes off. Both men unloaded on the Masks to drive them away from the platoons. It might already be too late.

Rhodes fired his scourge gun and released dozens of Vipers in rapid succession. He blasted as many Masks to pieces as he could hit. When that didn't kill them fast enough, he let the grid lines transform his fingertips into lasers.

Lasers flashed from all his fingers, sliced the Masks to pieces, and left their body parts littered all over the hillsides.

Their consciousness didn't go away, though. He felt them still trying to interface with Fisher—and all the SAMs.

The Strikers came racing back for another pass, and this time, they bombarded the Masks' position with punishing fire.

Dozens of scourge gun blasts erupted from Rio's wings. They punched into the ground running from one side of the battlefield to the other.

Those blasts detonated Masks, exploded their armor apart, and left swaths of mechanized bodies leading away across the valley.

Rhodes stalked down the last Masks. He let his fury off its chain and all his murderous bloodlust poured out at them.

He would kill them all. He would kill every last one of them for what they did to him, Fisher, and everyone else.

The Masks responded to the Strikers' arrival just as instantly. The moment the Strikers released the SAMs and changed them back, the Masks broke off fighting the platoons and turned all their firepower on the battalion.

Dozens of Masks rushed in on Rhodes and his people. Fusion blasts hammered Rhodes from all sides, but that sudden assault only brought the Masks closer inside his laser range.

He whirled from one side to the other bellowing his challenge at them. "Come on!" he roared. "Come on!"

They kept on coming until, without warning, a devastating flash burst in front of his eyes. He didn't see what caused it or even where it came from.

He fought the Masks one minute with dozens of them falling under his lasers. The next moment, he lay flat on his back staring up at the clear blue sky.

His connection to The Grid showed him the whole battlefield for miles around. Hundreds or thousands of destroyed Masks, dead soldiers, and demolished Ravagers dotted the planet's surface.

The Grid picked out his subordinates lying unconscious among the dead bodies. None of the battalion moved.

Each of them stared up at the sky without blinking, but The Grid returned their life sign readings. Everyone in the battalion was still alive and conscious. They were only stunned just like Rhodes.

He didn't see any living soldiers or even any Masks still standing. The Grid didn't return any life signs for anyone other than the eight battalion members lying among the dead.

Rhodes didn't see any SAMs, either. Fisher was gone and so were all the other SAMs. Everything else about The Grid looked normal.

Rhodes couldn't move. He could only lie here and stare straight in front of him while one of the Masks' invasion ships descended over the battalion from the high clouds.

He studied its spiky exterior. He would probably never get another chance to see one of them up close.

It descended right on top of him and opened some kind of hatch in its underside. Blinding white-yellow light poured from inside. He couldn't even blink to protect his eyes.

Some force picked him up and lifted him toward that hatch. He watched through The Grid as the same ship picked up each of his subordinates, carried them inside that ship, and then the hatch closed with all of them on board.

End of Book 2.

Keep Reading

Battalion 1 Series: Book 3: Echoes In The Machine

Just when Battalion 1 thought things couldn't get any worse, Captain Rhodes and his team find themselves prisoners of the Masks, a mysterious army of robot invaders. Fighting this overwhelming force is hard enough.

With the Masks razing the galaxy one solar system after another, the Aemon Legion is betting everything that Battalion 1 will be able to stop the Masks from killing billions of people and maybe wiping out the human race entirely.

There's just one problem. The same technology the battalion would use to fight the Masks recognizes them as its own kind. Now no one in Battalion 1 can tell friend from enemy. Is everyone in the battalion really a robot after all? Is anyone in the battalion human anymore—or are the Masks human after all?

With the lines between human and robot and friend and enemy blurring more and more by the day, Rhodes and his team will have to summon all their strength, intelligence, and grit to save not just themselves but whatever is left of humanity. The battalion just has to figure out a way to save their own lives and their sanity first.

You can find it at your favorite book retailer.

Sign Up Once--Get all Theo Mann's free books including brand new releases

S ign Up Once--Get all Theo Mann's free books including brand new releases

Commander Layton Raines was just doing his job when he got shot down on the battle defending his platoon's retreat. His whole life changes when he wakes up in the hospital implanted with cybernetic limbs, but Raines is nothing like anyone else who has ever gone through the Battalion 1 project.

With the fate of the galaxy hanging in the balance, the future will depend on the one man who has never been good with authority, following orders, or staying within the lines. With the mission in jeopardy and Battalion 1 pinned down by overwhelming odds, it will take a miracle to save their lives. It just might take a mutiny to throw out the rule book and forge a path no one has ever taken before.

Sign up at www.theomann.com to read it for free

About Theo Mann

I write 70 books per year—and yes, before you ask, all these books are my original creative work. Nothing written under my name is AI-generated or ghostwritten because I write better than AI and any ghostwriter out there.

People don't read fiction for entertainment or to escape from reality. People read fiction to see their humanity reflected in another person's character and story.

This is my promise to you. When you read my books, you'll see your own humanity reflected in the characters and stories. I take this commitment to my readers very seriously. My books are an intimate form of communication between us. I would never disrespect my readers by turning that over to a machine or another writer. This is my bond between me and you as my reader.

I write 20,000 words per day as my daily work output. If anyone with a public platform would like to challenge me to prove this in a controlled environment, feel free to contact me on this website's contact page.

I worked as a professional ghostwriter for fifteen years. Now I'm on a mission to set a Guinness World Record by writing 700 books over the next ten years and 1400 books over the next twenty years, all originally written by me. See my website for the full book list.

I'm also the author of *Proof for the Existence of God* and the *Crimes Against Fiction* blog. You can find all my nonfiction work at www.crimes-against-fiction.com.

If you have a story idea, or if you would like me to explore a series in more depth, or if you'd like me to explore a character by writing a spinoff series about that character or world, leave me a message on my website's contact page. I answer all reader emails, so ask me anything, tell me what you liked and didn't like, and let me know where you'd like your favorite series to go. I would love to hear your ideas and find out what you'd like to read next.

Find out more at www.theomann.com.

Also by Theo Mann (so far)

www.ingramcontent.com/pod-product-compliance
Lightning Source LLC
Chambersburg PA
CBHW060944030726
47503CB00003B/717